To all the *Cowboys* I've Loved Before

D. R. Graham is a multi-published author who lives in Vancouver, Canada. She worked as a social worker with at-risk youth prior to becoming a psycho-therapist in private practice. Her novels deal with issues relevant to young adults in love, transition, or crisis.

🐦 @drgrahambooks
f www.facebook.com/drgrahambooksauthor/
www.drgrahambooks.com

Other books by D. R. Graham

Put It Out There (Britannia Beach Series)
What Are the Chances? (Britannia Beach Series)
And Then What? (Britannia Beach Series)

Rank

One Percenter (Noir et Bleu MC Series)
The Handler (Noir et Bleu MC Series)
It Is What It Is (Noir et Bleu MC Series)
The Noir et Bleu (Noir et Bleu MC Series)

Hit That And You're Dead

To all the *Cowboys* I've Loved Before

D.R. Graham

A division of HarperCollins Publishers
www.harpercollins.co.uk

Harper*Impulse* an imprint of
HarperCollins*Publishers*
The News Building
1 London Bridge Street
London SE1 9GF

www.harpercollins.co.uk

This paperback edition 2019

First published in Great Britain in ebook format by
HarperCollins*Publishers* 2019

A catalogue record for this book
is available from the British Library

ISBN: 9780008328399

Typeset in Birka by Palimpsest Book Production Ltd,
Falkirk, Stirlingshire

To Integrity

Chapter 1

Della

And there goes my tea. Over the railing. Onto the library concourse. Shoot. "Sorry," I shout to the students walking below who had to jump back to avoid the spray of scalding liquid. Mortified that I could have maimed someone, I gather my transfer papers, stuff them into my bag, and rush down the stairs to clean up the mess before anyone slips.

No paper towels nearby. Awesome. Guess I'll have to use the silk scarf in my bag to soak up the tea. Actually, come to think of it, this isn't my scarf. It's my sister's. She's going to kill me. Unfortunately, I don't have a better option.

I should have known it wasn't going to be my day. There was no hot water in the shower at the sketchy motel I'm temporarily staying at. My car, although it made it through the seventeen-hour drive to get me here, wouldn't start this morning. I had to take the bus, which made me late. Then I showed up for my first engineering course, only to find out I wasn't even on the class list. Sorting it out meant waiting in line at the registrar's office for over an hour.

At least the tea didn't burn anyone. I sigh and pick up the paper cup to drop it in the recycling bin. I might as well throw the scarf in the garbage while I'm at it. It's soaked and stained beyond repair. And my phone fell in the trash with it. Of course, now, the phone is ringing.

I reach elbow deep into the bin to fish it out. Ew. Whatever that was, it's sticky. "Hello?"

It's my cousin Stuart, my saving grace. "Everley is able to meet you at the house to give you a key, but it has to be this morning. Can you swing that?"

"Oh. I don't know, Stuart. I have class. And I'd need to take transit." I twist my phone to look at the time. I'll be late if I try to squeeze in a visit before my next class. "Does it have to be right now?"

"Do you want to spend another night in that rat-infested motel?"

"No." Absolutely not. "Okay. Thank you for setting up a place for me to live. I'd be lost here without you."

"It's Stanford not New York. You'd be fine without me, but I'm happy to help you any way I can. Hold on a second." He speaks to someone away from the phone briefly before he comes back on the line. "Some sort of disaster has come up with one of the model's outfits. I need to get back to the studio. Do you still have the address for the house?"

"Yeah, somewhere. Thanks for everything." I hang up and search through my bag as I walk towards the bus stop. I wrote the address on the back of a receipt. Somewhere.

Stuart is a famous photographer who lives in San

Francisco now, but he graduated from Stanford and knows a lot of people here. Which is great since finding available housing at this time of year is a challenge. He's made arrangements for me to rent a room in a shared house with three other women who are post-grad Stanford students. The one named Everley has done some fashion modeling for him. They probably won't be the type of women I would normally be friends with, but it doesn't matter. I'm here to study not socialize. As long as they don't throw huge parties every night it should be fine to live with three strangers.

I hope.

I definitely don't want to have to go back to that disgusting motel.

Where did I put the address? Ah. Here it is, on the back of a Chili's receipt. I board the Palo Alto bus and ask the bus driver to let me know which stop I should get off at for the two hundred block of Coleridge Avenue. When we reach the next stop, he turns and waves. Wow. It's way closer to the school than I expected – probably should have checked how far away it was before I paid the bus fare. This could work out great. I could walk to class, save on gas and parking. I like it already.

I step off the bus and squint at the house numbers to figure out which direction to walk. Mental note: a blazer works for spring in Canada. Here, I'm suffocatingly over-dressed. The street is cute. Tree-lined. Wide sidewalks. Nice family homes. Tons of joggers—California types, but what-ever, at least it seems safe. And the fuchsia-colored flowers on the hedges smell amazing. The house that matches the address Stuart gave me is bigger than I expected. And despite the traditional Spanish style, it's more modern than I imagined for a student rental.

I walk up the brick path and knock on the door. Nobody answers, so I knock again, louder. There isn't a doorbell. In fact, I look around, duh, it's not even the front door. It's a side door to the garage. Smooth, Della. Hopefully a security camera didn't catch that air-head move. Before I enter the courtyard that leads to the actual front door, which is unmistakable since it's much grander and made from carved wood, I glance over my shoulder to check if any of the neighbors saw my dorky mistake. The gardener across the street might have, but he's pretending he didn't.

After I knock, rock music inside the house stops, and a few seconds later the door opens. Standing in the doorway, bathed in the glow of the California sun, is a shirtless, perfectly sculpted, slightly sweaty, long-haired, brown-eyed, dark-skinned, gorgeous specimen of a man.

He wipes a towel over his face and then extends his arm to offer to shake my hand. "Della?"

I blink repeatedly, stunned by the testosterone overload. Eventually, I raise my hand and clasp his. It's huge.

"I'm Easton."

"Hi," I eventually whisper, then clear my throat to regain composure. "Nice to meet you. Is Everley here? She was going to meet me, so I could get a key."

"I'm Everley."

"Oh." Didn't he say Easton? More importantly—"You're a—" I scan his physique again. "Guy."

"Yes ma'am." He chuckles and steps back into the foyer to open the door wider and invite me into the house. "Your cousin didn't mention that?"

"Uh." I step onto the terra cotta tiles hesitantly and glance sideways at him. There is no mistaking he's male, but his raven black hair falls to the middle of his back and is shinier than the hair of any female I've ever met. He is strikingly beautiful but definitely a guy. "Stuart said you modeled, and Everley sounds, um—" I stop myself before actually telling him his name is feminine. Based on his amused grin he already knows why I assumed he was female. "Is it Easton or Everley?"

"Everley was my mom's maiden name. I only use it for modeling. Easton Lewis is what everyone here knows me as."

"Oh." He's pretty enough to be an Everley, but Easton suits him better; homegrown and wholesome but also unique. And really cute. "Uh." I clear my throat to give myself a second to refocus. "The other roommates are female, right?"

His smile widens, but then he turns without answering and walks down the hall towards the back of the house. I follow, scanning the rest of the downstairs on my way to the kitchen. He pours two glasses of a green concoction from the blender. "Smoothie?"

I step up to the island and take the glass from him. "What's in it?"

"Kale. Papaya. Coconut milk. A scoop of peanut butter."

I sip at first but then tip it back. It's delicious. And if it's the reason his skin is that flawless, I'm completely willing to drink it, three meals a day. "So, you didn't answer the question. Is Taylor male or female?"

"Male."

"Bailey's a girl, though, right?" Please. Please be female.

Easton laughs and washes out the blender. "Bailey's sensitive deep down, but he won't ever show it to you. He's cowboy to the core. And nobody calls them by their real names. Taylor's nickname is Chuck. And Bailey goes by BJ because his last name is Jackson." Easton's thick lashes raise, and he shoots me a look that makes me gulp down the smoothie. "Your cousin didn't tell you he was sending you to live in a house with three rodeo cowboys?"

I shake my head slowly side-to-side and place the glass on the tile counter. "Nope. He left that part out. I'm sorry there has been a miscommunication, but this isn't going to work out." I glance at his etched muscles one more time.

"You don't have to worry about the boys. They'll treat you like a little sister."

"Thanks, but I can't live with three men. My parents are very old fashioned." And I am very not the kind of girl who could live with three guys. I mean, I assume I'm not. I've never lived with anyone other than my family.

He stares at me quietly as he comes up with a counter point. "Your parents don't need to know. Don't tell them."

"Oh, I can't do that. I try not to make a habit of lying. Well, except there was this one time with a friend, but it was to spare her feelings. I grappled with myself over the ethics, but I think omitting the truth was the right decision in her case. Not that you probably care about that. Sorry. I get sidetracked sometimes."

With his arms crossed he rests his butt against the edge of the countertop. "Maybe you could omit the truth with your parents. I'm desperate. We really need the extra person to cover the rent by this Friday or we're all out on the street. Is there anything I can say to convince you to stay?"

Hmm. With my feet still anchored in place I take a look around. The backyard has a pool. The appliances are stainless steel, gas stove. Everything is spotlessly clean. It's walking distance to the school. The rent is affordable. Easton is a piece of moving art. But three rowdy cowboys. No. "I don't think it's a good idea. I'm on a scholarship and can't afford to let my grades slip. If you guys are partying all the time like a frat house I won't get any studying done."

"They don't party here. They might stumble in at four in the morning, but you'll mostly have the place to yourself. We travel for rodeos almost every weekend."

I rub my hand over my face, torn. My dad really would flip if he found out I was the only female in the house. Mind you he's already practically disowned me for leaving in the first place. If I don't move in here I'll have to stay at the motel. And I'll have to do a house search to find a better place. Not that a better place in this price range probably even exists. This is exactly why Stuart left out the minor detail of them being male. He knew I'd turn it down flat if I knew. They're just roommates, does it matter what gender they are? I know what my dad would think.

I'm not sure what I think. Shoot. What to do. What to do.

Easton finishes his drink and says, "I need to hop in the shower. Why don't you hang out and look around? The room you'd be in is the first on the left at the top of the stairs. You'd have your own private en suite bathroom. The boys and I share the other upstairs bathroom. Laundry is in the garage. A maid service comes in once a week. We take turns grocery shopping."

I nod, letting it all sink in. It sounds perfect. He knows it does. His mouth makes a cute half-smile before he leaves the kitchen and heads upstairs. The shower turns on, so I wander around and peek out the patio door. Admittedly it would be relaxing to take study breaks out by the pool. The lush backyard is obviously maintained by a gardener. And there's a gazebo! Dining el fresco was something I was definitely looking forward to when I decided to move from Canada to California.

Despite how clean everything is, there is no doubt three guys live here. Six pairs of athletic shoes and a collection of cowboy boots are lined up by the back door. The barbecue is enormous, as is the stacked wall of empty beer cans next to the recycling bins. And they have a full universal gym, boxing bag, and huge free weights set up on the patio next to the hot tub. I wonder if they're all as fit as Easton. Probably. That would definitely be a distraction.

After checking out the laundry room in the garage, I tread quietly upstairs. Why does it feel like I'm sneaking around? Maybe because I keep imagining Easton standing naked in the shower. This is why my dad wouldn't approve.

He shouldn't approve. I'm going to completely fail all my classes if I live here.

Oh my. I swing the door to my room wider. It's ideal. I should leave before I fall in love with it. Too late. Why? Why are you so perfect? Walk-in closet. Queen-size bed that looks brand new. A solid wood dresser and matching desk. A huge window with a window seat and sunlight filtering through the leaves. Wooden California shutter blinds. Crown moldings. My own gigantic bathroom with a soaker-tub and separate shower. I have to leave.

As I step into the upstairs hall, Easton emerges from his room directly across from me. His hair is wet and tied in a bun at the back of his head. He looks just as good in jeans and a white T-shirt as he did in only athletic shorts. He smells amazing, like Hawaii. I absolutely need to leave.

"What's the verdict?" he asks as I make my way down the stairs in front of him, trying not to trip.

Once we're safely back in the foyer I turn and answer, "Uh, it's really great, but like I said, it's not going to work. Three men and me."

He nods, looking kind of disappointed as he reaches for a set of keys in a glass bowl on the hallway table. "That's too bad, but I understand. You have to do what's best for you." He opens the door for me and follows me out, then locks the door. "Do you want me to walk you back to school?"

"Um, yeah, okay. That would be nice. Thank you." My skin is tingling. What is that about? Apparently, the idea of walking with 'him makes me giddy like a fourteen-year-old. Get a grip, Della. He's just a dumb cowboy who happens to have stunning looks. We walk in silence for a while, which feels awkward, so I ask, "What are you studying?"

"I'm working on my MBA."

Oh boy. He's not dumb. My legs feel weird. Maybe I should take the bus.

"How about you, Della? What are you studying?"

Wow. The sound of my name coming out of his mouth is like melted chocolate flowing over ice cream. I'm already distracted, and I haven't even gone to one class yet. Guys like him are definitely experienced in the woman department. I wonder what he thinks about girls like me, AKA girls who went to an all-girls' private school and haven't had a lot of boyfriends. Or any, to be more specific. It's not like I've never had offers. Guys have asked me out, but when I was younger I refused all invitations to date because my father forbid it until I was sixteen. By then I was so terrified at the thought of getting pregnant or contracting an STD and having to tell my dad, that I basically avoided anyone who showed an interest. Once I was older and more open to the idea of a relationship, I just never met anyone I was that into. Definitely never met anyone even remotely as intriguing as Easton.

These are not great shoes for walking. It's really hot in Palo Alto. What was the question again? Oh yeah. "Studying post-grad. To do the engineering. I mean being an engineer. Environmental systems. Spring term entry. That's what I'm learning for or doing. I'm going to be that." Oh, my goodness, be quiet, Della. Abort. Abort the conversation. Change the subject. "You have very nice skin."

His eyebrows angle comically as we cross the street. "Thank you. It runs in my family."

Really? Gah. Complimenting him on his skin. How is that any less awkward? Ask him something normal. "Where are you from?"

"Here in California." He stops on the curb to wait for a light—fortunately—since I'm completely oblivious right now and would have definitely stepped out into on-coming traffic. "Mojave," he adds.

"Mojave? Like the desert?"

"Like the people."

"Ah." When the light changes, we cross and then cut through a small park. "So, you're a bull riding, Mojave Native American, super model, studying for his MBA."

"Bareback bronc rider, actually. And I haven't modeled in ages. The rest is true, though. And I'm also a rancher."

"Wow." I follow him along a path that shortcuts through another neighborhood. "You're very unusual."

He glances at me with an expression that's impossible to decipher. Hopefully he didn't take it the wrong way. Of course, he did. Who wouldn't?

"In a good way," I blurt out. "Unusual. Not the bad unusual. I didn't mean weird. Diverse. The opposite of everyday run of the mill. Interesting. Not dull like me." I'm an idiot. One second, I'm drooling over him, the next I'm putting my foot in my mouth. Just stop talking,

Della. Maybe if you're lucky you'll never run into him again.

He slides his index finger over his eyebrow in an uncomfortable gesture. "The guys don't know I used to model. Maybe we could keep that between you and me."

"Sure." Ugh. Now that I know it's a secret I have an impulse to whisper it to the first person I see.

We walk in silence the rest of the way to campus, then he stops in front of a building. He stares at me for a second before he says, "You seem unusual too."

As I'm wondering if he means the good kind of unusual or the bad, he hands me a key.

"The guys and I are leaving on a road trip tonight. We'll be gone two days for a training clinic. Stuart gave me your number. I'll message you mine. Think about renting the room. If you decide yes, then just move in and make yourself at home. If you decide no, drop the key in the mail slot. Cool?"

I nod. Yeah, cool, not really. Wait. What? I should just give the key back now. My hand isn't moving. Why can't I speak? He smiles and turns to bound up the stone stairs. He moves like an Olympian. Everyone in the vicinity watches as he waves back at me and then disappears through the front doors. A few of the females size me up, apparently because I was seen talking to the Mojave god. He must have Stanford celebrity status. Obviously he would. I mean look at him. And listen to him. And bask in his presence.

Okay, I'm still standing in the middle of the sidewalk

with my hand out and a key on my upturned palm. Move, Della. Carry on. At least pretend to be a normal human being. In a less than convincing attempt to appear cool, I slide the key in my pocket and pull out my class schedule to figure out where I'm supposed to be. What time is it?

Chapter 2

Easton

Chuck and BJ are already seated at the back of the lecture hall when I sneak in. Professor Cavendish isn't cool with students being late and, unfortunately, she just made eye contact with me. I wave apologetically and shoot her a sheepish smile. She's strict. It might not work. I pause halfway to my seat, waiting to see if she's going to kick me out or let me stay. Her left eyebrow raises in a cautionary way, but then she carries on with the lecture without giving me the boot.

"Impressive," BJ says around the toothpick that is perpetually propped at the corner of his mouth.

Chuck nods to agree with the impressiveness and pops an ice pack to apply to his injured shoulder. "Future generations will gather at the foot of your bronze statue as they recall the legend of Havie the Mojave: The only person in the history of the school to get away with being late to Cavendish's class."

Chuck is quintessentially redneck—mullet and lame-assed

hunting tattoos to prove it. BJ's more sophisticated, and he's black, so the other cowboys call us the Village People when we show up on the circuit together. I don't really care what they call us as long as we're taking home the money. And we usually do.

BJ waits until Cavendish turns around before he asks, "How'd it go with the new roomie? What's she like?"

I shrug, purposely evasive. I don't want him getting any bright ideas about dating or sleeping with her. "She seemed all right, but she's undecided. She'll let us know."

"Come on, Havie." BJ lowers his voice to a whisper after Cavendish shoots us a glare, "We need the money by Friday. If she's not in, we have to ask someone we know."

I shake my head. "No way. The last two guys were slobs, and I'm not letting a woman either of you guys have slept with or want to sleep with rent the room. You'll piss her off. She'll move out. And we'll be right back in this same position in a month. Or worse, you'll end up some buckle bunny's baby daddy and need to come up with child support too."

"Does that mean the chick you've picked is someone none of us would want to sleep with?" Chuck asks.

BJ's face freezes in a brace-for-bad-news grimace. "Is she hideous?"

"It doesn't matter what she looks like. All you should care about is whether she can pay the rent. And she's skittish about living with three cowboys, so don't scare her off if she does decide to move in."

"Gentlemen," Cavendish raises her voice to reach the

back of the room loud and clear. "Since you're going to be missing my next lecture for your little bronc riding adventures may I suggest that you listen during today's lecture?"

"Yes, ma'am," we all say in unison.

After an extended silence to drive home her point, she returns to lecturing and writing on the whiteboard.

BJ leans over and covers his mouth with his hand. "What color's her hair?"

"Brown," I say under my breath.

"Good brown or the ugly kind?"

"Shut up. Assuming that she's straight, you're not sleeping with her."

"You can't either then."

Chuck leans in. "Can I?"

"No," we both snap at him.

The woman sitting in front of me turns and shushes us.

BJ listens to Cavendish for a while, but the lecture is boring, so he swings his head over closer to me. "Does she have a nice body?"

"I have no idea. She was wearing dress pants and a blazer."

"Like a professor?"

"More like a Catholic schoolgirl. You won't like her. She's too conservative for you."

"Black? White? Asian? Latina? Or a Mojave princess?"

"She's white. Like fresh snow. Now, shut it before you get us kicked out."

Both BJ and Chuck swivel in their seats, staring at me with amused expressions.

"What?" I mumble.

"Why did you just describe her in a poetic way?"

I shake my head, annoyed. "It wasn't poetic. It was descriptive. In a factual way. She literally has the palest skin I've ever seen. And for all we know she wouldn't be interested in any of us anyway."

They both sink back into their seats, grinning. Like they know something I don't know.

After class, the guys and I walk to the deli for lunch. The freshman working the counter likes Chuck, so she gives us fifty percent off our sandwiches, which is cheaper than making them ourselves at home. I'm tired of the same thing every day, but money is going to be tight until we hit some rodeos. A half-priced turkey on rye is better than nothing.

We sit at a table by the window and BJ says, "Since we've never had a female roommate before, let's make a rule. What's her name again?"

"Della. But she hasn't agreed yet." I bite into my sandwich.

BJ pauses to give a woman walking by the eye, then continues, "Okay, if any of us sleeps with Della we owe the other two five-hundred bucks each."

Chuck laughs. "I don't even have a hundred bucks. I can't come up with a thousand bucks."

"Then don't sleep with her, dummy." BJ extends his hand towards me. "Are you in, Havie?"

He's got a scheming look in his eyes. Probably because he thinks the snowy skin comment means I have a thing for her. I don't. I barely know her. "Yeah, I'm in." I shake his hand. "All I want from her is her rent money."

Chuck looks confused. "Have we determined whether she's good looking or not?"

"It doesn't matter. Either you keep your hands off her or you owe us a grand."

Chuck squints into the sun as his brain wheels tick. You'd think he'd been kicked in the head by one too many broncs, but he's naturally like that. Book smart and life dumb. It's actually painful to watch him figure things out. "What qualifies as sleeping with her? Just so I'm clear on the parameters."

BJ checks with me, "Kissing? Heavy petting? Penetration? What should the line be?"

I shake my head to end the stupid conversation. "No touching. Period."

Chuck gestures in protest. "No way, man. We need to be able to shake her hand or give her a hug if she's crying or something. Penetration is the line."

"Fine," BJ says. "If any part of your body enters any part of her body you have to pay up."

"What if she initiates the sexual contact?" Chuck asks.

"Still counts," BJ says as he gets up to order a milkshake at the counter.

Chuck leans his elbows on the table, processing the situation. "What if she decides not to room with us? Is she still off-limits then?"

I don't answer because Della just walked in. She grabs a tray and loads it with a carton of milk and a salad. Her hair is the good kind of brown—long, thick and wavy. It's held back with a thin navy ribbon headband and she has dark-rimmed glasses on now, so she looks even more like a library monitor. Despite the modest outfit it's obvious she's fit. Probably a runner or tennis player. BJ has already spotted her and is checking out her ass. Chuck is about to notice her, too. He's not into good girls, but her big brown doe eyes, heart-shaped face, and the way she smells, like a mixture of vanilla and peppermint, will mesmerize him into giving it his best shot. One of them is going to spook her. Guaranteed.

Della steps up to the cashier where BJ is waiting for his milkshake. He says something to her that makes her cheeks flush. She responds quietly without looking directly at him and passes the cashier a twenty. When BJ points over at our table, Della turns and our eyes meet. I smile. Not in the 'trying to wheel her' way, but in the 'her looking at me actually made me smile' way. Uh oh. Maybe I do have a thing for her already. This is potentially not good.

She attempts to wave at me and tips her tray in the process. The salad bowl flies through the air and lettuce floats to the floor. The milk carton hits the ground hard and explodes, which makes her wince as the spray douses her and BJ in white droplets. "Shoot. I'm sorry," she says to him as she leans across the counter to grab serviettes. "It soaked your boots. I'm sorry. Let me wipe them off for you." She crouches down to clean up the milk.

"Don't worry about it, darlin'. Boots are made for getting dirty," BJ says as he makes eye contact with me. He points down at her and mouths, "Is this the new roomie?"

I don't want to answer because I don't know what he's going to do with that information. He can obviously tell from my non-reaction that she is, which makes him grin in a way that is only going to mean trouble. He helps her pick up the salad remnants and orders another one for her. He pays for it with what is likely his last ten bucks and then escorts her over to our table.

I stand to slide over a chair from the table next to us and offer her mine. "Della, that's BJ," I say. "This is Chuck." I shoot them both glares, intended to warn them to be on their best behavior, which they both ignore.

"Ah, Della," Chuck says. "We've heard all about you. Welcome to Stanford. Have a seat."

She sits cautiously and places the tray with the fresh salad and milk on the table. "Hi. Nice to meet you both." She glances at me and presses her lips together as if she's forcing herself not to say more.

"If you need help with anything, I'm happy to show you around," BJ offers before he raises his eyebrows at me.

"Thank you," she says quietly.

With all of us watching, she takes a sip of milk. She doesn't touch the salad, though, as if she's uncomfortable eating in front of people. Maybe I should get the key back from her. If I don't, I'll be leading a lamb to the wolves.

BJ leans back in his chair, sipping his milkshake, sizing her up, and literally licking his chops. "You have an interesting accent, Della. Where you from?"

"Vancouver, but I was born in Russia. We moved to Canada when I was eight. Then I moved to California yesterday, so here I am. How about you guys? I know Easton is from here. Where are you both from?"

"Chuckie's from Oregon. I'm a Texan born and raised." BJ watches as she finally picks up her fork and eats a small bite of lettuce.

"Do you prefer to be called Bailey and Taylor or BJ and Chuck?" she asks.

"Doesn't matter to me," BJ says. "Rodeo nickname. Real name. I answer to both."

She nods and glances at Chuck, waiting for him to answer.

With a straight face he says, "You can call me Big Poppa."

Her eyebrows angle together as she attempts to read him. I'm pretty sure he's joking, but honestly, it's not always easy to tell with Chuck. Either way, I shake my head to let her know that she shouldn't take him seriously.

"Are you going to eat this pickle?" He asks me after he's already taken it off my plate and bitten into it. "You know anything about Rodeo, Della?"

Her head swivels side to side. "No. Only that there are bulls and horses. And animal rights activists who claim it's cruel." She opens the package of salad dressing and it squirts onto the table. "Shoot," she mutters under her breath as she wipes it up.

BJ sits forward, defensive. "You think the animals are mistreated?"

"Oh. No. I don't know." Her cheeks flush from his confrontational tone. "I don't know anything about it. I've never even been to a rodeo." She clenches her eyes shut for a second as if she's trying to reset the conversation, then she glances at Chuck's wrapped shoulder and BJ's swollen eye. "It does appear to be cruel to cowboys, though."

I laugh. Chuck nods to agree and BJ relaxes back in his seat.

I like her. I don't know why. She's not the type I normally go for—awkward, eyes that are so innocent it makes me worry about her safety in the world, and really conservative. We probably have nothing in common. Then again, dating woman I have a lot in common with hasn't really worked out for me so far.

BJ pokes Della's arm to tease her. "Is shoot the worst cuss word you've ever said?"

She frowns and glances at me before she answers him. "I guess. Why?"

"Do you drink?"

"Like alcohol?" She immediately cringes and points at the milk carton as if she can't believe she didn't realize that was implied. "Obviously that's what you meant. Everyone drinks. Liquids. Milk. Water. I've had a glass of champagne. Once."

Chuck and BJ both laugh at her lack of experience. This is bad. She's a lamb. A cute, defenseless little lamb. They're going to eat her alive. And we definitely have nothing in common.

"Why'd you choose engineering?" I ask to prevent them from grilling her on anything that might embarrass her.

She pauses mid-bite and retracts the fork. "Um, honestly?"

I nod.

"Because my dad thinks women aren't smart enough to be engineers. I'm here to prove him wrong."

"Good on ya," Chuck says and gives her a fist bump.

"Hell yeah," BJ adds.

I nod again. Okay. I definitely have a thing for her. She can't live with us. I don't have an extra thousand dollars to give the guys.

Chapter 3

Della

Ew. What was that? Something just crawled across my face. I reach over and flip the lamp on. It's a cockroach. On my pillow. Gah! Disgusting. Get it off. No, no. They're everywhere. I hop up to stand on the mattress as a wave of giant shells scurry, like an insect army, across the floor to the bathroom and closet where it's dark.

And I'm done sleeping. Maybe forever.

Yuck. The hotel manager moved me to this room after I mentioned that last night's room didn't have hot water. Cold water is better than bugs. Why am I so itchy? I rub my palms over my arms vigorously. Do cockroaches bite? Do they carry disease? I'm going to catch the plague. Maybe I should call my dad and ask him what to do. No. Don't be a baby. Figure it out. Think. Well, one thing I know for sure, I can't stay at this disgusting motel. What time is it? Four in the morning. I don't care. I would rather be a homeless person.

I jump off the bed to zip up my suitcases and don't even

bother to change out of my pajama shorts or brush my teeth, which would horrify my mother. She doesn't even come downstairs for breakfast until she is fully showered and dressed for the day. I don't care right now. Well, maybe a little. It only takes a second to throw a sweatshirt over my tank-top before I leave.

My car is parked right in front of the door, so I toss my luggage into the trunk and pop the hood. I don't know anything about car engines. My dad always serviced it for me. But I'm going to be an engineer. I should be able to figure out why it wouldn't start yesterday. The engine wouldn't turn over at all, so that must be the battery, right? It might be a little tricky to get a new battery at four o'clock in the morning, if that's even what the problem is.

I could sleep in the car. Slightly uncomfortable, but infestation-free. Or, maybe that's not a good idea. The woman on the sidewalk who looks like a prostitute—not judging—is talking to a guy who could be a drug dealer— not judging. I sort of am judging. My guess is that this is not the safest place in the world for sleeping in a disabled vehicle.

I still have the key to the Palo Alto house. Easton said they'd be out of town for two days. I could maybe stay there and find a place before they get back. The guys were nice enough. Polite. Fun. All attractive, which is unrelated to this train of thought, yet notable. And they're easy going. They wouldn't care if I crashed there. But it sort of feels like taking advantage of them.

There really are no other vacancies near the school—at

least not any that would be better than the motel. A girl in my last class said there is a room for rent in the house she lives at. I wrote her number on the back of the deli receipt. It's actually cheaper than the Palo Alto place, but smaller, too. And a forty-minute bus ride to the school. Plus, it's her and two guys. So, not really that much more suitable. And it's a little early to call her up.

I pace as I think and become increasingly annoyed with my dad. My accommodation situation wouldn't even be an issue if he hadn't blocked the money in my savings account when he found out I was applying to Stanford. His name is on the account, but it's my money from my last ten birthdays, my job as a department store cashier, and my inheritance from my grandfather. It's not a lot of money but will cover my living expenses for a few years. So frustrating. And unfair. In fact, my sister never even had to use her savings because Dad paid for her entire nursing education. He also bought her a condo because she went to the school he wanted her to go to. Whatever. It's fine if he doesn't want to pay out of his pocket for me to take something he doesn't approve of, but the money in my savings account is mine. And, unfortunately, the scholarship funds haven't been deposited into my personal account yet. Sorting out the scholarship and banking issues will probably take several more one-hour line-ups. And possibly a lawyer to deal with my dad. I'm not looking forward to any of it.

I'm itchy.

The stores aren't open across the street. Hopefully the

restaurant on the other side of the parking lot opens at five. A sketchy looking guy sitting at the bus stop is staring at me. Maybe I should go into the office.

The fifty-something clerk is asleep behind the counter, so I sit on a chair next to the tourism pamphlets. They're so old. It looks like they haven't been restocked since the nineties. The coffee is burnt to the bottom of the pot, the plastic plants are covered in a layer of dust, and the ceiling has creepy holes in it, like a camera is hidden in it, or a creature. I'm for sure going to have nightmares about this place at some point.

The clerk snores himself awake and blinks groggily at me. "Hey there. I didn't hear you come in. You need something?"

"Do you have jumper cables?"

"Yeah."

"Really?" I shoot up out of the chair. I was half-joking when I said it and honestly didn't think he would. "That's fantastic."

"Are you checking out?"

"Yes. Please." I slide the key across the counter. He already made me pre-pay for the night so it's just a matter of signing a piece of paper and I'm free to go.

"I'll get my truck and meet you around front."

Yay.

It feels like I'm breaking and entering into the Palo Alto house. And, apparently, I am. Easton didn't mention anything about an alarm, but I hear beeping. Uh, oh. How long do they give you? Thirty, sixty seconds? I don't even know where the panel is. Shoot. I'm going to end up in jail, and none of us have any money to bail me out. Ending up a convict will absolutely support my dad's argument that moving here was a bad idea.

Okay, stop panicking. Where's the panel? It sounds like it's in the hall that leads to the garage. I sprint and quickly open the cover. 1234, nope. 0000, nope. 9999, nope. How many chances do they give you to screw up? At least there's no rent in jail. Think, Della. What would three cowboys choose as their alarm code? Boots? Horse? Bronc? Spurs? Or, how about 2057. The house address? Nope. How about the address backwards?

Ha. Bingo. It's disarmed. Woohoo. I'm a genius. Running man. Sprinkler. Booty bounce. Whoa, slip and hit my knee on the tile. Ouch. Okay, dancing is not my strong suit, not even celebratory jigs. I'm going to stop that now.

The light flicks on. "Hey."

Bah! Sweet Mother of Pearl. I gasp, clutching my chest to prevent my heart from leaping out of it. Easton fills the width of the hallway. When I notice the baseball bat on his shoulder I instinctually step back.

He chuckles and places the bat on the floor, leaning it against the wall. "Sorry. I didn't mean to scare you. I thought you were an intruder."

The sight of him causes adrenaline to gush through my veins. Not the bad kind from the thought of being mistaken for a burglar and attacked by a massive, muscular man with a bat. The good kind from only the thought of the massive, muscular man part. A man who happens to be smiling as if he's glad I'm the intruder.

"I didn't realize you'd be moving in so late." He smiles and glances over his shoulder at the clock on the wall in the kitchen. "Or early."

"I, uh, hi. Sorry. I would have called if it weren't so late slash early. Long story. I should have called, but I thought you were supposed to be out of town."

"I didn't go. My dad's not feeling that well after his last chemotherapy treatment, so I'm driving out there today to visit him."

"Oh. I'm sorry to hear that." I rub my knee where it's already starting to grow a lump and wonder if he witnessed me fall. "Do you think it's serious? Your dad?"

He shrugs and leans against the wall with his arms crossed. "Probably. He's a tough son-of-a-bitch, so if he's showing pain it's not a good sign." He glances at me and his eyes search my face as if he's trying to read my expression. "Sorry for cursing."

"Oh, no. Don't apologize." I wave my hands in an attempt to ease his unnecessary repentance. "You don't have to change who you are for me. I'm not a total prude." Except that I kind of am. Or, always have been. I guess I don't have to be.

He glances at the alarm panel. "You cracked the code?"

"Yeah. Eventually." I can't help but grin at my own cleverness.

"There you go. Women are smart enough to be engineers." He turns and walks down the hall towards the kitchen. "Since we're both up, you want some breakfast? I can make us an omelet."

Hmm. Yeah, breakfast with Easton would be good. But I was only planning on crashing here and then leaving. Sneak in a shower, maybe a dip in the pool. Make one of those smoothies. And then gone. That was the plan. Easton being here is definitely not part of the plan. My reaction to Easton calling me smart is also unexpected. He has some sort of magic effect on me. Everyone probably feels that way around him. That's why Stuart photographs him. He's got that something special. It. He's got it. Whatever it is. I like it. Which is why I am going to join him for breakfast in this very big, very empty house. Just the two of us. Alone. By ourselves.

Oh, grow up, Della. It's eggs with a guy, not sex.

"So, you decided to move in," he says as he clicks the gas element on. "I didn't realize it would be at four-thirty in the morning." He laughs. "Sorry I forgot to tell you the alarm code." His hair is woven into one long braid that trails down his spine. He's not wearing a shirt again, so every detail of his chiseled back is on display. Cooking half-nude. I guess he's not particularly concerned about splatter burns. He probably doesn't feel them. Like a super-hero, impermeable to the injuries of mere mortals. He turns to face me with the spatula poised in the air, as if he's waiting for something. Did I miss the question?

"Um, sorry, what did you say?"

"What made you decide to shack up with three men? I know it's not because you found Chuck and BJ irresistibly charming." He points at the fridge. "Cheese or no cheese in your omelet?"

"Cheese is good. I like cheese."

He smiles and leans into the fridge to take out all the ingredients. *Cheese is good. I like cheese.* He must think I'm odd. I am odd. And how am I supposed to tell him that I didn't actually decide to move in, I was just going to be a squatter for the night? He looks over at me again because, yeah that's right, I haven't answered the question yet. It's so hot in here. I pull off my sweatshirt and say, "Cockroaches."

His eyebrows angle together as he attempts to decipher my cryptic conversation skills.

"Cockroaches made my decision for me."

He places a bowl on the counter and stares at me with his mouth slightly agape. All of me. Not my face. My body. What's he looking at? Okay, I know I'm in my pajamas, and my hair's a mess, and my breath probably smells horrid, but I don't think it warrants actual shock on his part.

"What happened to your skin?"

I glance down at my arms. They're completely covered in red marks, like spider bites but all over in tracks. And they run along my chest. And, oh my goodness, all down my legs. What is that? I'm scarlet. It's a cockroach disease. That's why I'm so itchy. Even itchier now that I've noticed. My scalp is itchy now. I stand and jig around because it feels like insects are crawling all over me. "What is it?"

"It looks like bed bugs got you."

"Bed bugs? Are they still on me?"

He chuckles. "Probably not, but they might be on your luggage and in your clothes."

Yuck. Disgusting. Thank goodness I left my stuff in the trunk of my car and didn't track them in here. "Ugh. That motel was wretched. I probably have lice and tics and scabies, too. I should go."

"You don't have to go. Just have a shower. I'll make a Mojave remedy for you. It will take away the itch. You can wear one of my T-shirts and we'll put all your other clothes in the washing machine. The dryer should kill any that might have hitched a ride."

He's sweet. And calm. I feel better already. "I'm sorry. I know you didn't plan to rent to a dirty vagrant with communicable diseases."

"Chuck has worse."

My eyes widen and my expression makes Easton laugh.

"I'm kidding. I think." He laughs even harder and starts cracking the eggs, completely unfazed by my grossness.

I slink out of the kitchen and run up to the bathroom in my room. Well, not my room. The room that's for rent. The room that I'm currently contaminating, so probably obligated to rent even if I don't live in it. Oh, my gosh. Maybe my dad was right. Coming to Stanford was a bad idea and this is the universe's way of sending me the message. Hey, Della, go home. Who do you think you are? Quit.

Only, I don't want to quit. It's not that bad. Sure, it's only been two days and everything has pretty much gone wrong. It could be worse, though. In the grand scheme of things people deal with much worse hardships than broken down cars and unsanitary living conditions. But what if this is only the beginning and it does get worse? I can always drop out and go home. Think positive, Della. It could also get better.

I undress and step into the shower. The water pressure is amazing. Perfect for rinsing conditioner out. The guys probably don't fully appreciate this minor detail. Maybe Easton does. His hair is nicer than mine. I want to live here. And Easton is already making breakfast and a Mojave remedy. Plus, my clothes need washing. Hopefully dry-cleaning kills bed bugs too, otherwise I'm going to have to burn most of my wardrobe. Oh well, nobody dresses formally here anyways.

You know, come to think of it, my sister lived with Alex before they were married. My parents eventually got used to it—not until they actually got married. But still. Precedence has been set. Okay, I'm staying. Until things get worse.

Chapter 4

Easton

Visiting my dad at the ranch was rough. Partly for the same reasons it has always been rough between us, and partly because it's hard to see him struggling. When he was diagnosed with cancer I started going home more often to help out, and I thought maybe spending more time together would change some things between us, but it hasn't.

I'm sitting in my truck in the driveway of the Palo Alto house, trying to adjust back into my life as a student. Della's Volkswagen Bug is parked on the street, so she's probably home. I was hoping the guys would already be back. For some reason I'm hesitant to be here alone with her. Not some reason. I know the reason. It's because I haven't stopped thinking about her since I left yesterday morning. Her completely natural fresh-face, her klutziness, the inno-cent way her cheeks flush over everything, and the sexy way she looked wearing only my T-shirt while her clothes were in the wash. That damn near killed me.

Even my dad could tell there was something up with me. I denied it, but the fact that I kept talking about her probably didn't help convince him. The attraction is not good for the roommate arrangement. Neither is being alone with her.

A hand slams against my driver's side window followed by Chuck's ugly mug. He laughs because he startled me. "What's up, Havie?" Without waiting for a response, he carries on to the front door behind BJ. Glad to have them as a buffer, I get out of the truck and grab my bag from the back. I better figure out a way to keep my attraction to Della locked up, quick.

As I enter the kitchen Chuck breaks into a run and shouts, "Honey, we're home." He cannonballs past Della who is stretched out on a lawn chair in the backyard. BJ also jumps straight into the pool with his clothes on to cool off from their road trip. Della was reading a textbook but puts the book down and pulls on a long-sleeve beach cover-up over her head to hide her white bikini. She notices me over her shoulder and moves a towel self-consciously to hide her legs, which are still speckled from the bed bug bites.

"Hey," I say and pull up a chair next to her, trying to play it cool. Unfortunately, being close to her has the reverse effect. I've definitely never felt this way before. I'm in so much trouble.

"Hi," she says softly with a sideways glance and her trademark blush. "How's your dad?"

I lean back and run my hands through my hair as I watch the guys horsing around in the pool. "He's feeling better now. The chemotherapy takes a lot out of him, though, so I did some work around the ranch to let him rest until he got his strength back."

"What type of cancer does he have?"

"Non-Hodgkin lymphoma." I stare at my clasped hands for a while, then glance at her. "They caught it early, so hopefully it will turn out okay."

"I'm sure it will. How about your mom? How's she holding up?"

"Uh." I hesitate because Chuck and BJ don't even know anything about my mom. Not sure if it's because they never asked, or I never told. I lower my voice so only Della can hear and say, "My mom was killed by a drunk driver when I was ten. It's just my dad and me."

Della's lips press together sympathetically and the space between her eyebrows creases. Her eyes meet mine as if she's searching for something. Or maybe she's not searching. Maybe she already found it. "I can't even imagine what losing your mom as a child must have been like for you, but if you ever feel like you need to talk, I'm happy to listen."

Emotion rises in my throat from her offer. I don't know why. I'm not an emotional guy. But there's something about the way she said it. So genuine. "Thanks," I eventually say, after taking a deep breath to steady my voice.

Chuck swims over and folds his arms on the edge of the pool, looking slyly back and forth between Della and me. He can tell we're having a moment and it makes him smirk because he thinks he's got five hundred bucks coming his way. I stand to send the message that he's wrong.

"What do you guys feel like for dinner?" I ask to shift the intensity. "Your choices are pasta, rice, or oatmeal."

"Actually, my scholarship money came in today," Della says. "I was planning to do a grocery run and make you guys a proper dinner as a thank you. If you want me to."

"Hell yeah," Chuck says as he climbs out of the pool.

"Sounds good to me," BJ adds, still floating on his back.

I nod. "Sure. We're doing a Costco shop for all the big stuff after we get back from the rodeo this weekend, but there's a market down the street. Do you want me to come with you? We can pick up some things for the next few days, too."

Chuck and BJ exchange a raised eyebrow with each other.

Della nods and stands. "Okay. I just need to change. I'll meet you out front." She ducks by me and disappears into the house.

BJ throws a pool noodle at me. "What are you doing, idiot? She's been here a day-and-a-half and you're already on the verge of failing."

"What? I can't offer to go with her to the grocery store to show her what you guys like to eat?"

Chuck takes his boots off and dumps the water out. "Whatever's going on between you two has nothing to do with things you eat at the grocery store. I'll take my five hundred bucks in cash or check, whichever is more convenient for you."

"I'm not breaking any rules. I'm just being helpful," I say and turn to head inside.

"I want my winnings in cash!" BJ shouts as I walk away.

There are a lot of reasons why I shouldn't pursue anything with Della – including every complication that goes along with living together if it works out, or worse, if it doesn't work out – the money I'd owe them isn't even on the top of the list. Unfortunately, none of the reasons hold much weight when we're in close proximity.

She comes back downstairs dressed in a white blouse, white tennis shoes, and pink pants that are rolled at the ankle. Her dark hair is pulled into a ponytail and although she doesn't seem to wear makeup, her lips are shiny as if she put on some sort of gloss. I try to ignore that, and as we leave the house, I remind myself of all the reasons it would be a bad idea to pursue her. I have canvas grocery bags in my truck, so I offer to drive, then open the passenger door for her. Walking around the back of the truck to the driver's side, I mumble, "Come on, Havie. Stop acting like you can't take your eyes off her. It's a trip to Trader Joe's, not a date."

As I back out of the driveway, her gaze scans the interior of the truck, checking it out. I keep it clean, which she seems surprised by. "How far is the drive to your dad's ranch?" she asks.

"Close to four hours. It's near Three Rivers, California."

"Is that where you grew up?"

I nod and turn left at the lights. "Yeah. It's a nice area. I can take you there sometime."

She smiles and runs her palms along her thighs as if she's nervous or something. "I grew up in a village about four hours outside of Moscow. It's not a nice area. I won't take you there sometime. I mean, for your own sake. Not because I wouldn't take you if you wanted to go. I'm just sure you wouldn't like it there. That's all. I would take you. It's not sight-seeing worthy, though."

"Sight-seeing worthy or not, growing up in Russia is interesting. Is your extended family still in the village?"

"My dad's side of the family is. My mom's side of the family is actually former Russian aristocracy, so they fled Russia a long time ago. Her parents weren't thrilled about her marrying a poor country boy that she met at university." Her eyes widen as she glances at me. "No offence. I have nothing against country boys. Not that I have a thing for them, either. Just nothing against them. Or poor people. Love is the most important thing. Never mind. I don't know what I'm talking about."

I chuckle as she shifts uncomfortably in her seat. "Should we call you princess?"

She smiles, relieved that I wasn't offended by the poor country boy diss. "No. If we were in the nineteenth century I would have been on par with a more fully dressed Kardashian at best. Nowadays I'm just a middle-class Russian-Canadian immigrant." She winks. "You can address me as Lady Della if you like, though."

Being a descendant of aristocrats explains a lot, maybe not her goofy humor. That might be more a country pauper thing. I'm still smiling as I pull into a parking spot. We both hop out and I ask, "Do you speak Russian?"

"Yes, my parents both speak it at home, especially when they're mad at me."

I grab a grocery cart and follow her into the store. As she heads to the produce section, I chuckle at the image of her parents shouting at her. "I can't imagine anyone ever being mad at you."

"Oh, trust me it happens." Her nose wrinkles as if she's not proud to admit it but is too honest to deny it. "You don't know me well enough yet to know I can be very grumpy if I'm stressed. And I get PMS moody, not that you probably want to know that, but maybe you guys should know if you're going to have a female roommate." She pauses to choose avocados from the display and places them in the cart. "You said you're an only child, so if you haven't spent a lot of time around sisters or girlfriends. I mean, I'm sure you've had lots of girlfriends or have a girlfriend." Her eyes dart sideways to check my expression before she distractedly pokes a row of papayas one at a time.

Was that her way of asking if I'm single?

Before I have a chance to say anything she starts talking again like a racehorse out of the gate. "You definitely probably have a girlfriend, or maybe you like men. I'm sorry, I don't mean to assume or imply anything, or not imply anything."

She's unquestionably fishing for my status. And I could tell her. But that might unlock a whole load of awkwardness. For both of us.

"Sorry," she says after she notices that my mood shifted into something more serious. "I'm just trying, somewhat unsuccessfully, to say that women, some women, me, I get irritable sometimes." She picks a bundle of asparagus and a clamshell of cherry tomatoes. Then, in an oddly impressive way continues her animated gestures as she talks with her hands full. "Bottom line, living with me means you can anticipate some eye rolls and an occasional snappy tone of voice once a month. I apologize for that in advance. And if you ever get angry at me I'll remind you of this conversation in an I-warned-you way, which will likely only aggravate you more." She studies the firmness of a mango before making eye contact with me again. "And you'll likely end up shouting at me in Russian."

I smile and grab two lemons and two limes. "I'll steer clear of you once a month. And I promise not to learn any Russian."

"I have more flaws." She pulls a grapefruit from the display and scrambles to catch the others before they roll down the slope. "I'm completely uncoordinated, as you might have already noticed. You'd be surprised how angry a person can get when, due to clumsiness, you break or ruin something they love. Just ask my sister about her former diamond earring that is now in the Greater Vancouver Regional District sewer system thanks to a mishap that involved a public toilet and a bee. You don't need to know the details. I can be annoying when I'm in a chatty mood, which is almost always. Also, sometimes when I get nervous I jam my foot in my mouth and offend people by saying something inadvertently offensive or borderline stupid." She glances at me almost as if she expects me to confirm that one.

I add a bag of apples to the cart. "Well, nobody's perfect.

And it's entertaining for me when you do something embarrassing like your attempted touchdown dance that nearly blew out your ACL after figuring out the alarm code."

Her face turns almost magenta and she clenches her eyes shut as if she's attempting to erase that incident from either her memory or mine. She haphazardly tosses a head of lettuce, a bunch of carrots, and a bag of baby potatoes into the cart. Then, without saying anything, she speed-walks ahead and turns the corner into the cereal aisle.

Sexy and a goofball. Can't say I've ever met anyone quite like her.

Chapter 5

Della

All three of the boys are seated at the dinner table, laughing at a joke Chuck cracked. I think it included some sort of obscure sexual innuendo, so I don't really get why it's funny, but I'm smiling because they enjoyed the grilled fish and asparagus dinner I made. The brownies were a hit, too. They were Easton's choice of dessert because he doesn't like pie. Who doesn't like pie?

"Thanks, Della," BJ says. "Everything was really great. We have a new contender for best cook in the house." He smacks Easton's shoulder to give him a hard time.

I shake my head to turn down the title. "I only have three go-to options, and one of them is spaghetti, so don't get too excited."

They all laugh.

Easton's eyes meet mine for an extra beat before he takes the last bite of his brownie. Chuck jumps up from the table to clear the dishes. "Thanks for dinner, Della, but I gotta go. Janine is waiting for me. Date night. AKA Chuck gets lucky night." He loads the dinner plates into the dishwasher and then leaves.

"Chuck has a girlfriend?" I turn to look at both Easton and BJ, whoever wants to answer.

"When it suits him," BJ says as he gets up and clears the rest of the dessert dishes. "I have to jet, too. I've got a group project meeting on campus and I can't afford to drop anymore marks. Don't wait up."

He leaves, and I spin my fork around on the table, thinking about what BJ said about Chuck and Janine.

"You okay?" Easton asks.

I nod, not really. "Does 'when it suits him' mean he cheats on his girlfriend?"

Easton's expression makes it seem as if he wants to answer honestly but knows I won't like it, which technically is confirmation that it's true.

"Does his girlfriend know?"

"If she doesn't know about at least half of it, she's not that bright." Easton stands and walks over to the kitchen to hand-wash the pots and pans. He sneaks another brownie straight out of the pan and pops it into his mouth.

"I don't want to judge, but why would she tolerate that?"

He shrugs and places the pot upside down on the drying rack. "They've been dating for three years. And they're probably going to get married. Maybe they both want to live the best of both worlds while they're still young."

Part of that does make sense—take risks and experience life to the fullest so you have no regrets when you get older and settle down. But the other part is really hard for me to accept. How could you be physically intimate with someone you don't care about when it hurts the person you do care about? I have no experience to reference it against. Maybe I would feel differently if I were in their shoes. I ponder the ethics of it for a while, but then the fact that Easton's hair is loose distracts me. When he moves it fans out like feathers. Wild and delicate at the same time. Like visual poetry. I pick up my brownie with my bare hand and bite into it as I watch him clean the counter. Both are delicious.

After the kitchen is spotless again, he sits back at the table and offers me some wine.

"No, thank you," I say, referring to the wine. Then I study his face. He can obviously feel me doing it because he looks up, waiting. "Do you cheat on your girlfriend?"

His eyes remain locked on mine, and with the most intense expression I have ever witnessed in another person, he says, "I don't currently have a girlfriend. And I don't cheat on anything."

Whoa. Oh my goodness. Why does it feel like a supernova just blasted through me? My heart is palpitating. I think he can tell. He's looking at me so seriously. He can read my thoughts. Is that why the other guys left? Is it that obvious that I'm crushing on Easton? Do they not realize that leaving me alone with him is not actually doing me any favors? I'm sweating like a maniac. Maybe I should go for a walk. He'd probably offer to escort me. He definitely would, like a knight in shining armor.

"Homework," I blurt out.

His eyebrows raise, amused at my weirdness again.

"I have reading. Tomorrow's class. I'm going to my room. Reading in my room. For homework. Then sleeping." I stand and the chair almost topples over behind me, but he stretches his arm out and catches it before it falls. Then he pulls it back so I can attempt a more graceful exit. "Goodnight."

"Night." He chuckles before taking a sip of wine.

Unfortunately, he's probably watching me as I walk away. It's incredibly difficult to command my legs to function properly when I know someone is possibly assessing each step. The hypervigilance makes me overthink an action which is ingrained in most people by approximately twelve months of age but doesn't come particularly natural to me. Over-thinking is bad. Where do my hands normally go? Are they supposed to swing? They feel weird at my side.

Only I would forget how to walk.

I race up the stairs and close my bedroom door. Pull it together, Della. If you're going to live here, you need to get a grip. After several recovering breaths, I sit at my desk and open the textbook, then stare at the page for almost a minute before I realize the book is upside down. It's probably a good thing I didn't go to high school with boys. I'd still be there.

My phone rings. It's Stuart. "Hey, how's it going at Everley's?"

"Good. You didn't mention she's a guy named Easton, though."

He chuckles. "Yeah, well, little miss virtuous wouldn't

have given it a shot if she knew that ahead of time. He's great, though, right?"

"Yeah. He's great." So great. I stare in a dreamy way out the window, but since it's dark outside, all I see is my own reflection. Oh, man, is that a chunk of rice in my hair? How did that get there? "How are you, Stu?"

"Good. The reason I'm calling is because your dad contacted me."

"Ugh. So Annoying. I can't believe he bothered you. Obviously, the fact that I've been dodging his calls wasn't a clear enough message that I don't want to talk to him right now."

"He wants me to give him your address. I don't really want to get mixed up in any family drama, so if you want him to have it, you should send it to him. If you don't want him to have it, I'm going to tell him that."

"Why does he want it anyway?"

"I don't know. Maybe to forward your mail or show up at your doorstep and ground you."

"Great." I lean my elbows on my desk and rub the tension out of my forehead. "Did you tell him my roommates are men?"

"No. I didn't tell him anything. But you're probably going to have to call him."

"I'll call him so he knows I'm okay. Don't give him the address. I'll set up a post box he can send stuff to."

"All right. How are you for money? Do you need anything?"

"No. The student loan came in today. But thank you."

"Call your dad."

"Okay." I end the call with Stuart and dial my mom. She never answers her mobile phone because she can never find it. It's the perfect excuse for me not to talk to them. I leave a message to let them know I'm all settled in and promise to send the address. That should earn me another week or two before Dad hounds Stuart again. I also text my sister. We weren't really that close growing up because she's five years older than me. She's already married and has a kid now. But she supported me when I decided to go against Dad's wishes and pursue engineering instead of a teaching degree. She always caved into the pressure and did everything he expected her to do, which is why she completely understands how hard it was for me to come to Stanford. It's the one and only rebellious thing I've ever done, which is why I really don't want to mess up and give him reason to gloat. The last thing my sister said before I started off on the road trip was that she admired me. It still makes me feel warm and fuzzy when I think about it. She doesn't respond to the text. She must be busy with the baby, so I pick up my textbook.

Chapter two, paragraph one. Go.

Easton is still downstairs. It sounds like he's doing a load of laundry. Maybe I should plan to do all my studying at the library. That might work if I don't spend the entire time thinking about what he might be doing back at the house. I wonder if studying with him would be more or less distracting since my mind wouldn't have to drift very far. Who am I kidding? I'm just trying to come up with a justifiable excuse to ask him to study with me. Nice try.

He's coming upstairs. He went into his room.

Chapter two, paragraph one.

He crosses the hall to the bathroom, then the shower turns on.

Chapter two, paragraph two.

Shoot. Now I'm thinking about what he looks like with water cascading over his smooth, dark skin. Muscles. Long hair.

Chapter two, paragraph three.

Hmm. He made a sound, more like a groan, like he's straining. Or like he hurt himself. Maybe he stubbed his toe. That's something I would do. I did do it. This morning. But he must be okay. He just sighed in relief, like a huge stress was released. Ha. I wonder if he knows that when he stubs his toe it sounds like something sexy. Wait. I sit up straight, close my book, and stare at the wall that divides my room and their bathroom. Was it something sexy? Guys do that in the shower, right? No. Maybe. Oh my gosh. Did I just listen to Easton masturbating? Why am I whispering my thoughts? He can't hear me. But I heard him. I invaded his privacy. I stand and pace around the room frantically. I feel weird, like I should tell him the walls aren't exactly sound proof. But that would be even more awkward.

Oh no, the bathroom door opened. He crosses the hall to his room. I wonder if he streaked across naked or wrapped a towel around his waist. Uh oh. He's back in the hall. He's going back downstairs. Sit down, Della. Stop acting like a freak. Chapter what? Paragraph what?

He knocks on my door. "Hey, Della. Are you decent?"

Um, of course. What kind of question is that? "Yes. Are you?"

He laughs and opens my door. He's wearing shorts and a T-shirt, hair tied in a knot. I blink at him repeatedly, not sure how to act. "Sorry to interrupt your studies. I'm going to make tea if you want some?"

"Sure."

"And I was also thinking since the rodeo this coming weekend is only an hour away, you might want to come out for the finals on Saturday and see what we do. It's up to you. I just wanted to make sure you know you're always welcome."

I nod. "Okay. Thank you. That sounds fun."

He smiles, then steps back into the hall.

"I heard you stub your toe in the shower," I blurt out. "Are you okay?"

His expression gets stuck somewhere between about to laugh and complete bewilderment. Eventually he flashes an Everley super model wink and says, "I think I'm going to be all right."

After he leaves, I lean forward and bang my forehead against my desk, repeatedly. Stupid. Stupid. I'm going to die of embarrassment.

Chapter 6

Easton

Della joins us on the driveway as we're loading Chuck's truck with our rodeo gear, getting ready to leave for the final day of competition. "Morning," I say.

"Morning." Her nose wrinkles after looking down at her flip-flops, jeans, and white tank top. "I don't know what to wear to a rodeo. Is this all right?"

"That's perfect," BJ says. "You might want to bring a sweater for later, though. It can get cold at night."

"Night? How long does the event take? I thought it was eight seconds each."

He laughs. "There are a lot of events. Then we'll go for dinner. And there's a dance after. We'll be out late."

She inhales with a hint of frustration as if she feels that would have been useful information to have known before-hand. "I'll be right back."

I've got my new rigging stretched out in the garage, so I follow her inside to get it. Before I head back outside, I also grab a white cowboy hat that some girl BJ brought home once left here.

Della emerges from the house wearing a light-blue cotton dress that makes all three of us stare. No more bed bug bites to distract from her flawless skin. She changed into leather sandals and she's carrying a denim jacket. She also pulled her ponytail out, ready for an outing that includes a dance later. Damn. Heads are definitely going to turn at the rodeo.

"Is that suitcase handle thing what you hold onto the horse with?" she asks.

"Yeah. This one is new." I place the hat on her head and hand the rigging to her, so she can see what it feels like.

She tips the brim of the hat. "Thank you." Then she lifts the rigging to test how heavy it is. "Eight seconds doesn't seem very long. Is it really that hard to hold on?"

"Only when the horse is moving, darlin'," BJ says.

All of us laugh.

Della hands the rigging back to me and runs her fingers over the tassels of our chaps, which are laid out in the back of the truck. Chuck's are purple with yellow flames. BJ's are two-tone blue. Mine are red, black, and gold. "These are pretty."

"Which ones do you like the best?" Chuck asks.

She looks at him and notices the lightning bolts he got shaved onto the side of his head. They accentuate the ridiculousness of his mullet even more. "The red, black, and gold ones are my favorites," she says. "But they're all nice."

"Do you like my new haircut?"

"Uh." She studies it and her forehead creases. "It's different."

BJ smacks him in the back of the head. "See. Even the sweetest girl on the planet can't find nothing nice to say about that redneck mop."

"You don't like my chaps. You don't like my do. That hurts my feelings, Della," Chuck shouts as he gets into the driver's seat.

She blinks as if she's about to get teary eyed and then glances at me.

"He's kidding. It's not possible to hurt Chuck's feelings. And if people actually liked his business in the front, party in the back look, he wouldn't wear it that way." I open the back door of the cab for her and she climbs into the back-row seating behind Chuck. Then I walk around to get into the back on the other side. BJ takes the front passenger seat and we head out.

"Your truck is really nice," Della says to Chuck to smooth things over.

"It's too late for flattery, sweetheart. You already insulted my hillbilly hair."

"The truck really is nice," she says to me as she runs her hand over the leather seats. "I had no idea trucks could be this luxurious."

I feign a sad look. "So, you weren't impressed by my two thousand and five Silverado?"

"Yes. Or, I mean no, I was. Impressed." A scarlet hue rises up her neck onto her cheeks and the terror of offending me makes her eyes widen. "Your truck is nice, too."

"I'm just messing with you. Chuck's truck is a sweet ride. It's nicer than the rest of ours."

"Thanks, buddy," Chuck says and reaches back to fist bump me.

Pretending to be offended, BJ gasps and turns to glare at me. "You like Chuck's truck better than mine?"

"Chuckie needs to be the best at something. Can't you let him have the best truck?"

"No." BJ crosses his arms to sell the sulk.

Chuck holds his hand up to make us all be quiet as he sings the chorus of an old George Strait song, then he says, "Although I appreciate the compliment, Della. You can't compare a man's truck or cock to another man's truck or cock unless you're hoping for a fight."

"Watch your language, man," I say.

Chuck shrugs his shoulders apologetically. "Sorry for cursing. I should have said trucks and penises. Or is it peni? That sounds worse than swearing, if you ask me."

BJ takes a sip from his thermos, which is likely filled with vodka and orange juice. "You could use rig for both penis and truck."

Chuck points at him to agree. "Rig works. I like it."

Della's eyes dart cautiously between each of us. "I can't tell if you guys are joking or being serious."

BJ rolls his head to look at her over his shoulder. "We don't ever joke about trucks. Or penises."

I wink at her and whisper, "They're joking."

She nods, but her eyebrows are still cinched together from the worry that she's done something wrong. After letting her sweat it out for a while, BJ reaches into the back seat and offers her a piece of licorice to show her there are no hard feelings. She smiles and takes one for herself and one for me. "So, which one of you is the best at bucking?"

I chuckle at how her word choice sounds. I can't help it. BJ turns in his seat to face her. "What did you call it?"

"Bucking. Isn't that what you call it?"

"I call it a lot of things, darlin'. What do you call it, Chuckie?"

"Dirty rodeo, entering the chute, eight seconds of glory, backing the rig up, or bareback bucking works, too. No matter what you call it, I'm the best at it. I ride 'em like a pro."

Idiots. I should have known better than to invite Della along with them. It's going to be a long hour of juvenile jokes and sexual innuendos.

"They're talking about sex, aren't they?"

"Yes," I say, "We call it bareback bronc riding."

Since I'm the only one giving her a straight answer she turns in her seat to face me. "Are the horses wild?"

"Not in the true sense of the word, no. They're bred for bucking and raised in a pasture, but they have to be gentled enough to be trailered and loaded into the chute. Usually they're geldings or mares."

"What's a gelding?"

Chuck raises his hand to ask a question. "Is balls a swear word?"

I shake my head to ignore him, then answer her, "A gelding is a castrated horse."

Her face winces as if she can feel the pain. "And what happens if you all hang on for eight seconds? How do you decide who gets to win?"

"Judges score each ride. They look at your form and style—how well the horse bucks and how well you spur. If you don't mark his shoulders out with your spurs before his front legs hit the ground, or if you touch the horse with your free hand, you get disqualified. If the horse stumbles they might give you a re-ride."

"So, if today is the final round, which one of you is in the lead after last night?"

"BJ has the highest score right now. But we all have a chance to win it today."

"Good job, Bailey." She leans forward to pat his shoulder. "What's the best score you can get?"

He turns, still smiling from the compliment. "It's scored out of one hundred. Posting in the eighties is really good. If we post something in the nineties you should cheer your butt off."

"All right." She sits back to relax and adjusts the hat. "I'll do a back flip and land in the splits if any of you score in the nineties."

The boys go silent in the front seat, no doubt imagining her doing bareback bucking acrobatics in her summer dress.

There is no way someone as uncoordinated as Della could do a back flip. She obviously said it to pull their chains, which makes me smile. "Just make sure you don't really blow out your knee when you do cheer."

She laughs and shoves my shoulder playfully. "I wish you hadn't noticed that."

Chuck's eyes meet mine in the rearview mirror for a second, then he glances at BJ. They probably think it's only a matter of time before I end up handing over my rodeo winnings to them. It would be worth it, but what they don't realize is a girl like Della would never give it up that easy. I'd have to work damn hard to even have a shot with her.

Chuck turns up the music and BJ is focused on his phone, probably sexting. So, after driving in silence for a while Della turns to me. "What do you plan to do with your MBA?"

"Run the family cattle ranch. My thesis is on sustainable farming practices, so I'll probably get involved with speculative investments in that industry. What do you want to do with your engineering degree?"

"My main interest is water sustainability and regulation. I'd like to work on systems and infrastructure to make sure the world's water supply is protected and accessible."

As she passionately describes why she chose her field of study and enthusiastically shares her future ideas about ground water and aquatic ecosystems, a bunch of childhood memories that I haven't thought about in a long time flood my mind. Specifically, things about my mom. And the reminder of her takes me off guard. When Della stops to check my reaction, I don't know quite what to say.

In response to my speechlessness Della shifts uncomfortably in her seat, then blurts out, "We would die without water." As soon as the words leave her mouth she hits her forehead with the heel of her hand. "Sorry. I don't know why I said that. It's not a competition. Farming is important, too. We would also die without food, obviously. I wasn't trying to sound like my career with water will be more important than your career in sustainable farming. They are both cool, or important, or whatever."

She makes brief eye contact, probably completely confused by the fact that I'm borderline choked up about the unexpected reminder of my mom.

"Sorry." She fidgets with the strap of her purse and stares down at her hands. "I don't know why I jumped to assume that you disapproved. And it really doesn't matter if you do. You're entitled to your own opinions." She inhales sharply and then sighs as if she's disappointed in herself for getting defensive. "I guess I'm used to justifying my reasons with my dad and it accidently spewed out. Just ignore me."

I study her expression as she turns her focus to the passing scenery out the window. It's weird, right? What are the chances I'd meet someone who has the exact same passion as my mom? It could be a fluke. Or it might be significant. Why does it feel like a big deal? It's not. It's just a random coincidence.

"Hey." I reach across the cab and touch her elbow to get her attention. "The reason it took me a long time to react isn't because I was judging your goals. The opposite in fact. I was thrown off for a minute because my mom was a water protector. It brought up some memories of her as you talked about it. It's a good thing."

"Really?" Della smiles at the commonality. "That's really cool. What type of water protection activities was she involved in?"

"She was in charge of community education initiatives for water conservation in Three Rivers. She was also involved in a lot of national advocacy projects and even a few protests."

"So, I would have liked her?"

"Absolutely." I smile to myself as I check off all the qualities in Della that my mom would have liked. She would have loved her—actually—and not only because of the save-the-water ideals.

She spins in her seat to face me. "Sorry I misread your silence and jumped into defense mode."

"I get it. I had to defend my choice to pursue an MBA with my dad."

"Really? Why didn't he agree with it?"

"He runs the ranch on a high school education. My grandfather before him ran it on a seventh-grade education. He would have preferred if I skipped the MBA and offered an extra set of hands on the ranch all these years instead."

Her eyes track over my face as she decodes my expression. "If you don't need the degree, then why was it important to you to do it?"

Got to hand it to her. She has a way of cutting to the core. My real reason for getting an MBA isn't something I've ever talked about with anyone before. My dad likely knows on some level because he's experienced discrimination and racism his whole life, too. But his understanding of my motivation to gain legitimacy is unspoken, as is most of our relationship. "Let's just say you and I both have something to prove to people who don't believe we can do whatever we set our minds to."

She smiles and lifts her hand to give me a high five. "Cheers to proving the doubters wrong."

"Cheers to that."

"Hell yeah," Chuckie pipes in from the front. "Fuck the doubters."

"Language," both BJ and I say at the same time.

"Sorry. Screw the doubters. Poo on the doubters. Doubters are dumb." He throws up his hand to give up. "It loses its impact without the curse word. Sorry, Della, sometimes the F word is the only word that can adequately express how I feel about something. It's just a word. I personally find the word cellophane offensive, but I ain't gonna ask people to stop using it."

"I didn't ask you not to swear," she says in her defense.

"You wince every time someone does. And these two keep yelling at me for it."

"Sorry," she says quietly.

"Don't apologize, Della." BJ shoves Chuckie's shoulder. "Grow up, man. She's a lady. You should be the one apologizing."

Chuckie scoffs. "Sorry for being a country bumpkin who offends your sophisticated sensibilities, ma'am. But I am who I am. Get used to it. Or get out."

"That's real nice," BJ mutters.

I make eye contact with Della. "Ignore him."

She nods as if she plans to try, but I can tell she's uncomfortable with the idea of someone not liking her, even if it's someone like Chuck.

I lean over and gesture with my finger for her to move closer. "He's just testing you to see where your breaking point is. Don't let him get to you and you'll earn his respect forever," I whisper in her ear.

She nods again with the inspiration to do just that.

Della and I talk for the rest of the ride. Somehow, we move seamlessly from school to politics to travel. She's smart, well-read, and she's travelled to five continents. I've never been out of the US, so her stories about foreign countries are especially interesting.

By the time we arrive at the fairgrounds Chuck and BJ aren't even listening to us anymore—maybe because they really aren't interested, but more likely because they have a vested interest in Della and me getting close. We drive through the contestants' gate and park on the grass lot next to the outdoor arena. It's early, so I give Della a tour through the vendor and concession area while Chuck and BJ go get hotdogs. It's not quite lunchtime, but she and I also stop to buy pulled pork buns and ice teas, walking through the fairgrounds as we eat. Eventually we make our way over to the pens where the bucking horses are kept.

"Wow. They're impressive animals," she says as she leans her elbows on the fence. "Their muscles ripple like athletes." She watches them for a while, then turns to me. "What made you decide to be a bronc rider?"

I step in and lean on the fence next to her. "I didn't really decide. It was more of a natural progression. Growing up on the ranch I watched my dad and all my uncles break horses. I saddle broke my first horse all by myself when I was eight years old. Since I was getting bucked around every day anyway, getting paid to stay on a bucking horse was a bonus. And it's fun."

She sips her iced tea through a straw and the way her lips surround it makes my heart speed up. "What do love about it the most?"

"Love about what?"

She laughs as if she thinks it's weird that I lost the thread of the conversation. "Bronc riding."

"Oh." I've never directly been asked that question before. I push my hat back and watch the horses as I think about it. "Riding bareback on a wild horse is the purest form of horsemanship—it keeps me connected to my heritage."

She nods and smiles. "That is a beautiful way to describe it. Have you ever been seriously hurt?"

I shake my head to downplay the injuries. "I've broken my wrist three times. My lung collapsed last season, which hurt. And I had a bad concussion in high school, which made me temporarily blind."

She gasps and frowns. "Oh my gosh. You're crazy."

"Maybe." I rest my hand on the small of her back to guide her to start walking again. I have to pull her elbow to sidetrack her past a manure pile. "Watch where you're stepping."

"Oh. Ew." She hops over closer to me and wrinkles her nose. "Is that what I think it is?"

"Yeah. That's why we all wear boots. We'll have to get you some for next time."

Her cheeks light up like a pink sunset and the corners of her mouth turn up in the slightest smile as she keeps her eyes fixed on the grass. I'm not sure if she's embarrassed because she almost stepped in manure, or if she's happy about the inadvertent invitation to come along again next time. Maybe it wasn't inadvertent.

I stop in front of the back pen to show her the bulls.

"Yikes. They have horns." She stands five feet back from the fence. "Why in the world would someone try to ride a beast like that? Bull riders must have a death wish. Or they're not right in the head."

I chuckle. "Everybody in rodeo is not right in the head. But once it's in your blood you can't help it."

"Was your dad in rodeo, too?"

"Yeah. He was a bulldogger."

Her eyebrows angle dubiously. "What type of event do they do with dogs?"

"It's not with dogs. Bulldogging is what they call steer wrestling. The rider slides off a horse at full speed and wrestles the steer to the ground."

"Really? Is that a practical skill? Do you have to actually tackle cows on the ranch?"

"No. Not exactly." I chuckle. "Sometimes the ornery ones need to be wrestled with when we're branding. I'm better at roping them, though. I used to compete in the roping event when I was younger." I wink. "But the ladies like the bronc riders better."

The wink makes her bite her bottom lip. Damn, that's a move that's going to drive me crazy if she keeps doing it. I exhale and remove my hat to run my hand through my hair. She doesn't even know how sexy she is. Unfortunately, my body definitely does.

As we walk, she asks me more about rodeo and ranching. I'm not normally the chattiest guy in the world, but I like answering her questions because she's genuinely interested in the answers. And since I'm also more than interested in getting to know her better, we talk the entire time as I show her the rest of the fairgrounds.

When we return to the participants' lot, Chuck and BJ are both sitting on the tailgate, wrapping their riding arms. They're grinning at the way Della just looked up at me with her big doe eyes. Avoiding their eager-to-get-paid expressions, I turn to face Della. "I need to warm-up and get ready. Do you want to hang out here with us or head over to the grandstand to watch the barrel racing? It's going to start soon."

She glances at the stands and then over at Chuck and BJ. "I'm interested to learn about what you guys do for your pre-game warm-up, or whatever you call it. But I wouldn't want to be in the way if I stayed."

"You won't be in the way. You'll probably get bored watching us stretch, though. And you're definitely going to wish you didn't have to listen to Chuck's inappropriate jokes. But you're welcome to hang out here." I pull out a fold-up lawn chair from the back of the truck and set it up for her.

"I won't be bored, but I don't want to mess up anybody's routine by lingering."

BJ hops off the tailgate and slides on his leather vest. "Making lewd comments to girls is part of Chuckie's warm-up routine. And I personally perform better with an audience, so you'll be doing both of us a favor."

She looks over at me. "Are you sure I won't be in the way?"

"Positive. Sit down." I slide the chair over for her and then open my bag to grab my spurs and boot ties.

Chuck, who's only wearing his compression shorts, sits on the grass to stretch his hamstrings. "So, Della. Back to our earlier conversation about how you'll celebrate if any of us scores in the nineties; what kind of underwear are you wearing under that pretty dress of yours?"

"Shut up, Chuckie," both BJ and I say at the same time.

"What? That is a legitimate question. If she's going commando I'm about to have the ride of my life."

I shake my head and shoot her a you-asked-for-it look. Either she's inexplicably amused by his infantilism or she's trying to prove that he can't get to her.

Chuck and BJ both have good rides—seventy-nine and eighty-three. I'm up last. My horse is loaded in the chute. And I'm nervous as hell. I underestimated how having Della here would affect my performance. It almost feels like the first time I ever rode.

"Woo!" Chuck slaps my back and then hooks the latigo. "I hope Della is warming up for that commando back flip because I feel a ninety coming on. Show her how it's done, Havie."

Motivated by his enthusiasm I strap on my neck collar and climb into the chute. After pulling my hat down over my forehead I wedge my glove into my rigging, roll my fingers, and crack my arm back for a tight fit. Lean back. Heels up. Nod.

The gate opens and the world literally blurs. I pull my knees up and drag my spurs along the horse's shoulders, hitting his rhythm. The crowd roars because they can sense it's a good ride. Better than good. Eight seconds of ripping on a horse that's bucking like a champion.

The buzzer goes and the pick-up horse nudges next to me. I slide over its backside and land on my feet. As I tip my hat, I scan the crowd. Della is bouncing up and down in the front row and whistling with her fingers in her mouth. I point at her and then turn to watch the scoreboard. Too bad she was joking about the back flip because my score is definitely going to be at least a ninety.

Chapter 7

Della

The boys are so excited about how well Easton rode. They are literally hooting and hollering as we pile out of Chuck's truck and head to the front door of the bar. They ended up placing first, second, and third. Easton's ride was apparently close to perfect and they are all pumped up. I have no idea what a good or bad technique is. But, even to me, it was obvious Easton was in control the entire time. And the horse was so powerful. At the start of the event, when the first two riders in a row fell off—one on his head—I couldn't fathom why anybody would attempt to do something so painful and idiotic. Then Easton rode, and now, even though I have vicarious whiplash just from watching their heads being thrashed back and forth for an eternally long eight seconds, I can absolutely see why they love doing it.

The bouncer lets us pass without paying cover because the boys are rodeo contestants. The drinking age back home in Canada is nineteen, but in the three years since I've been legal, I've only been to a bar once before. It wasn't really my scene during my undergrad since I don't drink and can't dance. And the prospect of picking up a stranger was nearly panic attack inducing back then. It still is. That bar was a techno-type dance bar. This one is a rustic country bar that could pass as a barn.

A house band with a female lead singer is on stage playing something twangy. I don't know any country songs. Hopefully they don't all sound quite that down home. Chuck asks us what we want to drink and heads over to the bar. He walks somewhat oddly, like an arrogant penguin with swagger. It might be a combination of the cowboy boots and a bronc riding groin strain thing, but BJ and Easton walk normally, so more likely it's a Chuck thing. They hang out with me at a bar-height table that is designed for standing at. The band goes on a break and the DJ music they are replaced with is a million times better, even though I still don't recognize the songs. Two girls who must already know the boys come over to congratulate Easton. There is a lot of arm touching and shoulder hanging going on from their end. Flirting doesn't look too hard. I could do that.

Easton introduces me to them, but they're more interested in talking to him. Obviously.

"Do you want to dance, Della?" BJ asks and extends his arm as an invitation.

"Oh. Uh." No. That would be tragic. "I can't dance. I mean physically I can move my limbs, but it would more closely meet the definition of a seizure than any modern definition of dancing. Even if I knew the song, which I don't, it wouldn't make a difference. Thank you for asking, but no." I touch his arm to practice the flirty thing. It feels weird when I do it. I probably just creeped him out.

He nods to accept that I turned him down. And now there is an awkward silence.

"Really. Thanks for asking. I'm too klutzy. I would like to dance with you, but I lack rhythm. There is a good chance I'm tone deaf. One time at a family wedding I attempted the chicken dance with my sister and I knocked over a candle. It set the bride's dress on fire. Literally. Flames." I gesture with my hands to demonstrate the enormity of the inferno. "They had to use an extinguisher to save her life. It was awful. I was traumatized. So, yeah, maybe for your own safety and the longevity of the bar you should ask—" I point conspicuously over my shoulder at the red-headed girl who is talking to Easton.

"I can teach you how to dance, darlin'." BJ wraps his hand around mine and leads me out to the dance floor.

I reluctantly follow, mostly because I know it will draw more attention to me if I flail and attempt to escape. Once we are on the dance floor I survey the surroundings for flammable objects. The coast is clear unless we get too close to that long horn thing on the wall.

"All right." BJ faces me and rests his hands on my shoulders to make me square up. "I'm going to show you how to two-step. It's real easy, basically just walking."

"I'm not consistently good at walking."

He chuckles and slides his hat back slightly as if he's worried I'm going to knock it off his head. Probably a prudent move. "All you have to do is let me lead. Put your weight on your left foot."

After a half-second delay to confirm with myself which is my left foot, I shift my weight.

He shifts right. "The first two steps are quick. Then the next two are slow. Like this." He demonstrates on the spot and I copy him. "Now go ahead and turn in a circle by yourself – quick, quick, slow, slow. Quick, quick, slow, slow."

I don't know how to do that, so he does it. It's technically more of a square, but it's not actually that hard. It just feels a little embarrassing to do the four steps facing each wall of the room until I circle back to face him.

"See, you got it already," he says encouragingly. "Now hold my hand with your right hand and rest your left hand on my shoulder."

Wow. Holy cow. His muscles are simultaneously smooth and rock hard like the marble of a masterly carved Roman statue. No wonder the ladies are flocking around all the rodeo contestants. AKA specimens of the male physique. The giant flashy belt buckles they wear are like a beacon alerting the female species to the treasures that lie beneath the plaid button-up shirt.

BJ positions my arms properly. "Start by stepping back with your right foot. Quick, quick, slow, slow." He steps towards me and the momentum causes me to stumble because I forgot to step, but he stabilizes me so I don't fall.

"Sorry."

"It's all right. Let's try it again."

I glance across the bar at Easton. He's watching us with a smile on his face, even though the girl beside him appears to still be talking to him. Okay. I'm going to look like an idiot in front of everyone, but I want to learn how to dance. I exhale. Reposition my arms. And stare down at my feet.

"Don't look down." BJ lifts my chin with his finger. "Look at me, or over my shoulder. Your feet will do what they need to do without you looking at them."

"You have a lot of faith in my feet. You probably shouldn't."

He smiles and waits patiently for me to get set. "It's just walking to music, Della."

I nod and close my eyes. "Okay. Go." I step my right foot back. Quick, quick, slow, slow. I repeat the instructions in my head for every single step, and it only works with my eyes closed, but it's fine because he's ushering me around the dance floor in a circle. My knee bonks into his. "Sorry."

"It's okay. You're doing good."

I open my eyes and lose my timing. He pauses and waits for me. I glance at Easton again. He's still watching, but he isn't smiling anymore. Maybe he feels sorry for me. Or for poor BJ, who probably regrets taking on this assignment. And just got bonked in the knee again. I close my eyes again and repeat quick, quick, slow, slow as we dance, if it could be called dancing. Every once and a while he angles me slightly to the side, which I assume means we are side-stepping another couple. Or open flame. I don't know because I haven't opened my eyes. Whoops. That was his toe. "Sorry."

"Don't worry about it, darlin'. I get stepped on by hooves all the time. I can't even feel your puny little feet."

I open my eyes in an attempt to focus on his face while still moving. It maxes out my capacity for physical multi-tasking, but it feels rude to not look at him. "Thanks for being patient. How did you become such a great teacher?"

"I have two little sisters back in Houston. I helped my mom raise them."

"Oh. That's sweet. How old are they?"

"Ten and thirteen."

"Aw. They must miss you."

"Yeah." He nods and swallows hard. "It's been tough on them, but my mom wants me to finish my education. I only have one more year left, if I can keep my grades up. Then I'll be able to get a job and support them financially, so they can pursue their goals."

"That's very sweet. I guess that's why Easton told me you're sensitive deep down."

"He said that, did he?"

Oops. I shouldn't have spilled that. "He also said you're cowboy to the core. Tough. Manly. With a nicer truck than his."

He laughs and steers me clear of the long horn on the wall. "You've turned that boy into a gabby gossiper. How'd you manage that?"

"I talk too much. I don't know when to shut up. Evidently it's contagious."

BJ laughs again and spins me in a half-circle that requires my eyes to be closed to successfully execute.

When the song ends, he extends his arm across my shoulder and hugs me into his side. "You did it. Good job."

I open my eyes and smile as we walk off the dance floor unscathed. He invites me to step in front of him and steers me by my shoulders through the crowd. "Thank you for being my instructor. How's your knee?"

"I might need surgery, but it's all right. At least you can dance now."

"You have a very loose definition of dancing. I wouldn't go quite that far."

We both laugh as we return to the table. The two flirty girls are gone and Chuck is back, which might be directly correlated if he said something rude to them. "Rum and coke." He hands BJ a glass. "Virgin strawberry margarita for the new roomie." He hands me a towering pink slushie. "Nothing for me since I'm driving. And boring Corona for the big winner tonight." He points at Easton. "The rest of the rounds are on you, by the way."

I take a sip through the straw and the liquid burns my throat. "Whoa." I cough. "Holy cow. That's not a virgin margarita."

"Oh, really?" Chuck acts all innocent and feigns disbelief. "The bartender must have made a mistake. Sorry about that."

"Don't drink it if you don't want it," Easton says. "I'll get you another one."

I glance at him and then back at the mountain of crushed ice. My parents don't drink, which is why I never have. I could, though, I guess. I take another sip. Nope. Don't like it. "Sorry. It's not really my thing. But I don't want it to go to waste."

"It won't." Easton shoots a look across the table. "BJ can give it to the next girl he dances with."

There was something different about Easton's tone when he said that, as if it was meant to contain an underlying message. BJ smiles as if he knows exactly what the tone was designed to convey.

I slide the glass over to Chuck. "Thank you, but you should give it to someone who will appreciate it." I touch Easton's arm lightly but retract it the instant I realize I'm doing the flirty thing. I don't want to creep him out. "I'm just going to get some water. I'll be right back."

He nods, and as I'm walking away, he warns Chuck not to try to slip me alcohol again. It's not exactly a threat, but I'd take him seriously if he ever spoke to me in that tone. For someone who didn't grow up with siblings he sure has the protective thing down. My sister would like him for that.

The line at the bar is ten people long. Is it stupid to wait just to ask for a glass of water? Maybe they have Perrier or something that I could at least pay for.

"Hey." The girl behind me in line extends her arm to shake my hand. "You're Della, right?"

"Yes." I study her face, wondering when I met her. There aren't a lot of females in my classes. I would have remembered if I had introduced myself to her.

"My name is Janine."

"Oh. Chuck's girlfriend. Nice to meet you."

Her eyebrows lift in surprise as we move forward in line. "Chuckie called me his girlfriend? That's interesting."

"Oh, no, not exactly. Maybe I jumped to that conclusion. He was really excited to go see you for date night, so I thought you were his girlfriend. Sorry for assuming."

Her expression registers something halfway between shock and disbelief. "He was excited about date night?"

"Yeah. It seemed like it." Worried that I've already said too much, I step forward in the line and remind myself that less is more sometimes, especially in conversations with strangers.

"Well, that's a first. All he usually does is complain when he's with me. And I wouldn't say I'm technically his girl-friend since I've never heard him use that word in reference to me."

"Does he know you're here? We're just hanging out at a table over in the corner there."

"No. I just got here. But even if he did know I'm here he'd ignore me for a while. He likes to celebrate with the boys after a win. Then after they've had a few drinks he'll come over to find me and be all sweet and kissing up on me."

"Well, that's not what's going to happen tonight. I'm already intruding on their celebratory boys' night. You're welcome to come hang out with me. He'll just have to deal with it." When we finally reach the front of the line I shout over the bar to order a Perrier, then turn to Janine. "What would you like?"

"Vodka and cranberry."

I pay and hand her drink to her, very careful not to splash it on her white mini skirt. If I looked up the definition of country girl I would fully expect to see a picture of her. Big blonde curls. Baby-pink tank top with silver and turquoise jewelry. Brown suede boots. Golden tanned skin and a cheerleader smile framed by dimples. Cute in every sense of the word.

She holds out a ten-dollar bill to pay me back for the drink, but I wave it off. "It's my treat. You're my first female friend in California, whether you like it or not." Glad to have a gal pal, which is something I'm definitely more familiar with. I pull her by the elbow and escort her through the crowded bar. "Look who I found," I sing out once we reach the table.

Chuck, who was in the middle of a joke, freezes mid-gesture and the smile drops off his face. "Hey, babe. When did you get here?" He reaches over and hugs Janine while shooting Easton some sort of dagger expression.

Easton chuckles and moves closer to me to make room for Janine.

"So, you girls met," Chuck says with a tight smile that actually hints at a glimmer of panic. "That's fantastic. Great. Really. Really great. So glad you met."

Janine hooks her elbow around his but not in an affectionate way—more like a power move to take advantage of his obvious discomfort. "When you told me you have a new female roommate you failed to mention what she looks like."

"Did I?" He points at me and then wipes his forehead

with his sleeve. "That's what she looks like. Short. Sort of pasty."

"You mean beautiful." Janine smiles at me, then turns her head back towards him. "How did it go today? Did you make some money?"

"Of course I made money. I always make money."

"No, not always." She pats his arm in a way that is a little too forceful to be considered loving. "Sometimes you fall on your head and you can't remember that you didn't make money. And sometimes you hit your head so hard you forget where you live and end up sleeping in someone else's bed. Isn't that right, sweetie?"

"Ha. You're funny." Chuck coughs and scratches the back of his neck as he downs the now partially melted margarita he bought for me. "You want to dance, babe?" he asks Janine as soon as he's finished. Then without waiting for her answer, he stretches his arm across her shoulder and escorts her to the dance floor. She shoots a few directed warning glances at the other women in the bar and they all seem to accept that she has staked her claim on him and his buckle. It's an impressive demonstration of the power of non-verbal communication.

BJ pats my back in a consolatory way. "We try to keep Chuck and Janine separated in public. Otherwise it can get ugly."

"Sorry. I didn't know."

BJ and Easton both chuckle. "It's going to be an interesting night." BJ raises his glass to toast us. "I'm going to go ask a pretty girl to dance. You all have fun."

After BJ disappears into the crowd, Easton raises his beer bottle to tap my Perrier bottle. "It was nice of you to invite Janine over, although Chuck might not see it that way."

"I was trying to make friends with her. But I don't want Chuck to be mad at me for bringing her around. I have to live with him, so it's more important that he likes me. I was already not his favorite person."

"Chuck basically only likes himself. I wouldn't spend too much time worried about what he thinks about anybody if I were you."

I sigh. I want to get along with him. It's going to be difficult, though, if he's as selfish and mean as he seems. BJ and Easton seem like decent guys. Chuck must have some redeeming qualities or else they wouldn't be friends with him. Maybe they aren't close. "Do you consider Chuck a friend?"

Easton ponders the question for a few seconds. "He'd have my back if I needed him. I guess that's all that matters."

"Would you confide in him?"

"No, but I don't confide in anyone."

"Really?" I glance over at Chuck and Janine who are dancing precariously close to the longhorn. She's really good at the two-step. Not just the walking to music type that BJ taught me, but the spin around and lift your arms over each other's head type. "If you don't confide in anyone, what do you do when you're angry or sad?"

"I try not to let things bother me. Especially things I can't control."

"But you must still feel angry if someone is a jerk or something is unfair?"

His shoulder shrugs just enough to acknowledge that it's true at least some of the time. "It's rare that something gets to me, but when it does I just go for a ride. Horses always make you feel better without ever judging you or telling everybody else about your private business. And they don't expect anything in return."

"So, if I can channel a stallion vibe, you and I will get along just fine?"

He takes a slow sip from his beer and appears to be hiding a smile.

"What? Why is that funny?"

Eventually he cracks and laughs. "A stallion is a male horse—one that's not castrated."

I point at him with both of my index fingers as a challenge. "I could be a horse with testes if I want to be."

He buckles over, laughing even harder, and it takes him a few seconds to recover. He shakes his head as if he can't believe how weird I am. "Sure. Why not? You can be a stallion if you want, but I'm sure you and I will get along just fine without you being a horse. If you were a horse, though, you'd probably be an Orlov Trotter with a star-speckled coat."

"What's an Orlov Trotter, a pony with stumpy legs?"

"No." He glances at my legs as if he hadn't noticed before that they are disproportionately short for my body. "It's a Russian horse. It's one of the most beautiful breeds in the world."

Oh. Is that his way of saying he thinks I'm beautiful? I don't know how to react to that. Maybe he was joking. Maybe it's really a pygmy horse used in circuses. What if it actually is a beautiful Russian horse? Does he say things like that to all girls? Those other girls were acting like he'd maybe said something nice like that to them at some point. When a person makes you feel good about yourself it's addictive. There are probably Easton junkies all over California. What if he wasn't joking? I've never had anybody say anything quite that flattering to me before. Too much time has passed. He's going to wonder why I've suddenly become mute. Say something, Della. "Do you want to dance?"

His expression remains motionless as his brain adjusts to my random shift in gears. He's also taking too long to respond. Obviously it's a no and he's attempting to come up with a way to let me down easy. Ouch. Okay, apparently I read too much into the Russian horse compliment. He was just being friendly and talking to me because I don't know anyone here. The nice conversation wasn't supposed to be a gateway into close contact such as dancing. Or anything else. Message received. Is that what the rejection feels like to guys when I turn down their invitation to dance with them? If I knew it felt like a shank to the gut I would have maybe said yes to some of them, or at least said no with more sensitivity. I should ask a horse person what an Orlov Trotter is. It's probably a stumpy donkey. Why hasn't he answered yet? He watches my expression as my thoughts rocket through my brain at warp speed.

Eventually, he smiles and says, "I don't two-step."

"Me neither, technically. I don't even know why I asked. Sorry."

"I do dance, just not the two-step. We can slow dance at the end of the night if you want to?"

Really? Yeah. Ok. Awesome. Cool. Yay. The compliment combined with the promise to slow dance later have rendered me speechless, so I just nod and then drink out of my already empty Perrier bottle. When Chuck and Janine return from dancing he carries on to the bar as if he needs a break, or a shot. Easton excuses himself, too. Janine slides in next to me, looking happy.

"You're a great dancer," I say. "And Chuck is surprisingly graceful, too."

"Thanks. And yeah, Chuck has a lot of good qualities. If it wasn't for his personality he'd be a great guy. But he's no Havie. And just so you know, I've never seen Havie smile as much as he's been smiling tonight. The way he looks at you just makes my heart melt. I'm secretly jealous. Probably every woman in here wishes she were you."

Janine leans her elbow on the table and arches her back like a sexy pinup girl, which makes it more obvious that I'm standing here looking like a sixth grader at her first boy-girl party. I discretely glance around to see if I can figure out which one might be Havie. I've been so engaged in conversation with Easton I didn't even notice anyone else.

"Honestly," Janine continues, "I was concerned about Chuck having a beautiful female roommate. But since Havie has his eye on you it guarantees Chuck will steer clear. They would never compete for the same girl, and Havie definitely has dibs if you're interested, which you should be. Unless you're crazy."

I'm just about to ask her which one is Havie when Easton returns. Janine squeezes my arm and then leaves to go join Chuck at the bar.

Easton hands me a Perrier bottle.

"Thank you."

He nods and steps closer so we don't have to shout over the sound of the band who has started to play again.

"Do you know someone named Havie?"

He chuckles. "Yes. Why?"

I shake my head to downplay it. "Janine said something about him. I was just wondering who he is."

"Me."

The shock stuns me, and it takes at least five blinks to recover enough to say, "What?"

He leans in and speaks louder because he thought I just didn't hear him properly. "Havie's my nickname. It's short for Mojave."

I heard him the first time. My brain just couldn't process the information. My heart shifts into a dangerously fast rhythm as the development sinks in. Now, in addition to the content of the message I am also struck by the fact that his lips were in close proximity to my ear. Everley. Easton. Havie. How am I supposed to keep all his aliases straight? Janine said the way he looks at me makes her heart melt. Easton like-likes me?

Holy shiiiiish kabob.

I need to sit down.

Chapter 8

Easton

Chuckie started doing shots after Janine showed up. Now he's too drunk to drive home. BJ's also gooned. I've had four beers, which is probably under the limit, but I don't drink and drive. Hopefully Della doesn't mind being the designated driver. "You okay to drive us home?"

She looks over at Chuck's Ram Longhorn edition pickup and inhales stressfully. "It's so huge."

"That's what she said!" Chuckie shouts and then stumbles as he laughs at his own joke.

"Ignore him," I say and shove him into the back of the cab. Janine and BJ stumble in the back after him. "Don't worry, Della. It drives like a car. I'll sit in the front and navigate for you."

She presses her lips together as if she's weighing her options. Finally, she nods to accept the challenge. I hand her the keys and she walks around to climb in the driver's side. Shit, she looks so tiny behind the wheel. Maybe it is too big for her to handle. I take my hat off and hop in the cab.

"Treat her like a lover, Della," Chuck says from the back seat. "She likes to be caressed with a gentle touch. All of my women do." He pulls Janine close, trying to make out with her.

"*All* of your women," Janine snaps and jams the heel of her hand into his chest.

"Both my women. I meant both. You and Muriel." He squeezes his arm around her neck and pulls her in. "I've never sat in Muriel's backseat. Let's break it in, babe."

BJ groans and removes his hat to lean his head against the side window. "Gross, y'all. I'm sitting right here. Wait until we get home."

Della presses the start button and then glances at me as the engine roars to life. She clenches her eyes shut for a second, either praying or conjuring some bravery, I'm not sure which.

"What type of music do you find relaxing?" I ask.

"Classical," she says.

Chuck pretends to gag. "Muriel only plays country music and eighties metal. She'll break down on the side of the road if you play Beethoven."

"Silence is fine, too," Della adds as she shifts into reverse and shoulder checks about twenty times. "I can't see anything behind me."

"Use the side mirrors." I find a classical music station and turn the volume low to calm her down.

She turns out of the parking lot onto the street and clips the curb, which drops the back end. "Oops. Sorry."

"Don't worry. Alignment is overrated," Chuck mumbles.

Then he slides to lean on the door and Janine lays her head on his lap. Hopefully they'll fall asleep.

Unfazed by the curb drop, BJ is already passed out and breathing heavy. I point to the exit for the highway. "Take the northbound ramp."

Della signals and then grips the steering wheel at ten and two. It's probably a good thing she has to focus so intently on the road. Otherwise she might notice how jacked I still am from dancing the last song with her. It was only one song, but since something is definitely going on between us, I felt like a sweaty-palmed freshman at a high school dance. She was worried about messing up a step, so we stood still and hugged while swaying to the music. I can almost feel the warmth of her body leaning up against mine.

She makes me smile without even trying. She's refreshingly real. Honest almost to a fault, which I appreciate. She's been holding her own with Chuck despite his best efforts to offend. Every guy in the bar was giving her the eye. And her skin is so damn soft I can't stop imagining what it would feel like if her entire body was draped over me like a silk sheet. I don't know whether to thank her cousin for sending her over to the house or curse him.

Once we're on the highway, she relaxes and sneaks a glance in my direction. "What was the name of that song we danced to? Do you know?"

I definitely know it. It's always been one of my favorites, and now it's going to remind me of Della every time I hear it for the rest of my life. "*Tennessee Whiskey.*"

She points at her purse on the console. "Do you mind grabbing my phone and downloading it for me. I liked it."

"Are you sure you want me to go through your purse? Isn't that sort of taboo?"

"Why? Are you afraid you're going to come across a tampon or something?"

I gesture with my hand in an angle towards the windshield to make sure she stays right at the highway exchange. "I don't know what women keep in their purses. I was just taught not to go through one."

"I give you permission. And don't worry. All you'll find is my phone. Some cash. The key to the house. And a lip balm. Sorry for being boring." She releases the steering wheel with her right hand only long enough to toss the purse onto my lap. "The password is my birthday month and day. 0605."

"You're not boring." I check over my shoulder. They're all asleep in the backseat. "And you shouldn't say your password out loud in front of these guys. Do you have any idea what pranks they'll pull on someone who has an unlocked phone?"

"They're asleep. And I trust you."

Our eyes meet briefly. Normally, it would seem strange for someone to say they trust a person they had just met, but it doesn't feel like we just met, and there is nothing normal about what's happening between us. I unzip the purse and slide the phone out. The 5th of June. I commit that to memory and unlock the screen. "There's a message from your dad here." I turn the phone upside down on my thigh, so I won't be tempted to read it.

"What's it say?"

"I don't want to read it. What if it's private?"

She signals to change lanes and pass a slow-moving car. "It likely says something like," she lowers her voice to a deeper register in an attempt to sound like her dad, "Send me your new address immediately or I will have my lawyer contact the registrar's office."

He sounds like an asshole. I flip the phone over and read the message out loud; "Sweetheart, I'm worried about how you are doing. Please call so I can hear your voice and know you are all right. We love you and miss you already. Please stay safe."

Her posture sinks slightly as she sighs.

"Why haven't you called him?"

"It's complicated." She removes the hat I gave her and places it on the console between us. "I left my mom a message. Maybe they didn't get it."

I wait to see if she wants to elaborate, but she doesn't say more, so I open her music to buy *Tennessee Whiskey*. "I need your account password, too. Do you trust me with that? I might buy hundreds of songs and a year's worth of movies with it."

"It's Tabitha. That's my niece's name."

I open the account and download the song. "You're an aunt? How old is she?"

"Fourteen months. She's so adorable." She points at her phone in my hand. "There are pictures of her on the photo stream. You can look if you want."

I open her photos, and the first one that pops up is a

picture of me fully extended on my ride today. She caught the buck at exactly the right moment. The next photo is of me loading into the chute. There are a few of the other guys and the last one is a professional looking shot of me taping my glove to my wrist. She added a filter on it that makes it look gritty and cowboy tough. I glance at her and her eyes shift away from the road for a second to meet my gaze. "These are really good. You're talented."

"Thanks." Her cheeks turn rosy and she concentrates back on the road. "Photography is one of my hobbies. And you are a model, so it kind of makes the picture taking part easy. I'll have to ask my mom to send my nice camera down, so I can take some high-quality shots for you guys. The phone camera can't really do the action shots justice."

"They look good to me." I keep scrolling until I get to the shots of her niece. She is cute. And the way Della is smiling in the last shot makes my breath catch in my throat. What the hell is wrong with me? I don't understand what's going on. I've been dating since I was thirteen, hooking up since I was fifteen, and I was even in love once when I was seventeen, but I've never felt like this before. Shit. It's crazy, but even if I could stop it, I don't think I want to. I check over my shoulder, worried that everyone in the truck can tell I'm falling hard for Della.

"Congratulations again," she says. "You rode so well today. Do you know what you did differently? If you can figure it out maybe you can replicate it for the next rodeo. Oh!" she gasps and excitedly taps the steering wheel with her palm. "You know what it probably was? Your new suitcase handle. It must be a good one. Based on how many guys fell off before the eight seconds, I assume it's probably not that easy to repeat something like what you did today, but if the secret is the gear, you'll be riding like that every time. You seemed so in the zone. That's what they call it when an athlete performs optimally, right?"

"Yeah. I was in the zone." But I'm positive it had nothing to do with the new rigging. I roll the window down a crack for oxygen. Good thing I won today. I'm definitely going to owe those guys a thousand bucks if her feelings are mutual. It seems like she is at least attracted to me, but she's not the type to sleep around casually, and she might consider a serious relationship too much of a distraction from school. I'm going to be out for the count if she turns me down, but it will also be torture to be around her if I deny my feelings. I'm not sure how to handle the situation. "Merge left. You can stay in the carpool lane for the rest of the way." I exhale, hoping I sound normal. I don't feel normal. I'm wrecked already and I haven't even kissed her. Maybe I never will. I want to. I shouldn't. This is bad.

"Do you mind the nickname Havie?"

"No. Why?"

She shrugs and then shakes her head, flustered, as if she wants to backpedal. "I don't know. I was just wondering since you said it was short for Mojave. I wanted to make sure it wasn't a nickname you considered disrespectful or derogatory."

"Calling me Mojave isn't an insult. I'm proud of who I am."

"Yeah, of course. I didn't mean to insinuate that it was a demeaning term." She blinks hard, almost wincing, and grips the steering wheel as if she wishes she could erase the entire conversation. "Sorry. I don't think you should be ashamed to be identified by your heritage. I just like to check with people to confirm what they prefer to be called. Because in high school, I became friends with a girl named Tootie. I thought it was her real name. Even the teachers called her Tootie. And I went around introducing her to everyone, including my parents, as Tootie. And like six months later she broke down in tears and told me her name is actually Elizabeth. Being dubbed Tootie all started in elementary school after she accidentally farted during a presentation in front of the entire school. Breaking wind was embarrassing enough. Then the nickname stuck all the way to college, which was mortifying, and she didn't know how to make it stop. So anyway, if you ever meet my good friend Beth, don't let on that you know she's the infamous Tootie."

I laugh. "You can call me whatever you want. If I don't like something I'll tell you."

"Okay. Cool." She exhales and her posture relaxes. "Could you use my phone to download a picture of an Orlov Trotter for me, please? I want to see what type of beast you compared me to."

I search for one with a star-speckled coat, then hold it up for her to look at.

"Oh," is all she says.

What does "oh" mean? I turn the phone to look at the

screen, wondering why her smile dropped off her face. Apparently, comparing a woman to a horse is a bad idea. If she knew it was a type of horse I've always loved she would probably be less offended. But I'm not saying that to someone I've known for less than a week. Especially not in front of these guys who will never let me forget it. I slide her phone back in her purse and close the zipper. I want to tell her how I feel. I shouldn't. Or maybe I should. Maybe it's better to just lay it all out on the table. Or not.

We drive for a while with only the classical music filling the silence, but then a car merges in too fast from an on-ramp and crosses three lanes before swerving back into the second lane. "Hang back from that guy. It looks like he's been drinking," I say.

She nods and eases off the accelerator to slow down. "Did they ever charge the drunk driver who killed your mom?"

I turn my head to stare out the side window. It's not a bad thing that she's interested and cares enough to ask, but I don't like to talk about it. I'm surprised I even told her in the first place. Only people who knew me back then know what really happened. I can't not answer her, though. Whatever. Just say it, Havie. "Yeah. He went to prison for two years."

"Two years. That's it? Doesn't seem fair to take a child's mom away from him and only have to serve two years."

I nod and check over my shoulder again. Everybody is still out cold. "He'll have to live with the guilt the rest of his life. That's punishment enough."

"Not if he doesn't feel guilty."

I run my hand through my hair and avoid looking at her. "He feels guilty."

Her head turns to study me. I can feel the stare as she lets the comment sink in. "You know for a fact he feels guilty?"

"Yeah. Hey, I'm starving. Do you mind taking this exit, so we can hit a drive-thru?"

She obviously knows I purposely dodged the subject but lets me get away with it. She signals and exits off the highway.

Chuck and Janine woke up at the drive-thru and ordered cheese burgers. They stay awake for the rest of the ride home, so Della and I stick to small talk and steer clear of anything too deep or personal.

She parks on the driveway and smiles at herself, proud of the accomplishment of getting us all home safely. BJ is still passed out and tumbles out onto the grass when I open the back door. Chuck hooks his elbows under BJ's armpits and I grab BJ's ankles to carry him into the house. We toss him onto the couch instead of lugging him all the way upstairs to his room, which he'll be ornery about when he wakes up in the morning with a kink in his back.

Janine and Chuck head up to his bedroom, whispering and giggling. I follow Della up the stairs and stop in the hall. She pauses at her door and turns to face me. "Thanks for inviting me. I had a really great time."

"Thanks for coming."

"I'm sorry for bringing up your mom. It obviously makes

you uncomfortable. I have a knack for asking a person about the one thing they really don't want to talk about. Just tell me to stop talking next time I make you uncomfortable. It will definitely happen again at some point. I can guarantee that. I won't be offended if you just shut me down. I would rather know I'm treading on a touchy subject right away before I inadvertently bother you. The last thing I meant to do was upset you."

"I know. You don't need to apologize for caring. It's hard to talk about what happened, but that's mostly because I've never talked about it with anybody before you. It's not that I don't want to tell you. It might take some getting used to, though, if you don't mind being patient with me."

The compassion in her smile ticks another box for me. Things are going to be too weird if I don't come clean. It's impossible to be this attracted to a person and then just walk away at the end of the night like she means nothing. I can't do it. Or I can't not do it. I have to do something. I glance down the hallway. Chuck and Janine are being loud with the bedroom antics. "Is it all right if I come in for a minute?"

"Um." Her posture stiffens with pure trepidation over having me in her room at two o'clock in the morning. "Sure." Her voice wavers as she steps inside and swings the door wider to invite me in. She continues to hold onto the doorknob in a death grip.

This isn't going to go well if she's worried that I'm trying to put the moves on her, so I attempt to ease her discomfort. "I just want to tell you something. Is it okay if I'm completely honest with you?"

"Of course." She closes the door and leans her back against it to face me.

"I like you," I say bluntly.

Her eyes widen and she blinks slowly like a stunned bunny.

"I don't like game playing, so I'm not going to pretend that I don't think you're awesome. You are. And I'm dying to ask you for a goodnight kiss. The problem is that the guys and I agreed it wouldn't be a good idea for any of us to date the new roommate. I don't want to do anything to screw things up and jeopardize our living arrangements, but I also don't want you to think I'm not interested. I am. Very interested. And the reason I rode so well today had nothing to do with my new rigging. I was showing off for you. I realize now that it sounds arrogant to assume you might want to date me in the first place. Maybe you never would have considered it anyway, but in case I had a chance I thought I should clarify exactly why I'm not taking the next step. I want to, but it's probably best if we just stay friends. Because of the circumstances. Sorry. Or not sorry, depending how you feel about it. Now I'm the one rambling."

She blinks repeatedly and her mouth drops open slightly, but no sound comes out.

"So, yeah. That's all I wanted to tell you." I study her face to read her expression. Since she hasn't fully decided how she feels about the disclosure, it's impossible to read her reaction. I wait for a few more beats, but she's not any closer to coming up with a response. Maybe I should let her sleep on the news to process it. We can talk in the morning. If she wants to. She might not want to. I might have just screwed things up. Badly. "Are you okay?"

She nods almost indiscernibly and grips the doorknob as if it's what's keeping her upright.

She opens the door and I step out into the hall. "Goodnight."

She nods again and then closes her door.

Chapter 9

Della

I couldn't sleep after Easton left my room. I tried, but my heart was racing too fast. I took a shower to calm down, which didn't help, so I ended up listening to *Tennessee Whiskey* on repeat and stared at the ceiling above my bed until the sun came up. My sister met her first boyfriend at her summer job at the mall when she was fifteen and, even though they would work an entire shift together, she would come home and they would talk or text all evening, too. I never understood that crazy insatiable desire to stay connected with a person, until now.

I appreciate that Easton just came out and honestly told me he likes me. It eliminates any guess work and potential for miscommunication. But that's the problem. I now know for an absolute fact that he likes me. What am I supposed to do with that information? Part of me wants to move out just so we could go on a date. Part of me knows as soon as he tries to kiss me and finds out how laughably inexperienced I am, the relationship will end before it even starts. Maybe Easton only likes the idea of me—a virginal, homeless damsel sleeping conveniently across the hall. Or maybe it's a competitive thing with the other guys and he likes the idea of beating them to get the girl.

Or maybe he really likes me. I'm a good catch. I'm smart. I'm funny. I'm pretty. I'm also a complete dork with zero sexual experience. What's not to love? I want to tell him I feel the same way. I'm going to definitely do it. I think. At some point. Maybe it would be easier if I didn't say anything. We could just carry on living together and be friends. That would be best for everyone. Except I really do like him. I should talk to him. At some point when my brain doesn't feel like it's about to explode. I need to go for a run first. It's only five o'clock. Who cares?

I jump out of bed and dress in shorts and a running top. I don't know my way around the neighborhood yet, but I can head over to the campus. I tie my hair into a ponytail and open my bedroom door. Easton's door opens at the same time. He's shirtless. Hair braided. Boxer briefs bulging. Huge scar up the side of his upper thigh. Stop staring. I force my eyelids shut to give the impression that I'm functioning properly, but since the unnatural blink feels more like a combination of a wink and a wince, I assume he's not convinced I'm normal.

An amused expression lights up his face before he says, "Hi."

Not ready to talk to him. Head literally about to blow. Can't breathe. "Morning." I avert my eyes and point at the stairs. "Just leaving. Have to run. Going running. See you.

After. When you're dressed. Gotta go." I sneak a glance at his face. He's smiling. He's so gorgeous. I'm going to definitely move out, so I can find out what it feels like to press my lips against his. Or maybe I can talk him into letting me stay and kiss him. I point at his leg to pretend like I wasn't staring at his lips. "You didn't mention femur surgery on your list of rodeo injuries."

He glances down at his thigh. "That one's not from rodeo. It's from the car accident."

"Oh. I didn't realize you were in the car when it happened." I want to ask him more about it but standing in the hall in his underwear at five o'clock in the morning is not the right time or place. Even I know that, so I settle for, "Sorry."

He reaches up to unbraid his hair and says, "I'm driving out to help my dad again today. Would you like to come with me?"

Yes. Absolutely. Wait. Did he change his mind about us being just friends? No, he probably means as friends. Does it matter? He wants to spend the day with me. Say yes, Della. No, it's not a good idea. I don't want to get too attached. I'm already too attached. And I'm behind on my schoolwork because of yesterday. I need more time to sort out my thoughts. "I would love to, but I have some reading to do and an assignment I have to finish. I should probably stay here."

"Bring your work with you. I have chores to do on the ranch for a few hours. You can get all your studying done there."

When does he study? He must be really smart and get by with winging it. Maybe he doesn't sleep. Obviously, he doesn't, we only went to bed a few hours ago. But he's too pretty to not ever sleep. My eyes wander over his bare upper body. There is no doubt I want to go with him. It will be weird, right? Meeting his dad. Seeing where he grew up. Hanging out, just the two of us, for the entire day. Actually, friends do things like that. Boyfriends and girlfriends do things like that, too. Is he trying to confuse me?

Chuck's bedroom door opens and he steps into the hall, groggy and adjusting his boxer briefs, which he might already be aware are not as bulging as Easton's. Hence the fancy truck. He has a roughly drawn tattoo of something that vaguely resembles a deer head on his left chest and a trail of what looks like mouse droppings angling down his abs. Maybe they're misshapen animal footprints. "Sup?" he says before he cuts past Easton and disappears into the bathroom.

"Think about whether you want to come to the ranch while you're out on your run," Easton says quietly to me. "I'll make breakfast. You can decide after we eat."

"Okay," I squeak out, then spin around and rush down the stairs. I already know what my answer is.

I only ran for twenty minutes and we left by six while everyone else was still asleep. We made good time to Three Rivers. The ranch is another half an hour out from here. Easton's truck is not as showy as Chuck's, but that's what I like about it. It's genuinely country and not pretentious at all. Like him.

It's attractive to me that Easton is comfortable being judged on his integrity and how he treats people rather than shallow and trivial things like a brand new, over-the-top truck. Although I know nothing about rural living, I've always been drawn to that down-to-earth quality in others. Rich, poor, from the city or the country, doesn't matter, people who are secure with who they are don't need to show off. Our family was poor when we first arrived in Canada. The only reason my sister and I were able to attend a private prep academy was because Dad's boss was on the board of directors at the school and granted us financial bursaries. It didn't take long for me to figure out that the most conceited and superficial girls at our school were either the other bursary girls who were insecure and trying to prove something, or the few rich girls who had nothing else redeeming going for them besides mommy and daddy's money.

In many ways, Easton is completely opposite to me—not that it was my goal to find a questionably coordinated, suburban, Russian-Canadian immigrant exactly like me. But maybe compatible values are all that matters. Not that I'm one hundred percent sure. I don't even know what it's normally like to hang out with someone who is romantically interested. My only experience hanging out with guys my own age was with my two cousins who were more interested in their video games than talking to me. I'm fairly sure it's not always this comfortable. I can't explain it, but it feels like Easton was custom made for me. Like my soul's counterpart, my yin to his yang. His mac to my cheese. No, not his bacon to my eggs. Don't ever say any of those things out loud, Della.

"We need to stop here," Easton says as we approach a small one-street strip of shops in the middle of nowhere— a gas station, a hair salon, a deli, and a place called Mathers General Store and Diner. He slows down and parks on the side of the street. "Do you like root beer floats?"

He's wearing a baseball cap instead of his cowboy hat today. It's a whole different type of sexy – not better or worse – just different. I mean, he would look hot in whatever he had on, but the ball hat is doing something to me. Or maybe it's the fact that he didn't shave and has a sexy scruff thing going on. Or the white T-shirt that pulls tight over his chest and biceps. Or the thick metal belt buckle. Wait. What was the question? "Of course, I do. Who doesn't like root beer floats?"

I climb out of the truck and follow him into the general store. The left side of the store is set up with grocery shelves. And along the right side is a long fifties-style diner counter and stools. He sits down on the end stool and spins to face me as I sit next to him. His legs straddle either side of my stool. "I didn't want to assume you like root beer floats. You didn't think there was anybody who doesn't like pie until you met me."

"True. The pie thing is odd. I get not liking one type of pie, like lemon meringue or mincemeat, but all pies doesn't make any sense. You like blueberries. You like apples. What difference does it make if they're baked into a sweet, warm, crumbly crust?"

"The crust is like an ice cream cone. Dry and unnecessary."

I shake my head. "I'm always surprised to discover how many weirdos there are in the world. I suppose root beer float haters are no exception. I'm not one of them, though."

He laughs and waves through a window opening to an attractive older woman in the kitchen. Her red and gray streaked hair, freckles, and Bohemian clothes give her a Sissy Spacek vibe. "Easton!" She smiles and rushes out through a swing door, then leans over the counter. Easton stands to hug her. "Welcome home, darlin'. How you been?"

"Good. Thanks. This is Della. Della, this is Crystal. She's been like a second mom to me, keeping me out of trouble."

"Yeah, and that was no small feat," she laughs. "Nice to meet you, Della." She pulls out two fountain glasses without even asking for our orders and fills them with soda and scoops the ice cream from a tub. "Has your daddy been honest with you about how he's feeling?"

Easton shrugs and slides over the first glass for me. "Not really. He tells me he's fine, but he's always got a list of things for me to do when I come home to help him out."

"Well, you and I both know he's as tough as a cornered rattler. He'll bounce back soon enough." She points at me. "And a visit from your pretty girlfriend oughta cheer him up."

Easton looks over at me and smiles. I wait for him to correct her, but he doesn't.

"Go on then," Crystal says with an encouraging hand

gesture. "Give it a try. If it ain't the best root beer float you ever tasted, I'll close up shop and retire to Mexico."

I dip the straw in and take a sip. Easton watches my mouth expectantly. Oh, my goodness that is delicious. I pause only long enough to say, "Wow," then suck back another straw full of bubbly, creamy goodness. "Don't retire. This is definitely the best I've ever had. And I practically consider myself a float connoisseur."

"That's good since Easton has broken up with girls for the single reason that they didn't like my root beer floats. You pass the Crystal test."

Easton nods to agree and dips his straw through the foam on top of his float. A customer enters the store, so Crystal leaves us at the counter to go help the woman.

"That's a weird reason to break up with someone. But wow. Oh my gosh. Why is this so good?"

Easton chuckles. "The secret is her homemade ice cream. It's basically crack. You won't be able to stop dreaming about them from now on."

"Thanks a lot. If I knew your plan was to bring me out here to the middle of nowhere and turn me into a drug addict, I might have said no."

"Might have said no?"

Probably still wouldn't have said no. Definitely would have still said yes. I raise my eyebrows at him but continue drinking so I don't have to answer.

He finishes before I do and then watches me drink.

"Crystal thinks we're dating," I say once I'm finished.

He shrugs again as if her believing that doesn't bother

him. "I haven't brought a woman around since I moved away. Everybody is going to think we're dating. You can correct them if you want, but that will only make them gossip more with speculation. Either way you're still going to be the talk of the town."

My ears heat up in an uncontrollable embarrassed flush that has its roots in a fourth-grade rumor mill fiasco that left me emotionally scarred for life and apparently horrified to be the topic of anyone's gossip.

Easton chuckles. "Relax. It's a one-street town."

Okay. Yeah. What's the big deal? It's the good kind of gossip. I don't mind everybody assuming we're dating if he doesn't. I'd rather I was actually dating him, but I'll take it. My red-hot ears are still on the verge of producing steam. Not sure how to turn that off. Change the topic! "Should we pick up something for lunch? What does your dad like?"

His face creases in a reluctant expression. "He loves the roast beef on rye sandwiches from the Dudnik's deli across the street. You have to get them, though."

"Why? Are you banned form the deli or something?"

"Sort of." He stands and digs into the pocket of his jeans to give me a twenty. "Order two roast beefs on rye and whatever you want. I'll meet you back at the truck."

"How do you get banned from a deli?" I mutter to myself and shake my head as I walk to the door. "Bye Crystal." I wave. "Nice meeting you."

She waves over the customer she's helping. "Bye Della. Have a nice visit at the Lewis place."

Two other customers look up from what they were doing

and eyeball me. Then they look over at Easton. Okay. I see how gossip in a small town works. I'm probably going to be pregnant with his illegitimate baby by noon. I leave and cross the street to the deli. The owner is a short, stocky Russian guy. I greet him in Russian, assuming he's the Mr. Dudnik of the Dudnik Deli, and you'd think he just met royalty or something. He calls his wife out from the back storage room to meet me, and they both shower me with double cheek kisses. All because I said good morning in Russian.

While the owner makes the sandwiches from scratch I look around, wondering what Easton could have possibly done to get banned from the deli. I really don't believe he's the type who would steal. Maybe he was different when he was younger. Crystal did say it wasn't easy to keep him out of trouble. But that doesn't sound like the Easton I know.

Mr. Dudnik takes forever making the sandwiches and telling me about which part of Russia they are from. Apparently not a lot of Russian-speaking customers stumble into a sandwich deli half an hour outside of Three Rivers, California. Go figure. Maybe Easton didn't get banned. Maybe he purposely sent me in knowing that the guy talks too much. Not judging. I talk too much. But he's killing me. Eventually he wraps the sandwiches and stacks them in a paper bag, with the precision one would use for packing a sandwich for royalty. Then he tries to give them to me at no charge.

"No. That's very generous of you, but I insist." I hand

him the twenty and bolt out the door before he can protest. Easton isn't at the truck yet, so I sit on the tailgate to wait.

A striking woman with long, dark hair to her waist walks up and stops in front of me. Then she extends her arm to shake my hand. "Tracy."

"Della." Is that normal in a small town? People just randomly walk up and say their name. It's very friendly. But honestly, a little strange.

Her eyes scan down and narrow as if she doesn't approve of what I'm wearing. What's wrong with white capris and a pink peasant blouse? This isn't exactly Manhattan. She's wearing jeans and a button-up shirt. Not grounds for the critical look on her face. "Is this Easton's truck?"

"Oh. Yeah. I think he's running an errand or talking to someone he knows. He'll be back in a minute."

She nods slowly, still taking me in. But doesn't say anything.

"I take it you know him."

"Yeah, I know him. Tell him Tracy says hi." She turns and walks away.

All right. Nice talk. There's definitely a story there. I don't want to know it. Well, I mean I do. I'm just fairly certain I'm not going to like it all that much. I have a very strong impulse to shout; "He told me he likes me and that I'm awesome and he was dying to ask me for a goodnight kiss because I'm as beautiful as an Orlov Trotter," but some things that pop into your head are better left unspoken, as my sister has reminded me at least a million times in my lifetime. Tracy turns the corner at the hair salon and disappears.

After five minutes, when Easton still hasn't shown up, I open the deli bag and unwrap my turkey sandwich. It's not that disgusting, slimy processed meat. It is actual shaved chunks off a home-roasted bird with cranberry sauce. Fresh out of the oven bread. Mmm. It smells good. And it tastes amazing. Easton appears from around the corner of the deli, smiling and carrying a blue shop bag.

"Sorry to keep you waiting. I had to pick up a fishing reel for my dad." He holds up the hardware store bag, then points at the sandwich. "It's good, right?"

"Yeah. As good as the float. Why can't you go in the deli?"

"Dudnik doesn't like Native Americans."

My mouth opens and the partially chewed piece of sandwich drops out onto the ground. Ew. Did I just do that? I spit out food on the sidewalk. "Sorry." I hop off the tailgate and scoop up the glob of food with the napkin, then throw it in the garbage can. "What? He's a racist? Why would you ask me to buy his sandwiches?"

"They're the best in town. Maybe the best in California."

"Easton. I can't eat the sandwich of a racist."

He chuckles, completely unaffected. "Guaranteed you eat food prepared by racists all the time. You just don't know it. Besides, I don't care what that guy or any other bigot thinks of me."

"Hating someone because of how they look is wrong."

"That's his problem. I like his sandwiches."

I shake my head and storm back to the deli, throwing my sandwich in the trashcan on the sidewalk.

Mr. Dudnik looks concerned that I'm back so soon. "Is everything okay with the sandwiches?"

In Russian I say, "Yes. I just came back to tell you how delicious they were. They were even better than my grandmother's."

He smiles proudly and rushes out from behind the counter to press the twenty-dollar bill into my hand, insisting that he doesn't want a daughter of the homeland to pay.

"Thank you," I say in English and pocket the money. "I will definitely be back. My fiancé is Easton Lewis. You must know him. He grew up near here. His father still lives here. The Lewis ranch. They are Mojave, as in the first people to ever inhabit the land. Now that we are going to be married I'm sure we will be visiting regularly. I will be sure to stop in and say hello each time. Hopefully it won't be too long before I'll be able to bring our half-Russian, half-Mojave children in to enjoy your sandwiches, too. Thank you, again."

His eyes widen and his mouth drops open in a dumbstruck way. Speechless is good.

Spinning around, I resist the urge to lecture him in Russian before I leave.

Outside, Easton is leaned against his truck with his arms crossed. "I don't need you to fight my battles for me."

"I didn't." I hand him the twenty. "I told Dudnik how much I enjoyed the sandwich. He insisted there was no need for a fellow Russian to pay. And then I let him know my Mojave fiancé and I would definitely be visiting the deli regularly once we are married because we want our future mixed-ethnicity children to experience small-town hospitality and home-cooking."

Easton smiles and stuffs the twenty back into his pocket. "That will get the town talking. Good job."

Ah, man. My ears are ablaze again. "Speaking of town talk, who's Tracy?"

The amused expression disappears from his face and he scans the street looking for her. "My high school girlfriend. We broke up after my first year at Stanford. Why?"

"She came over to say hi while I was sitting on the tailgate, waiting for you."

He opens the door for me. "What else did she say?"

"Nothing. She asked if this was your truck and then told me to say hi to you before she walked away." Leaving out the fact that her tone was hostile enough to make me wince, I hop in the cab and he shuts the door for me. His expression is difficult to read as he walks around the front of the truck and gets in the driver's side. "Is she Mojave?" I ask as he takes his hat off and slides it onto the dashboard.

"No. She's half-Mexican and half-Norwegian."

"She's beautiful."

He nods and turns the key in the ignition. Then he turns his head and flashes one of his model smiles. "She might slash my tires once she hears that you and I are getting married."

"You're joking, right?"

"Partly."

Which part? I slouch down and scan the street for any

sight of her. "Maybe you should clear up the rumors for her benefit. And our safety."

He shakes his head, unconcerned as we drive past all signs of civilization. "We broke up because she cheated on me. Whom I'm friends with, whom I date, and whom I marry are none of her business. She made her choice. I don't care what she thinks."

I sit up straight and stare at him, completely dumfounded. Why in the world would anyone cheat on him? There can't possibly be someone better out there. She's such an idiot.

"Okay, no more talking about two-timing Tracy and the racist Russian. They don't mean anything to me." He points across the road to an open pasture. "That right there means something to me. That's where our property begins. It extends over those hills out in the distance and farther than the eye can see on the other side."

The stunning vista stretches across the entire horizon. A small river with a craggy stone bank cuts through the meadow and follows the curvy foot of the green, rolling hills. Bigger mountains tower in the background. "Wow. It's gorgeous."

He nods and then turns off the main road, through an arch with the words 'Lewis Ranch' welded in iron. We carry on along a gravel road, which is sort of like a driveway but five minutes long. The house is literally a rancher—a one level log house with gabled windows in the attic, a metal roof, and a covered porch that runs along the entire front. They even have rocking chairs. It's really charming, like the setting of a movie based on a Nicholas Sparks novel.

As Easton pulls up and parks in front of a red barn that is adjacent to the house, he says, "I have a room up in the loft of the barn where you can study. That's where I stay when I'm home. It has a desk, bathroom, drinks in the fridge and snacks in the cupboard."

"Okay." I get out of the truck and spin in a full circle to take in the majestic surroundings. "I love it here already."

A fluffy black and white border collie runs from behind the barn and greets Easton with wiggles and figure-eights through his legs. "This is Brewster," Easton says to me before addressing the dog, "This is Della. She's nice. You'll definitely like her." He raises his eyebrows and flashes a grin at me as he rubs Brewster's ears.

"He's cute. But I'm not a dog person."

"What?" Easton feigns shock and exchanges a look with Brewster. "Did you hear that, buddy? She doesn't like dogs. I know. I know. You're no ordinary dog. Just be yourself. There's no way she won't eventually fall for you."

"I don't want to hurt his feelings, but his chances of winning me over are slim. I'm really more of a goldfish person."

Easton shakes his head at Brewster. "What can I say? She's weird. Don't try to figure her out." Brewster barks once as if he understands, then runs off and disappears behind the barn.

I grab my backpack, which is full of textbooks. Easton scoops the deli bag with the other two sandwiches from me. "Do you want me to meet your dad?"

"Yeah, later. He said he would be out clearing brush until this afternoon."

"Shouldn't he be resting?"

"He won't until the work's all done, so I better get at it." He points to the stairs that lead up to the loft and then opens one of the horse stalls. "The keys are in the truck if you need to go back to the general store for anything. You can also go into the main house if you want to. Make yourself at home. Ranch hands will be coming and going, so don't be alarmed if you hear something down here or see guys around. If there's a problem, you can call me. I'll be back around five." He grabs the saddle and other leather things I don't know the name of to prepare the horse.

Is it weird that I don't want him to go? He's like home-made ice cream. I'm going to slip into withdrawal as soon as he's out of my sight. He stops buckling the saddle strap thingy and looks over at me with one of his model smiles. Oh shoot. He knows what I'm thinking. Maybe he's thinking the same thing. I want him to love me as much as he loves Crystal's root beer floats. That sounds strange, but it's true. I need to break free from his gravitational pull before I do something stupid like volunteer to get on a horse and ride the range with him. I step up onto the bottom stair and say, "I'll miss you." Ugh. Stupid. Not the right thing to say. I don't know what the right thing to say is, but it isn't that. I wince and then spin around and run up the stairs to the loft.

Chapter 10

Easton

Fixing the downed fence took longer than I had hoped, and it's after six o'clock by the time I get back to the loft. Della's curled up asleep on my bed, which makes me want to join her. Wondering what she was doing back here alone was all I thought about while I was working. Being in bed was definitely one of the scenarios that had occurred to me—not the best train of thought considering I'm attempting to keep things platonic. Not that inviting her to spend the day here and meet my dad can be considered platonic. I glance at the empty bag of peanut M&Ms and three Mountain Dew cans on the desk next to her pile of books. At least she got some studying done. Avoiding the squeaky floorboards on the way to the bathroom, I strip down and hop in the shower.

There's no question I'm going to need to hire another ranch hand. There's too much work for Dad to do while he's not feeling well, and I can't come out every weekend. But, unfortunately, I don't have the funds to hire another hand right now. I could take a modeling gig, which means heading to San Francisco or LA and more time off school. It also means time away from Della. Shit. I can't believe she's even a consideration that's crossing my mind already. I'm in deep.

I wrap a towel around my waist and step out of the bathroom. She's awake and sitting cross-legged on the bed. "Hey," I say as I unzip my bag and pull out a change of clothes.

"Hi. I thought maybe you were a ranch hand helping himself to a shower."

I step back into the bathroom to dress but leave the door open so she can hear me. "I should have clarified that they aren't supposed to be hanging around up in the loft. How many of them came up for showers while I was gone?"

"Only two. And one of them spoke Spanish, so I'm not one hundred percent sure what he said when he stroked my hair lovingly."

I laugh and step back into the apartment. "If that really did happen it's probably better that you don't know what he said."

She hops off the bed and slides her feet into her canvas tennis shoes. "Please tell me it's almost time for dinner. I'm starving."

She moves closer and stands right in front of me, like hugging distance. Kissing distance. Pick her up and carry her back to the bed distance. "Uh. Yeah, it should be almost ready. My dad's cooking up the fish he caught."

Her eyes track across my chest and her top teeth rest

against her bottom lip as if she's thinking the same thing I'm thinking. My heart is pounding so hard it's making me light-headed. We need to go to the main house before I reach over and touch the exposed skin between the waistband of her pants and the bottom hem of her blouse. She's killing me.

"Uh, so just to give you a heads up, my dad and I have a complicated relationship."

"Okay." Her eyes angle up at the ceiling in a squinty, perplexed way as she tries to figure out what that means. "Is there something specific you want me to say or do?"

"No. Just don't take the tension personally."

She focuses on my expression, trying to read more into what I mean by tension.

A part of me wants to tell her everything, but I don't know how to explain without going into the whole history, which would take forever, so instead I say, "Let's go eat." I place my palm on the small of her back and let her walk ahead of me down the stairs.

She slows as she passes the horse stalls and pats each of their muzzles. "Which one is your favorite?" she asks.

"My favorite horse died last year. I was the only person he would let ride him. His name was Shitake, but I called him Shithead." My palms fly up in apologetic defense. "It's not really swearing if it's his name."

"Why do you guys all think I can't handle a swear word?" She props her hands on her hips, offended. "I'm not that fragile."

"Oh really? If it doesn't bother you, then say his name."

"Shitake." She laughs and tugs my hand to lead me out of the barn and across the yard to the house. Ah, man. Even holding her hand sends me over the rails. I should have taken an ice cold shower.

Dad is on the porch, smiling at us as we approach. I haven't seen him smile like that in years. Since before Mom died. And he actually put on a shirt that he had to iron. "Della, this is my dad, Jack. Dad, Della."

She steps up on the porch and hugs him as if he's already family. I haven't even gotten that much action from her yet. Jesus. I'm jealous. "Nice to meet you, Mr. Lewis."

After taking a second to recover from the shock of being hugged by a stranger, he says, "You can call me Jack."

She sways her head from side-to-side as if she's considering the prospect of addressing him informally but isn't entirely convinced she'll be able to do it. He's completely bald right now from the treatments, but it probably doesn't strike her as strange since she didn't know him when he had hair like mine.

"Come on in. Dinner is ready." He leads the way through the living room and then pulls a dining room chair out for her. "Normally, it's just me, so I eat in front of the TV. But I actually set the table for tonight's meal since Easton said he was bringing his girlfriend for a visit."

"I said I was bringing my roommate for a visit." I sit down beside her and shoot him a glare.

"Roommate, right." He nods as if he's received the message before he disappears into the kitchen. I doubt clarifying the distinction will make a difference. I haven't brought a woman around since Tracy, so he knows it's serious. Not serious the way he thinks. Serious as in I just got a thrill from holding hands with her. If things progress, I'll be hooked and reeled.

He returns from the kitchen, carrying the platter of rainbow trout. It's his specialty, served with green beans and potatoes from the garden. Hopefully she doesn't mind that it's drenched in butter. He serves it up and sits down to watch Della take her first bite. Her eyes widen as the butter hits her palette. It's the best part.

"Seriously?" She swallows and looks over at me. "Why does everything taste so good here? This fish is outstanding."

"Fish always tastes better fresh."

She places her palm on her chest and faces Dad. "This is amazing. Thank you for going to the trouble to catch it and cook it. I'm so grateful."

"Anytime." He smiles and digs in. It's weird to see him acting friendly. Really weird. He hasn't willingly socialized with anyone in over a decade. He can barely even tolerate eating at the same table as me, let alone being forced into conversation with someone he's never met before.

"Oh, wait, I forgot to ask what you would like to drink?" He makes a motion to get up from the table, but I beat him to it.

"I'll get it, Dad."

He settles back down. "I'd offer you a glass of wine, Della, but I don't keep booze in the house."

"It's fine, Dad. She doesn't drink." I head to the kitchen to check what he's got in the fridge. Milk and apple juice.

Neither is all that appealing with fish. I find a can of lemonade concentrate in the freezer, which isn't really a better option, but I make that in a pitcher. I pour her just a plain glass of water, too, in case she doesn't like lemonade.

When I return, they are deep in conversation. I probably shouldn't be surprised. She cracked the code to get me talking, and he's basically the source I was cloned from. But what I'm witnessing is a miracle in the dining room. It hasn't felt this light in the house since Mom was alive.

I hand the glass of water to Della and place the jug of lemonade on the table. She thanks me, and I nod but then get back to eating, trying not to interrupt the roll of their conversation. They talk about everything from the cattle to Mojave traditions, and they eventually end up discussing his cancer. She probably has no idea how rare it is to hear him chatting openly like that.

"Well, you look really great," she says to him. "The treatments must be working."

He pours himself a lemonade and leans back in his chair. "I don't feel quite myself yet, but if I get enough rest it doesn't slow me down too much."

"Being out in the fresh country air must help with the recovery. It is so beautiful here. Has the ranch belonged to your family for generations?"

"Only as far back as my father. The house I grew up in is on the north side, we rent it out now. I built this house before Easton was born, even before I got married. Before— before a lot of things."

Sensing the change in his mood as his voice trails off,

she reaches over and places her hand on his wrist in a sympathetic gesture. "I was very sorry to hear about the accident."

I almost choke and have to grab for the jug of lemonade.

She glances at me to check if I'm all right before finishing what she was saying, "I'm sorry for your loss, Mr. Lewis. It must have been horrible."

He nods. Conversation over.

Della notices his wall slam down and clenches her eyes shut in regret. After a deep, remorseful exhale she goes back to eating in silence. She's probably berating herself, but it's not her fault we don't talk about the accident. Maybe if we had talked about it we would have moved on by now. Or not. Who knows? I reach over under the table and squeeze her hand to reassure her.

To erase the uneasiness I say, "Della is studying engineering, Dad. She wants to work with water systems."

"That's great. Water's important." He stands and clears the platter and his plate to the kitchen.

Della's head rolls to face me as she whispers, "I am so sorry."

"It's fine. There's a giant elephant in the room. It's not your fault for pointing it out." I finish my fish, then pour another glass of lemonade. I wish it was alcohol.

I can sense the wheels turning in her mind as she puts together all the pieces—the way Dad reacted to the topic, the no alcohol in the house, my discomfort. She appears to have lost her appetite and pushes the potatoes around the plate with her fork. Maybe I should have mapped out the landmines for her before we got here. Or maybe it's good to have someone hold a mirror up and show him how the past is still affecting him and our relationship. I have to hand it to her. She made more progress with him over one meal than I've made in a decade.

After some clunking around in the kitchen Dad comes back into the dining room, wearing orange oven mitts and carrying a dish that's hot right out of the oven. He's obviously decided to press the restart button on the night, so I help him out. "Wow, Della. My dad only makes apple crisp for special occasions. You should feel honored."

"I do." She watches him as if she hopes he'll look over at her with a forgiving glance. To my complete shock, he does. It's subtle, but it's the most forgiveness I've seen him express. Ever. Satisfied that she's back on good terms with him, she relaxes and reaches over to scoop out three servings of apple crisp. "So, Easton tells me you used to be quite the bulldog," she says.

"Bulldogger," I correct her.

"Oh, right. That's what I meant." She sneers her lip in a mock cowboy face and jerks her arms to mimic the motion of twisting the steer's neck. "A cow tackler."

Dad and I both laugh. I stretch my arm over the back of Della's chair as she continues to entertain him with her animated story telling. It's good to see him happy. But it also stings a little to have confirmation that his normal sullen mood can be lifted—just not by anything I've ever done.

After dessert, I clear the table and start the dishes. Della excuses herself to make a phone call. She steps out onto the deck and through the screen door I hear her say, "Hi, Dad." Then she moves to the end of the porch and the rest of the conversation is muffled.

"She's a keeper," Dad says as he wraps the leftover potatoes. "You better be careful."

I'm not sure if I'm more thrown off by the fact that he's talking to me about something other than the direct operation of the ranch, something that involves emotions, or by the comment itself. "Careful about what?"

Dad leans against the counter and crosses his arms. His mood is darkening again now that Della isn't close enough to blow away the storm clouds of our past. "Never mind."

He doesn't have to say it. I know what he's worried about because we had a huge blowout over it when I was dating Tracy. He thought she and I got too serious too young. It turned into a heated argument about my future and the choices I was making. When I pointed out that he and Mom were married and had me by the time they were eighteen he broke down. It was the first and only time I ever saw him cry. It scared the shit out of me. And although I don't agree with his philosophy of being miserable and lonely for the rest of my life as an attempt to avoid the heartbreak of losing someone I love; his concerns probably aren't unjustified. Della and I barely know each other. There are a lot of complicating factors. She's a year behind me in school. Her family lives in Canada. Shacking up together and dating could end in disaster. Damn it. What if he's right?

He slaps my shoulder. "Forget I said anything. I like her and I appreciate your help. Thanks for coming out."

Silence and fighting are the only two modes I'm used to with him. Everything about tonight is new territory. I drain the sink and fold the towel to hang it on the handle of the stove. "You know I don't mind coming home, but I can't do it every weekend and also keep up with school. I can quit rodeo, but that money helps out."

"I'll be all right."

"You should be taking it easy. I'm going to hire another hand."

He shakes his head. "With what money?"

"I earned some winnings. I'll figure out the rest."

He inhales as if he's going to protest, but then he doesn't. That's also a first. It's probably the closest to asking for help he'll ever get. "All right, son. I'm going to turn in. Tell Della I said goodbye. And bring her around again."

I nod, and he clutches my neck briefly in a cowboy brand of affection before he heads down the hall to his bedroom. I don't know what Della did to him or how she did it, but I just saw a glimpse of my old dad—the one from before the accident. I finish stacking the dishes in the cupboard and turn the lights out, then open the screen door to check if she's finished her phone call. She's sitting on Mom's rocking chair, looking out at the view. Brewster's got his head propped up on her foot.

"Hey," she says and relaxes back to rock.

"Hey." I lean on the porch railing. "Looks like you made a new friend."

Her eyes roll in a gesture of reluctant surrender. "Every time I move my shoe out from under his chin he just scooches over and places it down on my foot again. He's relentless."

I swear it looks like Brewster is smiling smugly. I laugh and sit down on the bench next to them. "How'd the phone call with your dad go?"

"Good. He still wants me to come home, but at least he's not angry anymore."

"My dad was tired, so he went to bed. He told me to say goodnight to you, and he wants you to come over again."

"Phew." She exhales and combs her fingers through her bangs to push her hair back from her face as she relaxes. "I thought I blew it by bringing up your mom."

"No. You knocked it out of the park. Seriously. He's a different man around you." I offer her my hand. "You want to go for a walk before we head back? There's something I want to show you."

She slides her foot out from under Brewster's attempt to claim her, then reaches over and wraps her fingers around mine as she stands to join me. I wish a relationship with her didn't have to be complicated. Or, on second thought, maybe that's why it appeals to me.

The sun is low and the sky is dusky as we walk around the barn, but I know the way by heart and have negotiated the path in the dark plenty of times. She follows me up the incline to the ridge of boulders that overlook the valley. Once we reach a grassy spot I guide her to sit and we hang our legs over the edge. She inhales deeply as she admires how the river runs through the basin and the hills frame the panorama like a painting.

"It's breathtaking," she whispers.

The mesmerized expression on her face. Now, that's breathtaking.

Without looking at me she says, "Your dad was the drunk driver who killed your mom, wasn't he?"

I close my eyes as the accident replays in my memory. It doesn't haunt me anymore, like it used to, but it still feels like a sledgehammer to the chest when I do think about it. "Yeah."

The sky turns a bright orange and then transitions into purple hues. "I'm sorry," she says softly.

"Yeah. Me too."

Her hand gently lays over mine. "You must have been so angry at him. How did you get over that?"

Staring out at the sunset, I seriously consider the question. Unfortunately, I'm not proud of the answer. "I haven't."

She nods with empathy and understanding, then tucks her knee up and turns until she's facing me. "Who took care of you while he was in prison?"

"I was in hospital for the first three months afterwards. Then I lived with my grandparents for the two years of his sentence and the year after that when he was still too messed up to come home."

Her gaze tracks across my face, reading my expression. Surprisingly, it's not pity in her eyes. It looks more like admiration. "I guess that's why you turned out so strong."

Man, she has a way about her. I want to say thank you, but it will choke me up if I try. Instead, I reach over and gently run the back of my hand over the contour of her cheek.

She smiles and then scoots over closer to lean up against my shoulder to watch what's left of the sunset. "Thanks for sharing your family history with me."

"Thanks for caring."

The stars appear one at a time and she sighs. "I love it here."

"Me too." I squeeze my arm around her and rest my cheek on top of her head briefly. "We should get going, though. We have a long drive ahead."

She nods but doesn't seem ready to leave yet. Her fingers tighten around mine and she stares down at our intertwined hands. "I've been thinking. All day. Well, actually, all day and all last night. Because there is something I want to say to you. Obviously, I could have said it before now, but I've been waiting for the right moment. I hope this is the right moment. If I'm wrong, sorry." She inhales and then lifts her chin and meets my gaze. "Okay. Here goes. I think you are an amazing person, already, and I don't even know everything about you. I've never met anyone even remotely as intriguing as you. And the thing is—I don't know how to put it exactly. You know last night when you said you were dying to ask me for a good night kiss? The truth is I was dying for you to ask me for a good night kiss. And we don't—"

I cut her off by leaning in to kiss her. She initially stiffens as if she wasn't expecting it, but when I slide my hand up the side of her neck and comb my fingers through her hair, she relaxes and her lips soften against mine. She tastes like apple cinnamon crisp, which guarantees I'm never going to be able to smell those scents again without remembering this moment. It takes all my strength to restrain myself from laying her back right here in the grass. I don't want to spook her by rushing things, so I ease off and smile. She doesn't move, as if she's stunned.

"You okay?"

"Yes. Thank you." She tucks her hair behind her ears. "I just want to take it all in. I never imagined my first kiss would be so perfect and I don't want to forget anything."

What? "Your *first* kiss?"

"Um." It's too dark to see, but I can tell by her tone that her face has turned scarlet. "Yes. Unless an eighth-grade truth or dare peck on the lips at a birthday party counts."

Whoa. First kiss. I didn't see that coming. This needs to go even slower than I thought.

Chapter 11

Della

I'm such an idiot. When I told Easton it was my first real kiss he immediately withdrew. Although he held my hand as we walked back to the barn to get my books, and he's made small talk during the drive, he hasn't said a word about the kiss. And we're almost back in Palo Alto. I lean my head back and clench my eyes shut. It was such an amazing moment and I ruined it. But who am I kidding? I was bound to screw up my chances with him at some point. I just didn't expect the collapse to happen so quickly. Maybe it was better to crash and burn right out of the gates. Painful and embarrassing, but at least it saves me from suffering a slow demise. It really was the perfect first kiss, though, with the perfect guy. I'm glad about that. Even if that's all it will ever be.

Easton pulls into the driveway and parks the truck. He glances at me as if he wants to address what happened but doesn't know what to say. To save him the discomfort, I hop out of the truck and rush up the path to unlock the front door of the house. Based on how dark and quiet it is inside, BJ and Chuck must be either out or already in bed. I remove my shoes and head upstairs. Maybe we can start over in the morning and pretend the kiss didn't happen? Or maybe there will be an awkward tension between us for the rest of our foreseeable future?

As I reach out to turn my bedroom doorknob, Easton catches my other hand in his. And just like that the awkward tension is over. "Is it all right if I come in for a minute?" he whispers into my ear.

Tingling all over from his touch, I nod and step into my room. In one smooth motion he spins me around, closes the door behind us, and presses me against the wall. Wow, maybe talking isn't what he has in mind. His thumb lifts my chin until I'm looking directly at him before he says, "I was hoping maybe I could steal a goodnight kiss. How do you feel about that?"

"Okay," I breathe out, almost inaudibly, insanely excited.

He smiles and gazes into my eyes for a few extra heartbeats before he leans in and presses his lips to mine. They are strong and soft at the same time, like his hands, which slide up my neck to cradle my head. A warm sensation travels down my throat and into the core of my body where it transforms into a slow, deep pulse. His lips move with mine and his hands travel from my neck down the side of my body, until he reaches my hips and pulls me even tighter up against him. I don't know if I'm doing it right, but it feels good, at least to me. Really good. Fan-freaking-tastic good. The blood rushes out of my legs and I'm worried they won't be able to support my weight much longer, so I dig my fingers into his shoulders to hold myself up.

If this is what his goodnight kiss does to my body, I don't know if I can handle anything more ambitious. Although, I'm not opposed to trying. The rush through my veins is literally euphoric. I want to go further. Be bold, Della. Take a risk. Go for it. The bed is less than an arm's length away. No, don't mess it up by getting in over your head. Stick to the level that most thirteen-year olds have already mastered. But he will want more than that. He's a grown man. His fingers glide across the skin between the bottom of my blouse and the waistband of my pants, then linger seductively as if it's something he's looked forward to all day. He clutches the fabric of my blouse as if he wants to take it off. I could handle that, I think. But he doesn't do it. His eyes close tightly for a second as he musters the strength to do whatever he's about to do next. Eventually he releases the fabric of my blouse and his fingers intertwine with mine. Then he lifts my hand to kiss the back of it.

"Goodnight, Della."

Wow. I can't swallow. I'm dizzy. How could something as sweet and innocent as a goodnight kiss do so many things to me? He's good. Like phenomenally good. Is it weird that I'm already looking forward to tomorrow night? And every night after that. "Night," I finally choke out.

He's amused by how dazed I am and chuckles as he steps back. Before he turns the doorknob, he leans over and gives me another quick peck on the cheek. "Sweet dreams. See you in the morning."

My head nods like a bobble head. After he's crossed the hall, I close the door and lean my forehead on the wood, trying to catch my breath. I love him already. Well, not love-love. Yet. But the infatuation part is firmly established. And by established, I mean pulsating. Ironically the first person I've ever been interested in sexually is a complete gentleman who literally left me yearning for more. I've never even wanted anything before, now I want more? If he keeps leaving me hanging like this, I wouldn't put it past myself to beg. Seriously, on my knees, pleading with him not to leave. Surprising, and possibly slightly pathetic, but true.

I spin around and flop down on my bed as the endorphins course through my blood. Too bad it's too late to call my sister. She was fairly experienced at dating before she met her husband. Not sleazy or anything, but she kissed her fair share of boys throughout her teen years. She never shared any of the juicy details with me because I was so much younger than she was, but I could tell how much she liked a guy by how long they stood out by the back shed.

Maybe she is awake. The baby doesn't usually sleep through the night, and I've seen Yulia online late sometimes. I sit up and grab my phone out of my bag to text her: *Are you sleeping?*

Her response is immediate: *What's wrong? Are you okay?*

I can almost feel the frantic big-sister panic in her typing. *I'm fine. I just need some advice.*

One o'clock in the morning advice must mean boy advice.

Yeah. Can you call me?

She calls without even saying hello first and blurts out, "You have no idea how long I've been waiting for this call. My little Dee Dee is finally ready for the sex talk."

I prop up the pillows to get comfortable. "Don't get too excited. I don't know if I'm quite there yet. I did have my first real kiss, though."

"Are you on birth control?"

Whoa, apparently this crash course on the birds and the bees is moving from zero to sixty. "No."

"Okay, you have to find a doctor at the school clinic or wherever and get a prescription and some condoms, like tomorrow."

"We kissed. That's all. I'm fairly sure unwanted pregnancy and STDs aren't my priority."

"You want to be prepared. Just in case. Go tomorrow. Trust me. What's his name? What's he like?"

"Easton. He's very sweet, smart, and sexy."

"The three Ss. That's good. Is he a student?"

"Yeah he's studying for his MBA. He's also a rodeo cowboy and a rancher and a model." I wince in anticipation of her reaction to what I'm about to divulge. "And he's my roommate."

"Holy shit, Della. Does Dad know?"

I hop up and head to my bathroom to get ready for bed. "No."

She laughs in an appreciative way, as if my predicament is the most entertaining thing she's been a part of in a while. "Don't tell Dad unless it lasts like six months or a year. And just because I told you to go on birth control, doesn't mean you should give it away easy. Make him work for it to make sure he's not just a jerk trying to sweet-talk you into bed."

"Easton is one of the good ones," I say into the speaker as I put my phone down on the counter to wash my face.

"So you think now, but they don't show their true colors at first. Anyone can act romantic, adoring, and respectful in the beginning. Hold out."

"I thought most people expect sex on the second date," I say as I change into pyjama shorts and a tank top.

"How are you supposed to assess a person's character after two dates? I recommend at least a month. The ones who are only hoping to get laid will give up and move on to an easier target. If Easton is still sweet and loyal and chivalrous after waiting a month, he deserves to get in your pants. And if he's willing to hold out, you should probably keep him because guys like that don't come around very often."

"Really?"

"The world is full of horn-dogs and self-serving assholes, Della. You probably won't meet many other guys who compare."

I sit back down on the end of my mattress and rub my palm over my face. "That puts so much pressure on me to not screw up."

"Not really. Screwing up is actually a good test to see how he handles it. No one is perfect, and you want to be with a partner who can accept that."

"It was only a kiss. You're talking like I'm going to marry him."

"I met Alex when I was your age, remember? You kind of bypassed all the practice dating and jumped into the big leagues."

I nod and let that sink in. I should have started dating when I was twelve, so I'd be a pro by the time I met Easton. Maybe a seasoned veteran is a better choice of phrases than a pro in this case. Although both sound a little worn and used. Amateur, rookie, newbie. Ooh, I like newbie the best. It implies fresh on the scene but not necessarily incompetent. Although, there is a strong possibility I will be incompetent. "How will I know if I'm doing it right?"

"What? Sex?" She laughs. "It's not like all those cheesy teen romance novels you used to read where it's clunky and awkward. A monkey can do it. Literally. Monkeys do it."

"That doesn't help."

"Don't worry, he'll do most of the work. But don't just lay there. They all like oral, so Google that."

"Yulia!"

"What? You asked."

We continue to talk for almost an hour, not just about Easton and sex but about school and BJ and Chuck, too. I can hear the baby fussing, so I reluctantly call it a night. "Thank you for the tutorial. I should let you go. It's getting late and I have class tomorrow."

"Any time. Just take it slow and be safe. That's all you really need to know."

"Those are two things I can handle." I climb under my covers and turn out my lamp. "Night."

"Night."

After I hang up, my thoughts immediately drift to Easton. Is he still awake? Is he thinking about me? Would he be willing to officially become boyfriend and girlfriend even though he and the guys agreed none of them should date me? Is he aware that we are at an age where the person you date might potentially be the person you marry? Will my inexperience, combined with the extent to which he fills out his boxers, be a problem? They all like oral?

I pull my phone out and Google it. Oh my. How am I supposed to sleep with that image in my head?

Chapter 12

Easton

Della and I have been taking it slow for two weeks, and it requires every ounce of restraint in me to sleep alone in my room each night, knowing she's right across the hall. I don't mind, though. Having to wait actually has me more fired up than I've ever been over a woman. Her laugh, the way she glances at me from across the room when she doesn't think I'm looking, her sweetness towards every single person she encounters, the smell of her hair in the morning—everything about her does something to me. The guys know we spend a lot of time together, walking to class and studying at the coffee shop, but they don't know about the hand holding and goodnight kisses that have progressed to on-the-bed, half-clothed, make-out sessions. Hopefully I'll eventually owe them some cash, but so far, no lines have been crossed.

She's coming with me today to a rodeo in Oakdale. BJ decided not to enter because he has an assignment due on Monday. Chuckie's out, too. He claims his collarbone is bugging him, but I've seen him ride with a torn bicep. The injury's only an excuse. The real reason he's bent out of shape is because Janine's been hanging out on campus with some guy who looks like a surfer. And he's in a particularly foul mood this morning.

"Would you like me to make you some breakfast, Taylor?" Della asks Chuck as she and I finish the Eggs Benny she made. "These were pretty good if I do say so myself."

He slams the cupboard door and pours himself a cup of coffee without answering her.

"So, no?" she asks.

His eyes roll slightly before he turns to leave.

She stands to clear her dishes and says, loud enough for him to hear down the hall, "I was just trying to be nice."

He turns around, but not in a hey-I'm-sorry-you're-right-I-was-being-a-dick way. He wants to get into it with her, so I stand. He glares at me as a challenge before he lowers his voice and says to Della, "Listen, sweetheart, I'm sick of the bullshit sunshine that's always blowing out your uptight little ass. So, give it a rest. If I don't feel like talking, I'm not going to talk. Get used to it."

"Back off," I say to him.

"It's okay, Easton. I can handle myself," she whispers. Her cheeks blush from the confrontation, but she remains calm as she continues, "I know you're upset about Janine, Taylor, but it's not fair to take it out on me. We can talk about it if you want to."

"I don't give two shits about Janine. She's free to hook up with whichever ass-wipe she wants to. Being the president of your little high school chess club probably made you feel so damn smart, but don't fool yourself into believing that you know everything about me after living here for a couple weeks. And don't kid yourself into believing we're friends. I hate to break it to you, sweetheart, but a twenty-one-year-old prude who has a pathetic PG-rated school girl crush on her roommate because he was the first guy she met after she left her mommy and daddy's house doesn't know shit about anything, especially not my relationship with Janine. So, go give your unsolicited advice to someone else."

Her giant doe eyes blink slowly as she attempts to keep her composure. "I didn't offer you advice. I offered you breakfast. But since we're on the topic, you didn't treat Janine right. You deserve what you got. And you have nobody to blame but yourself."

He aggressively leans in, less than an inch from her face, and says, "You need to learn when to keep your mouth shut, you snotty little bitch."

I shove Chuck's shoulder to make him back away from her. He throws his coffee in the sink, spewing it all over.

Della flinches but doesn't move and doesn't say anything as I move to stand between them. He postures as if he wants me to hit him so he'll have an excuse to fight, which is exactly why I don't. He can't take me anyway, and he knows it.

Once he realizes I'm not going to take the bait, he scoffs and walks backwards. "Pussy. I'm outta here."

After the front door slams behind him, I turn to Della.

She's already wiping up the coffee from the floor. "You okay?"

"I was president of the debate club, not the chess club," she mumbles to herself as she wrings the towel in the sink.

"Don't take anything he said personally. He's an idiot."

Her eyes widen in a humorous expression and she points at me. "Remember when I tried to explain how I have a knack for triggering rage in other people? Exhibit A."

"That wasn't your fault. His asshole genes made him do that. And he wouldn't have actually hurt you, which doesn't make what he did okay. But he would never hurt you."

"I know he wouldn't." She sighs. "Do you think he meant outta here as in to cool off? Or outta here as in moving out?"

"Doesn't matter. I'm not okay with him talking to you like that. I'm kicking him out, whether he likes it or not."

After loading the breakfast dishes into the dishwasher, she says; "But we need the rent."

"I plan on taking home some rodeo earnings this weekend. I'll figure something out for the rest."

"The money isn't the only issue." She leans her elbows on the counter. "The three of you are friends and see each other in class and at rodeos. I would feel better if I could work it out with him, if you don't mind."

"No." I shake my head. "He can't act that way around you."

"I agree. I'll tell him it was out of line. But we should give him a chance to redeem himself. It's not fair to have a one-strike policy. And I really don't want to be the reason that your friendship ended with him."

I step closer and pull her in for a hug. BJ and I have always put up with Chuck's tantrums, mostly because both of us can kick his ass if he steps too far out of line. But with Della in the house it's not cool. Chuck needs to be accountable for his behaviour. Suffering the consequences is the only thing that even remotely has a chance of drilling through his rock-hard hillbilly head. "He's the problem, not you. I'll talk to him."

"If he's ever really going to respect me, it would be better if he and I came to an agreement. Let me talk to him before you do anything. Please," she says into my chest.

"I'll think about it."

During the drive to the rodeo in Oakdale, I made my decision. Chuck's outburst was not acceptable, and my plan if he hasn't already done it by the time we get home, is to pack up all his stuff and leave it on the front step. Unfortunately, we're not going to get home anytime soon. On my final out, the horse's hoof came down hard on the side of my knee after my ride. Now we're sitting in emergency, waiting to be seen by a doctor. I had hoped it was only a hematoma, but the paramedic at the event insisted I needed to see a doctor.

"Can I get you something from the vending machine?" Della asks.

"I'm fine. Thanks." I adjust the ice pack and then turn my head to wink at her. "Sorry you have to hang around waiting for me. I'm sure a hospital is the last place you want to be right now."

Her cheeks blush as she shakes her head to disagree. "What? You like waiting for hours in emergency?"

"No. But I want to be where you are. And this is where you are." She clasps her hands together and squeezes them between her knees. "So yeah, I'm happy."

I nudge her ribs with my elbow. "That's a romantic thing to say."

"I know." She swings her feet back and forth like a bored kid. "Weird, right? This whole day has been awful—waking up to someone with an anger management problem directed at me, then a terror-filled afternoon of witnessing what I thought was you being killed by a one-thousand pound animal in a manure-covered arena, and now an evening of torturously long wait times in an airless facility that smells not so faintly of urine and vomit—and there is nowhere else I'd rather be."

"It means you like me."

"Hmm." She smiles and picks up a magazine to flip through the pages. "The question is, do you like me enough to overlook the facts that I single-handedly drove away one of your roommates with my inability to keep my mouth shut and somehow jinxed you with my presence into being stomped on by a vicious bucking horse that evidently despises people, thus leaving you in dire financial straits and presumably a fair amount of pain?"

"I'm a cowboy, I don't know what pain is. A dose of the truth is exactly what Chuck needed, and you're the only person who's had the balls to give it to him. I still scored an eighty-seven on that ride. And my sense of smell is not that good because of all the concussions I've had, so the urine and vomit doesn't bother me." I lean over to kiss her neck and then whisper in her ear, "And in case you're wondering, I more than like you."

Her head turns and her gaze locks with mine. It has seriously been a shit day and I don't care because she's with me. I want to sleep with her so badly right now. And even though she has never been with anyone before, I can tell she wants it, too.

"Lewis. Easton Lewis."

"That's you," Della whispers without breaking eye contact with me.

"Is it?" I wave to let the nurse know I heard her, but I don't look away from Della.

She nods to answer my question and her eyes shift to stare at my mouth, telegraphing her thoughts. "The faster you finish with the doctor the sooner we can get home. And, you know, share a goodnight kiss. Or more."

With that implied promise, I literally pop up on one leg and hop to meet the nurse who called my name. I don't know how much Della's ready for but getting home to find out is now my main goal.

Della glances at me from across my truck cab as she drives us home. "You've been so quiet. What did the doctor say?"

"She wants me to see a specialist. I almost definitely need ACL surgery."

Her hands grip the steering wheel and she focuses on the road. "At least it's not a broken bone."

"This is worse. Broken bones heal faster than ligaments."

"Oh." She glances at me again, gauging my foul mood. "I don't know the right thing to say."

"Nothing," I mumble. I'd rather not be in a shitty mood around her, but I'm pissed. There's a waitlist to even get an appointment with the specialist. The recovery from the surgery, once I get it, will take months. No rodeos. No money. And with Chuck out of the house and Dad needing to hire someone for the ranch, the timing couldn't be worse. Not that there would ever be a good time to get injured. It goes with the business, but it's still frustrating as hell.

Della gives me space to be grumpy for the rest of the drive home, which I appreciate. She parks on the street in front of the house and leans over to kiss my cheek. "I'm sorry you're injured and won't be able to ride or help your dad for a while."

"Thanks."

"If it makes you feel any better, I had an idea while we were driving. Well, actually, I had about a thousand ideas but only two that you'll likely be interested in given your current state." She hops out of the truck and jogs around the back to get the crutches they gave me at the hospital. "I was thinking you could call Stuart and see if he can line up some modeling jobs for you."

"I've been out of that game for a long time."

"But you could get back into it," she says with enough enthusiasm for both of us.

"They don't like to book rodeo cowboys who are likely

to show up with a black eye or missing teeth." Crutches annoy me, so instead of using them I carry them as I limp up to the house.

"Yeah, but Stuart told me that you had a ton of potential and if you had been willing to focus on the modeling you could have done really well." She opens the door and swings it to the side to let me in.

"I don't love it, Della. I love bronc riding. I only modeled back then because it was fast, easy cash. I didn't want to focus on it."

"Okay, I respect that. But a few photo shoots will make up for the money you'll be missing at the rodeos. Only while you're injured and can't ride anyway."

I smile and wrap my arm around her shoulder. "Okay. You convinced me. What was the second idea you thought I'd like?"

Her eyebrow arches before she laces her fingers with mine to lead me upstairs. It's obvious by her half-smile and the way her head is spinning to check for BJ and Chuck that she's about to do something sneaky. She hooks her fingers over my belt buckle and tugs to silently invite me into her room. I don't know what she's got planned, but I can tell I'm going to like it. She steps closer and rests her index finger on my chest, applying enough pressure to guide me backwards towards the bathroom.

"You need a shower."

I nod, hoping she's getting at what I think she's getting at.

"Do you mind if I watch?"

I remove my shirt. "You want to watch me shower?"

She nods and leans back against the wall. "I have very much enjoyed our nightly make-out sessions. And I can't even express how much I appreciate the fact that you have been patient with me and taken things slow over the last few weeks. However, we are consenting adults, and I'm ready to take our relationship to the next level. Not all the way, but up one notch. If that's cool with you."

"It's definitely cool with me."

She glances down as I drop my jeans and boxer briefs. Her mischievous expression transitions into a cute combination of intrigue and apprehension as she studies me. All of me. On full display.

"Your knee is very swollen."

I laugh at the fact that's what she decided to focus on. "I can't even feel it."

She exhales slowly as if she's attempting to maintain composure, then she spins around and enters the bathroom ahead of me.

"Do you want to join me?" I ask.

Her gaze scans down my body before she quickly returns to the safety of eye contact. "Maybe." She hops up to sit on the counter, ready for the show. "Later."

I step into the shower and turn the water on. Shampoo commercials in showers, gay men's magazine spreads in waterfalls, western wear print ads in rivers—I've modeled in a lot of water over the years. It's going to be a good show. Her eyes widen and her mouth drops open slightly as the water cascades over my body.

Once I'm fully lathered, I gesture with my finger to invite her to come closer.

After a slight hesitation, she slides off the counter and crosses over to stand up next to the shower glass.

I open the door. Then, to my surprise, she makes the first move. She reaches in the shower and grabs the back of my neck to pull me in for a kiss—open mouth, the perfect amount of tongue. Her other hand slides up my thigh until she's touching me. I go hard against her palm, and she flinches back at first, but then as we kiss, she relaxes and squeezes the tip softly.

"Is it okay if I touch you?" she asks as she looks down at my entire extended length resting in her palm.

"Definitely."

"Am I doing it right?" she asks as I dip forward to kiss her neck.

I lift her up by the armpits and place her in the shower in front of me to show her how to form an 'o' with her finger and thumb around the tip and then guide her other hand further down to the base of the shaft. With my hands over hers I show her how much pressure and twist I like. Then I vary the speed, so she'll get the hang of changing the stroke up. Her hair and clothes are soaking wet, which turns me on even more. She concentrates so intently on getting it right that a crease forms between her eyebrows. It's cute.

I reach for the bottom hem of her blouse and pause to check if she's okay with me removing it. She nods and then lifts her arms over her head. The clasp of her light pink bra unlatches with a quick flick of my fingers and the satin straps slide down over her pale shoulders. She covers her chest with her arm self-consciously as she drapes the bra over the glass, then she slowly gets more comfortable and lets her arm drop away. I lean in to leave a trail of kisses from her shoulder, along her collarbone, and down the slope of her breast. Then I take her nipple in my mouth, briefly. She closes her eyes and exhales as if my touch is the most incredible thing she has ever experienced, which is another huge turn on.

Her hand slides back down to fondle me. All my weight is centred over my left leg, and I have to hold onto the shower door for balance, but I don't care. She kisses my chest and then lowers down to my abs as she continues to work both hands. I drop my head back as she hits exactly the right rhythm. Just the thought of her taking me in her mouth nearly sends me over the edge. Then she does it. Her lips slide around the tip and her tongue dances across the sensitive skin. "Holy shit," I say under my breath as the sensation travels into my body. She glances at me with apprehension, maybe because she misread my initial shock for dissatisfaction. To reassure her and encourage her to keep going, I wink and caress the side of her face. Everything she's doing feels awesome, more intense than ever before. Partly because I've been waiting for a while, but mostly because it's her. She moves from a crouch to kneel on the tile and her hand slides around my hip to grab my ass as she lets me slide deeper into her mouth. I'm already there, so I pull out. Every muscle in my body tenses and then I release with a shudder.

Della reels back, almost startled by how fast I came. Then she pauses, unsure what to do next. So, I ease her back up to stand against the wall tiles and rest my palms above her head.

"Sorry. I didn't expect it to go that fast. Did I do it wrong?" she asks.

"You did good. It went fast because I want you so bad."

"Really?" She searches my face with a wide-eyed expression, as if she's worried that I'm only saying that to make her feel better.

To prove I'm serious, I consume her mouth with mine and caress her breast. Her fingers dig into my back as she drags them down from my shoulders to my waist. She draws our hips closer together and I lift her skirt until I'm pressing up against the crotch of her underwear. It makes me hard again. "Are you ready for your turn?"

"Um. We're talking about oral sex, right? I'd like to try it. Yes. I'm not sure if I'm ready for real sex, though. Partly because, have you seen how large you are?" She points down between my legs and widens her eyes in a hilarious expression.

I laugh, which I probably shouldn't do when she is already insecure about her inexperience. "We'll only do what you're ready for. Let's move to the bed."

"Okay." She removes her wet skirt and underwear.

I turn the water off and open the shower door to grab two towels. "I'd carry you, but with my knee screwed up and your natural lack of coordination, we might end up back in emergency."

"Walking is fine," she laughs before she scuttles into the bedroom, clutching the towel around her body.

I chuckle and then follow behind her.

"Is it okay if we keep the lights off?" she whispers.

"Yeah," I say and reach for her through the dark. She drops the towel and wraps her arms around my neck. "Say stop or slow down whenever you want to, okay?"

Although I can't make out much more than her silhouette I see her nod.

I slide my palm along her waist, then over her hip. "Stand with your feet a little farther apart." She widens her stance and then gasps slightly as I trail my finger between her legs, dipping inside her just for a second. She raises up on her toes to kiss me and guides my hand back to invite me to do it again.

"You like that?" I whisper as I slide two fingers in and out of her, slowly.

"Yes," she whispers and drops her head back, which lifts her breasts irresistibly. I take one nipple in my mouth while still alternating between sliding fingers inside her and applying gentle pressure to her clitoris. She's wet and her breath is raspy in her throat, which makes me even more eager to make her come.

My knee is killing me, though, so I pause long enough to lift her up and place her on the bed. "Bend your legs." She does and I dip down to kiss along her inner thigh. "Is this okay?" I ask.

"Um yeah. It feels like you're doing it right."

I chuckle. "I meant are you okay with what I'm doing?"

"Oh. Like consent. Yes. I consent. What you are doing is consensual. Everything you have done so far has been fine, as in you had consent. And it was literally fine too, as in it feels great. Not that I have anything to compare it to, but I'm sure if I did it would still be the best thing I've ever experienced. It hasn't been a month yet, though. My sister said, ugh, never mind. I'm Sorry. I'm being weird." She groans and covers her face with her arms. "Can you please just keep going so I'll stop talking?"

"I like it when you talk." I smile and then kiss my way down from her knee, sliding my fingers inside her again. "Say my name."

"Oh my goodness." She arches back from the pleasure of being simultaneously touched on her breast, kissed on her clitoris, and fingered. Her hands clutch at the sheets and her hips buck. "Which name?"

"Whichever one you want to say." I lick in a straight line between her legs, then swirl the soft, flat side of my tongue like I'm tasting the icing on a cinnamon bun. That one does it for her.

"Havie," she whispers as she quivers against my lips.

The way she says it sounds so damn hot. I thrust my tongue inside her and tease her clit lightly between my fingers. Her breath catches again almost as if she's about to cry, so I pause. "Is this okay?"

"Consent. Consent. Holy shit. Easton. Don't stop."

Amused that I made her curse, I laugh and then get to work. Well, it's not work. Discovering everything about her body is like wandering through a pristine wilderness that has not only never been touched by anyone else, it has never even been seen. I want to stay in the moment forever, suspended in its perfection. But I also want to take her to the brink.

Her breathing is rapid and quiet moans roll in her throat, so I figure-eight the tip of my tongue over the surface of her clit. And she's there. A tiny whimper escapes from her lips as she throws her head back and comes in several waves. It's so beautiful to watch her completely undone.

I've been with virgins before, but I didn't really know what I was doing back then. Based on her reaction, I'm going to assume she appreciates my current skill set.

"Wow. Holy cow. Thank you." She flops back on the pillow and combs her fingers through her hair as she basks in the lingering euphoria. "I might want that to be my goodnight kiss every night from now on."

"Fine with me." I slide up to lay next to her and lace my fingers with hers.

She lifts our intertwined hands and kisses mine. "Sex is even better than that?"

"It's all that and more."

She inhales deeply as if the thought of more is hard to comprehend. Her head turns on the pillow to face me. "Do you want to sleep in my bed tonight?"

I kiss her forehead. "Yes. If you're comfortable with it."

"I'm a heavy breather, according to my sister."

"It won't bother me. I can sleep through a tornado." I reach over to arrange the other pillow under my head.

"My hair gets really messy when I sleep. I don't wake up looking pretty."

I chuckle and make her roll onto her side so I can spoon up against her back. "Me neither."

After lying peacefully in my arms for a while, she says, "Easton?"

"Yeah."

"Don't worry. I'm not going to talk all night. Although quite a bit of adrenaline is still pulsating through my veins and I'm probably too excited to sleep. But I'll be quiet so you can sleep. I just want to tell you that I like everything about you."

I smile and give her a squeeze to pull her tighter to my chest. "I like everything about you, too."

She's quiet for about a minute but then rolls over to face me. "Sorry. One last thing. Are we dating? Or are we just friends who happen to kiss each other in a really sexy way?"

"What do you want us to be?"

Her finger touches my lip first and then she leans in to kiss me. "I want to be your girlfriend."

I slide my hands up her neck to cradle her perfect face with my palms. "Della, would you do me the honor of agreeing to be my girlfriend?"

Her eyes widen with excitement but instead of agreeing she says, "I don't want to cause more problems in the roommate department. Do you think they'll mind?"

"BJ will be happy because I'll owe him five hundred bucks. And as far as I'm concerned, Chuck doesn't live here anymore."

"I told you I want to try to fix that. And if I can, it would be better to spend that money on hiring someone to help your dad. We don't have to tell them."

I nod. "We'll see. Don't worry about it right now."

She rolls over again to snuggle her back up against my chest. And she's quiet for less than thirty seconds before she says, "You're my first boyfriend, by the way."

I laugh and whisper, "I figured that. Now, go to sleep so we can do this again in the morning."

She nods, fluffs up her pillow, and is quiet for ten seconds before she lunges out of bed. "I have to pee."

She runs nude to the bathroom, and I can't stop smiling. She's definitely one of a kind. I already can't imagine my life without her in it.

This is exactly what my dad tried to warn me about.

Chapter 13

Della

Easton and I explored each other's bodies again once we woke up. I'm not quite ready for going all the way, but thanks to the extensive research I did on giving head, I think he's happy with how far things have progressed so far. After we showered, he made sure Chuck isn't home and then he left to run some quick errands to pick up an anti-inflammatory prescription at the pharmacy and to transfer money at the bank for his dad. He gave me five one-hundred dollar bills to give to Bailey, who is already downstairs eating breakfast.

"Morning," I say as I slide the cash across the counter.

BJ looks up from his cereal bowl and smiles. "You guys sealed the deal?"

"Let's just say that Easton feels he owes you some money." I pour myself a glass of orange juice, proud of the fact that I took the leap. "That's all I will be sharing."

"Congratulations."

"Thank you." I bite into a muffin and then sit next to him at the bar. "How's your assignment coming along?"

"Not great. I'm only half done and it's worth forty percent of my mark."

"You still have the rest of the weekend to work on it."

"The timeline isn't the only problem. I'm on academic probation. If I don't get at least a B on it, I'm going to get expelled."

"Really?" Wow. Flunking out is serious. It would be a huge blow, not just to him personally, but to his mom and sisters back home, too. I'm vicariously anxious for him. "Is there anything I can do to help?"

He shrugs and swirls his spoon between his soggy Cheerios. "How much do you know about international trade barriers?"

"Nothing. Easton probably does, though."

He stands and walks over to the sink to dump the milk from his bowl. "He's already helped me get this far, and he has his own assignment due on Monday."

"He does?" I shake my head, wondering where he'll find the time to do everything. I'm a distraction, obviously. Not just to him but to myself, too. Last night and this morning were amazing, but we can't lose focus on our academics. We need to talk about how to balance everything when he gets back. Maybe I should run things by my sister for a second opinion.

The front door opens, and I assume it's Easton. Instead, Chuck walks into the kitchen. "Hey, Della. Sorry I was a dick to you yesterday. No hard feelings?" Without waiting for my response, he opens the fridge door, grabs the milk, and drinks straight out of the carton.

BJ glances at me and then back at Chuck, probably trying to figure out what the apology was for. Saying sorry was a big step for Chuck, I can tell by his uncharacteristic discomfort. I want to accept his peace offering. Easton won't be as forgiving, though, especially if Chuck is all talk and no action. He eventually turns around and checks my expression to see if we're good. The cautious apprehension in his eyes sells the case that he's genuinely sorry, but I'm not sure if it's because he has nowhere else to live or if he actually feels bad for acting the way he did. Before I have a chance to respond, he spots the cash on the counter.

"What's this?" He picks up the pile of hundreds and fans through the bills. "Lottery win? Proceeds of prostitution? Gambling?" Then it hits him like a bolt through his brain. His face breaks into a huge grin and he points at me accusingly. "Penetration?"

The vulgar word slams into my chest and literally makes me wince. My face and neck feel like they've turned blotchy and my pulse pounds in my ears.

He waves the money in front of my face. "Is this here because Havie dipped his wick in your wax? Rammed the cob in the corn hole? Lowered the anchor in the dinghy? Parked his rig in your garage?"

"Leave her alone, man," BJ says as he snatches the cash away from Chuck.

Chuck laughs and hops up to sit on the counter. "Which orifice did he penetrate?"

"Shut up," I say quietly as I stand and tuck the stool in.

"Ooh. The S word. Listen to little Miss Priss with the

potty mouth. What's wrong? You're naughty enough to let him penetrate you but too delicate to talk about it afterwards?"

"Stop saying that word."

"Which one? Penetrate?" He laughs again. Obviously his apology was only intended to secure his roommate status.

"It's none of your business."

"Yes it is. I have five hundred bucks coming my way too if Havie penetrated you."

"You don't live here anymore. He doesn't owe you anything."

Chuck's mood flips like a switch. He hops off the counter and steps into my personal space to intimidate me. "If anyone needs to move out it's you. Everything was fine before you got here."

"Step off," BJ warns him.

Chuck eases back but hostility still vibrates off him. "I've lived here three years. You've lived here three weeks. You slept with one of us, which goes against the roommate agreement. You need to go."

I'm about to cry but suck back the humiliation, anger, and fear. Staring at him with a flat expression, I wait until my voice is steady enough to speak. "Easton and Bailey can decide which one of us needs to move out."

He glances at BJ who, at this exact moment, doesn't appear to hold a supportive vote for Chuck. After mumbling a completely offensive curse word, Chuck throws the entire carton of milk in the sink and it explodes. "Fine." He points at me. "But you let Havie penetrate you, so if they kick me out, I want my five hundred bucks before I leave."

A woman gasps behind me and I whip around. To my absolute horror my mom and dad are standing with Easton in the archway. Mom's hand is clasped over her mouth. Dad's face is creased and tomato-coloured. I have never seen him look so furious.

Easton points at Chuck. "Get out. Now."

Chuck smiles and lifts his eyebrows at my parents in a fake nice-to-meet-you way, which nobody but him appreciates. Then he grabs a muffin off the plate on the counter before he walks down the hall. Once the front door shuts behind him, everyone turns to look at me.

"Hi," I say through a trembling forced smile.

Dad clutches my elbow to escort me to the sliding door and out into the back yard. Mom follows behind us and closes the door, leaving Easton and BJ inside. Dad obviously wants to say something but based on the size of the vein bulging at his temple, he's not calm enough yet.

"What in the world is going on?" Mom asks as she hugs me. "What is a Havie?"

Unfortunately, her embrace makes me emotional and I have to fight not to get choked up. It feels as if I'm regressing back to a twelve-year-old little girl who's terrified to disappoint her parents. I can't break down in front of my dad. "They were just joking around," I say.

Neither of them buy my attempt to play it down, probably since I don't buy it myself.

"You live with three men?" Mom asks, completely in shock.

"What are you doing here?" I ask to avoid answering her question and throw the focus back on them. "How did you even get my address?"

Dad sits down on a patio chair and rests his elbows on his knees like a basketball player who has to take a break on the bench because he's about to pass out from exertion. "The bank called about your savings account and wanted to confirm the address change."

"And you took that as an invitation to fly down here and barge in on me unannounced?" I snap.

"Della." Mom rests her hand on my arm to try to settle me down. "We were concerned. We just wanted to make sure you're okay."

I shake my head and pace next to the pool. It feels like I'm being sucked back into my old unwaveringly obedient and pleaser self. I need to stand up for myself. "I told you on the phone how I am. Have you forgotten that I'm an adult? I don't need my mommy and daddy to check up on me. Thanks anyway." Evidently, I don't know how to stand up for myself without going on the offensive and sounding like a petulant teenager.

"Apparently you do need us to check on you." Dad stands and gestures animatedly with his hands. "You're living with three men and one of them was speaking to you in a disgusting manner and insinuating that you are some sort of prostitute. This living arrangement is unacceptable."

"It's not something you can control, Dad. I make my own choices. I pay my own rent."

He inhales deeply and the tendons in his neck tighten,

which makes me legitimately worried that I'm going to give him a heart attack or a stroke.

"Why did the one with lightning bolts in his hair say he wanted money?" Mom tries to sound compassionate, but her dismay is seeping through. "Oh, *myshka*, have they taken advantage of you, sexually?" she whispers.

I roll my eyes and sit on the patio chair, legs crossed and foot bouncing with frustration. Frustrated that they are treating me like I'm incompetent. But more frustrated that I'm essentially proving them right by having a hissy fit. "No. Nobody is taking advantage of me. It's just a silly bet. I told you I was fine. That's all you need to know. I can handle myself."

Mom pulls up a chair next to me and places her palm on my knee. "One small girl is no match for three bulging men like that."

"Easton and Bailey are complete gentlemen, who are both studying for their MBAs and take care of their families back home. Taylor is immature and rude, but he would never hurt me, and he's moving out anyway."

The sliding door opens and BJ steps out onto the patio with his arm extended towards my dad to shake his hand. "Sorry to interrupt. Bailey Jackson. Nice to meet you Mr. Koskov." He rotates to his right and shakes my mom's hand, too. "Mrs. Koskov. Welcome to California. Unfortunately, I have to head out to get some studying done but enjoy your visit. You've got a great daughter here." He smiles and then gives a little wave before stepping back inside.

Easton obviously already met them outside when they

arrived, which is why they ended up landing right in the middle of Chuck's tirade. Easton makes eye contact with me through the window as if to ask what I want him to do next. I'm not sure. It's definitely not the right time to introduce him as my boyfriend. But if they got to know him they would be less worried. Mom would instantly like him. Dad, not so much.

Before I have a chance to decide how to handle things, Dad says, "I'm very disappointed in you, Della. Let's go, Polina." Then he disappears into the house.

Ouch. The word disappointed coming from my dad is the equivalent of stepping off a curb and getting blindsided by a bus. He's only said it to me one other time in my life, when I was sent to the headmaster's office in the eighth grade for skipping school with some older students who smoked weed and then got caught shoplifting. I didn't try the pot and went back to the school by myself when they decided to go into the shop, so I didn't get suspended, but I still haven't recovered from my dad telling me he was disappointed.

Mom watches him leave but doesn't get up to follow. She ardently studies my expression. "Are you happy, sweetheart?"

"I was until my parents showed up unannounced, trying to tell me how to live my life. And embarrassed me in front of my roommates."

"I'm sorry about that. You're right. We should have called first." She squeezes my hand. "But you don't have to pretend everything is okay if it's not. Don't suffer just so you can stubbornly prove something to your father."

"I'm not pretending or suffering. It's a nice house. Easton and Bailey are really sweet. I can walk to school. My classes are interesting. And the weather is great. I love it here. I'm sorry that Dad is having a hard time accepting that I've grown up, but what am I supposed to do about that? I'm an adult, whether he likes it or not."

She nods slowly and examines my face for any sign of unhappiness. If she's paying attention, what she will notice is how ecstatically infatuated I am. Not that me falling in love for the first time would be any less concerning for her, but I'm probably the happiest I've ever been. "Okay. You do seem fine. And other than the one with the lightning bolts, the boys do seem decent enough. Just be careful." She pats my arm. "We're staying in a hotel not far from your school for the week. Why don't we give your dad the day to calm down, then we can meet up later?"

Glad to postpone everything for long enough to come up with a game plan, I agree. "Okay." I stand and give her a hug. "I'll call you later."

I walk her to the front door and watch as she gets into the rental car. She waves as they drive away, but Dad doesn't even look at me. Which really isn't fair. He came in with a preconceived notion that I wasn't safe, and he wasn't open to changing his mind. Chuck didn't exactly help with that first impression, but still, my own parents should have faith in my ability to judge a person's character and make good decisions. They should trust me.

And I should probably act like an adult if I want them to treat me like one.

Easton steps up behind me and circles his arms around to hug me. "You okay?" he whispers into my hair.

I shake my head as the frustrated tears that I've been holding back since Chuck showed up swell to the surface.

Chapter 14

Easton

Della's parents have been in California for a week. They spent the last two days in San Francisco and are back in town for one more night before they fly home to Vancouver tomorrow. She invited me to dinner with them at a high-end Italian place, but she told me right up front that she didn't think the timing was right to tell them about us dating. It takes some of the pressure off, but I still want to make a good impression. I don't want them to be disappointed when she does eventually tell them about us.

Della coached me beforehand to let me know that her dad is interested in sports, but I've tried everything, including tennis and Nascar. He hasn't given any conversation starter much more than a brief answer. If Della didn't seem so desperate to change his mood, I'd just accept that he's naturally quiet and not worry about trying to engage with him. It's obvious by her nervous sideways glances and excessive serviette folding that she wants him to like me, so I keep trying. It's not until I ask him about his sailing hobby that he finally becomes more engaged.

Her mom warmed up to me earlier this week when I took them on a tour of the campus. She's a lot like Della, actually. Funny and sweet, and she's knocked over the salt shaker with her elbow three times since we sat down at the table. She already knows a lot about me – the important stuff, except how my mom died. And she's as curious about rodeo as Della is.

Mr. Koskov notices when I do things like pull the chair out for Della, and I'm sure he's judging my character based on things like how I address the waiter. He's also been watching how Della touches my arm when she's talking. Even though he hasn't asked any questions, Mrs. Koskov has been firing them at me, and he listens intently to all my answers as if I'm being evaluated at an interview. Although I'm nailing the interview, he's acting as if he had someone different in mind for the job. Good thing Della is in charge of hiring for the position.

Della shoves my shoulder playfully. "Is it all right if I tell them about how you used to model for Stuart under an alias?"

I chuckle. "You just did."

"I know." Her eyebrows dance up and down. "Did you like how I did that? I'm so crafty."

I nod and smile as she tells the story of how she thought she was moving in with three women. When she gets to the cockroach and bed bug part, her dad's demeanor changes. Maybe because she's hilarious when she tells stories, or maybe because she's proving to him that she really can handle herself. He actually chuckles at the part about cracking the alarm code and the failed touchdown dance.

Mrs. Koskov reaches over to give Della a hug and tips her water glass over in the process. "Oh shoot," she says, just like Della always does, which makes me smile.

Her dad casually soaks up the spilled water as if it's a second nature reflex that he doesn't even have to think about because it happens so often. "So, Easton, AKA Everley, where do you plan on settling down after you finish your degree?"

Della's eyes pop open in a mixture of excitement because her dad finally addressed me in conversation, and apprehension for exactly the same reason.

"My family owns a cattle ranch a few hours from here, near Three Rivers."

He nods, but his expression gives no clue to what he thinks of that. It's possible he asked simply to make friendly conversation but given the fact it's the only thing he's directly asked me all week, I'm going to assume he's worried there's a risk Della might never move back home.

Mrs. Koskov studies her husband for a second, then she glances at Della, who physically deflates from her dad pointing out the biggest glitch in any plans we might want to make in the future. Her mom's face lights up as she puts the pieces together, and she says, "Well, Easton, if you ask me, you are very fortunate to have property here. I love California. It reminds me of the south of France." She places her hand on her husband's arm. "When the girls were young we spent the entire summer in Corsica. It was so beautiful and relaxing. Do you remember how much we loved it there, darling?"

He nods and takes a sip of wine.

She faces me and says, "We've always had dreams of retiring there. Who knew California is basically the same thing? And it's only a two-hour flight from Vancouver."

"American food doesn't compare, not even close," Mr. Koskov mumbles in a grumpy protest.

"Pfft." Mrs. Koskov flaps her hand at him and rolls her eyes hilariously. "You cleared your giant plate of American food just fine. And living in Europe would mean being at least a ten-hour flight away from both the girls and any other grandbabies that might arrive in the future." She points at Della in a cautionary way. "Not from you, yet. I meant your sister having more kids. You need to finish school first."

Mr. Koskov inhales sharply as if the thought of his baby Della having kids one day literally makes his chest hurt.

Della's eyelids flutter in rapid blinks almost like she's having a seizure or something. In her defense it is too much to process. We just started dating. I reach under the table and squeeze her leg, which does seem to calm her. She places her hand over mine and laces our fingers together for the rest of the meal.

When the waiter drops off the bill, I reach for it and say, "I've got it."

Mr. Koskov shakes his head in protest and hands a stack of cash directly to the waiter.

I don't want to argue with him, so I simply say, "Thank you."

"Yes. Thank you for dinner." Della stands and hugs her dad. "And although I was slow to warm up to the idea, thank you for coming down to visit."

He stands and kisses her forehead, helps her with her jacket, then stretches his arm across her shoulder to walk her out. I pull the chair out for her mom and she fires off a few more interview questions as I escort her to the foyer. The questions are all geared towards determining the suitability of a suitor, so if she doesn't already know that Della and I are dating, she suspects it's a possibility.

Della and her mom head to the restroom together, leaving her dad and me to stand outside the restaurant as we wait. As soon as we're alone he says, "When we first arrived, I was interested by the tone you took with the obnoxious roommate with the ridiculous haircut."

I nod, not sure where he's going with the comment.

"You defended Della without hesitation. Am I correct to assume the nature of your relationship with my daughter is more than just roommates?"

I nod again. There's no point in denying it. The last thing I want is to come across as a liar. "Yes, sir. That's correct."

After a hesitation that leaves sweat dripping down my traps he says "Well, she seems happy." He reaches over and shakes my hand. "Make sure she stays that way."

I nod again, and he walks away to go get the rental.

All right. That was huge. Della and her mom join me and they both seem curious to know why I'm grinning.

Della reaches over and quickly squeezes my hand to signal that she's happy things went well. Mr. Koskov pulls up to the curb with the rental car while Della hugs her mom again.

"We'll call before we show up next time." She turns and rests her hand on my arm. "Nice meeting you, Easton." Her voice lowers as she adds, "You two make a really beautiful couple."

"Mom," Della protests.

Her mom kisses both her cheeks. "Don't sound so shocked. You two aren't fooling anyone." She glances over her shoulder at Mr. Koskov. "Your father approves, too, so don't let him tell you otherwise."

Della looks as excited as I feel to know we got the thumbs up. I open the car door for Mrs. Koskov and then wrap my arm around Della's waist to pull her close as we wave goodbye. Once they've turned the corner, Della turns to face me and casually drapes her arms over my shoulders. "Nicely done, Mr. Lewis. You were a big hit. You should be very proud of yourself since they've never liked any of my sister's boyfriends, not even the one she married. He still has to sit at the kid's table every Christmas."

I laugh because I can vividly imagine that.

She leans in to kiss me. "How do you think they figured out that I have a major thing for you? Is it really that obvious?"

A breeze catches her hair and blows a strand across her cheek that I sweep away and tuck behind her ear. "Your dad knew because of the way I told Chuck to get out on the morning they arrived."

"Mmm. That was very chivalrous. But, for the record, I was holding my own."

"I know you were." I slide my hands down to rest them on her hips. "Your dad also said you seem happy. He told me to make sure you stay that way."

Della lifts to her tiptoes and kisses me again. "Do you think you can handle that assignment?"

I nod and touch the tip of my nose to hers. "I'm going to give it all I've got."

"Yay." She spins around, which makes her dress flip up in a flirty way. She steps off the curb to head to the truck and looks over her shoulder with a sexy pout. "Do you have too much homework to kiss me goodnight tonight?"

I rush to catch up to her and smack her ass. "I'm willing to pull an all-nighter."

"For which part, the goodnight kiss or the homework?"

She stops next to the passenger door of the truck and I ease her up against it, leaving a trail of kisses down her throat. "I already finished my homework. My schedule's wide open for the goodnight kiss."

Her teeth dig into her bottom lip seductively as she pulls me by the belt buckle closer to her. She slides one hand up to clutch my neck and whispers, "Good. Because I'm ready."

Damn. I have never been so excited to hear someone say that in my entire life. "Are you sure?"

She nods and then spins around to open the door and hops in the truck.

I don't even get this jacked when I ride broncs. Once I sleep with her there'll be no going back for me. I'll be all in, and she'll own me. Which means she will also have the power to destroy me. It's like bronc riding, though. I can't go in thinking about the possibility of being killed. The gate's already wide open. All I can do now is hold on tight.

Chapter 15

Della

Easton lights the candles on his windowsill, which smell deliciously like grapefruit. Then he turns on music. The song has a slow, sexy groove that I like. His bedroom is slightly smaller than mine, but his gorgeous, wood-framed, king-sized bed is spacious and the crisp white duvet is so fluffy and inviting. The goodies he bought at the pharmacy are lined up on top of his dresser, so I pick a bottle of lubricant and a box of ribbed condoms, then place them on the bedside table. My hands are trembling. Not in a bad way. Just in a fear meets excitement way—like right before the rollercoaster drops, or the moment you step out of an airplane to skydive. I really did parachute once to prove to myself that I could overcome smaller doubts and fears. It was a tandem jump with an instructor and I screamed the entire way down, but it was thrilling. And I survived. Obviously.

I spin to face him. "Have you ever parachuted out of an airplane?"

His eyebrows angle in amusement from the randomness of the statement. "No. I'm not a huge fan of heights."

I nod, wishing I was better at proper conversation instead of just odd blabbering. "You're always so calm. How do you do it?"

"I guess when the worst thing possible has already happened to you, everything else is minor in comparison."

Makes sense. Breaks my heart. He's amazing. I want to be with him so badly.

"I'll be right back." He winks, quietly opens the door, and disappears into the hall before he heads downstairs.

Okay. Not sure if he expects me to undress while he's gone, I just stand in the middle of the room, hugging myself like a dork. I can't believe how amazing dinner went with my parents. The fact that they immediately liked him is such a relief. Not that their disapproval would have changed how I feel about him. I'm just shocked that everything has been so easy. Easton's integrity undeniably exudes from him, and my parents would have to be oblivious not to notice, but they gave Yulia such a hard time about Alex. And Alex is a solid guy, too. He's no Easton, though. Maybe they trust my judgment more than Yulia's? Nah, that's not it. Easton won them over with his no ma'ams, yes sirs, and protectiveness. Plain and simple. He's so awesome.

Wait. I should probably brush my teeth.

I swing his door open and leap across the hall to my room. It would probably be a good idea to make it back to his room before he does so he doesn't think I got cold feet and ran away. At super-human speed I brush my teeth, swish a capful of mouthwash and run the brush through my hair to smooth the fly-a-ways. Gah, on second thought, maybe I should hop in the shower really quick. Just a rinse.

Shoot. I forgot to bring my towels up from the laundry room this morning. Still wet, I snatch my cute baby-pink sleep dress out of the dresser drawer, clutch it to my chest and literally split leap back across the hall, stark naked. I can't be positive who, but someone is definitely coming up the stairs. I only caught a flash in my peripheral vision as I streaked by. Hopefully it's Easton. Oh my goodness, what if it isn't? Oh well. Too late now. Whoever it was is probably laughing so hard he rolled back down the stairs.

The door inches open. Easton slips quietly back in with a bowl of strawberries and chocolate squares in one hand and an open bottle of champagne in the other hand. He's smiling as if he wants to burst out in hysterical laughter but is purposely holding it back to be respectful of my feelings. "I liked the nude ballet show," he says with a chuckle as he places everything on the bedside table.

"It was inadvertent, but I'm glad you enjoyed it. I mean really glad it was you and not someone else who happened to see it."

He nods and his eyes scan my body. "Private shows are the best kind."

"And I didn't wipeout. Although sprawling on the floor naked could have potentially been strangely erotic."

He laughs and removes his shirt, then switches the music track to *Tennessee Whiskey* and extends his hand. "Would you like to dance with me, funny girl?"

I nod and step in to lean my head against his bare chest. His arms wrap around my body tenderly as we sway to the music. His heart is beating faster than it normally does, maybe he's a little bit nervous and excited, too. It might just be from running down to the kitchen and back upstairs, though. He doesn't seem to get nervous about anything. And he's done this before, so it's probably not as exciting after the novelty has worn off. Or maybe it is. What do I know? My heart feels like it's doing cartwheels, partly because of the warp-speed freshen-up session, but mostly because there is no place I'd rather be than in Easton's arms.

Woo. I'm nervous and excited. My fingers have gone numb, so I shake them to get the feeling back.

"You okay?" he asks.

"What if I'm bad at it?"

He laces his fingers with mine. "Remember the first time you saw me ride?"

I nod and inhale deeply.

"Sex is like bronc riding. You go in prepared but then turn your brain off. No fears. No analysis. Just feel the rhythm and let your instincts take over." He kisses the back of my hand. "Hopefully you have the ride of your life, but if for any reason you're not feeling it, you just jump off and try again another time."

"Okay." Feeling more relaxed, I rest my arms on his shoulders as we dance. "I hope it's like your ride that night. Let's try to get in the zone and score in the nineties."

He laughs. "First time out, might be tough to score that high, but we'll give it our best shot."

I'm so lucky. I don't understand why people ever break up. If this is what it feels like to be in love with someone, who would ever throw it away? Maybe they don't want to. Maybe it just unravels and there is nothing they can do to stop it. The feeling must fade over time. Or maybe the person changes. I hope neither of us ever change so much that I don't feel this safe and this happy. I don't want to ever forget how I feel in this moment.

I press my lips to his chest, then reach down to unbuckle his belt. "Can you believe this? A month ago we didn't even know each other. We clicked immediately. Meeting your dad went great. My parents basically like you better than they like me. You think my dorkiness is funny. And when you touch me it feels like heaven. It's all so perfect. I never expected being in a relationship to be so easy."

"It isn't usually this easy."

I stop swaying and tilt my head back to meet his gaze. "Why do you think it's different this time?"

"Because it's meant to be," he says with absolute, steadfast certainty.

The seriousness of his tone ignites every nerve in my body and renders me speechless. My heart stops for a fraction of a second and tears build along my lashes, the overwhelmingly happy kind of tears. I'm lost for words, so I pop up on my tip toes, grab his face, and kiss him. Hard.

Without hesitation, he swoops me off my feet and carries me to the bed. Seeing me laid out and nude on his bed makes him smile in the most irresistibly sexy way. He drops his jeans to the floor and kneels on the mattress to leave a trail of kisses along my inner thigh. They tickle. But not as much as the chilled champagne bubbles he dribbles along my abdomen. His tongue slides across my skin to lick the champagne in an insanely effervescent sensation that makes me squeal. He smiles and then places a square of chocolate in my mouth and rolls a strawberry over my lips. The chocolate melts on my tongue and his eyebrows lift seductively as he slides the strawberry across my collarbone and then touches its flesh to my nipple. It is ridiculously sensual and I'm glad I waited for the right guy to share the experience with. He sips champagne straight from the bottle before he bites into the strawberry, then he feeds the rest to me. My teeth pierce the fruit and the juicy sweetness bursts into my mouth. So delicious.

Propped on my elbow I sit up and reach over to guide the champagne bottle towards me. He tips it into my mouth and the bubbly liquid slides down my throat in a tingly bliss, which he follows up with a deep kiss. I am so ready. And so is he. His smooth, fully erect penis brushes against my thigh as he reaches down with his hand to touch me between the legs. His fingers dip inside me and he groans.

I swing my arm up and over my head, searching blindly with my fingers for the box of condoms. It takes me a few attempts to get it open and to separate one packet. He's going down on me as I do it, so there's no real rush. Although I am eager to do more. This is good, too. Oh my. Yeah. That feels amazing. Wow. What was I doing? Condom. Right. My eyes clench, partly because my brain doesn't work great when he does that tongue trick, but also because my body moves on its own in unexpected back arches and toe curls. It's just so, wow.

Once I catch my breath and regain a semblance of brain function, I tear the foil wrapper and guide his chin so he'll slide up and let me roll the condom on him. I'm confident with all the technical parts because I diligently researched proper condom use and even practiced with a banana. I'm still a little worried about what comes next, though. Nobody really has great stories about losing their virginity. I want him to enjoy it, which is why I want to be good at it. Is it weird to be a perfectionist about sex? Yes. Is it also weird to be thinking instead of just being in the moment? Yes. Come on, Della. This is it. Get a grip. It can't be that difficult. I just need to remember what my sister said. Monkeys do it.

"You okay?" Easton asks softly after he kisses my neck and applies a decadently cool and slick layer of lubricant between my legs.

"Yes. Very okay. But please just do it so I'll stop thinking."

He laughs and flips me over onto my hands and knees, then pulls my upper body up so we are both on our knees and my back is pressed to his chest. His right arm reaches around my hip to stimulate me from the front and then he enters me from behind, pausing to whisper in my ear, "Is this okay?"

It feels stretched and full, and I'll need him to go slowly, but it's not painful, so I nod.

His left hand cups my breast and his right hand taps gentle, rhythmic pressure to my clitoris as he slides deeper inside me. Every fibre in my body trembles from the high. I could easily come just from him being inside me, but I don't want it to end so quickly, so I inhale and focus on prolonging the moment.

"You ready to take things up another notch?" he asks in a smooth, sexy voice between leaving a trail of kisses down the side of my neck.

"Yes," I breathe out and guide his hands to caress my breasts. His hips buck behind me and he thrusts, getting deeper each time. His breathing deepens as the pace quickens and when it feels as if he's getting close, I drop forward to brace myself with my arms on all fours. Arching my back, my hips lift so he can push even deeper. I love how it feels to be that close to him. Not just physically but emotionally. Everything about him is inside me now.

"Yes. Yes. Yes!" I'm yelling. I can't help it. I don't care. It feels too good to care. His fingertips dig into my flesh as he squeezes my butt and when my orgasm releases, my muscles tense around his entire length, making him groan in pleasure. He's made me come every time we've been together, but this time is different. It's like three orgasms crashing in from different locations simultaneously. He thrusts one more time with a sexy rumble in his throat and then he clutches my hips towards him as he releases.

Spectacular. That is the only way to describe it.

He remains perfectly still for a couple breaths, then kisses between my shoulder blades and slides out. I collapse to the mattress and roll over onto my back. He's smiling. That's a good sign. He removes the condom and wraps it in a tissue, then slides down to lay beside me. I kiss him and stare into his eyes, which are sparkling from the flickering flame of the candles.

"Thank you," I whisper.

"Thank. You. That definitely scored in the nineties."

"Are you just saying that so I won't be embarrassed?"

"No." He laughs. "Couldn't you tell it was great?"

"Well, yeah. For me. It was mind-blowing. Way better than skydiving, which up until now was the most invigorating and life-changing thing I'd ever done. But I don't know how it was for you. Truthfully."

He leans in and presses his lips to my ear. "It was unfuckingbelievable. Sorry for cursing."

The smile on my face stretches so wide it makes my cheeks hurt.

Best.

Night.

Ever.

Chapter 16

Easton

At three-thirty in the morning my phone rings. Della is asleep next to me, so I slide out of bed carefully to avoid waking her. It's Phil, a friend of my dad's.

"Hey, kid. Sorry to wake you but I thought you should know your dad's in the hospital."

"What happened?"

"They don't know yet. He didn't come in by dark so a few hands went out to look for him. His horse stood by him, which helped them find him quick. He was confused as if he'd been knocked unconscious. And he was dehydrated. He might have been thrown. Or maybe it was something to do with his condition."

Shit. I sit on the end of the bed.

"He was pissed off they took him to the hospital, so that's probably a good sign. The doctors are running tests right now."

"All right. I'll be there as soon as I can. Thanks for calling."

"Yup."

I end the call as Della sits up, clutching the sheets to her chest. "What's wrong?"

I stand and kiss her on the forehead. "My dad's in the hospital. I'm going to head out there."

"Oh, no. I'll come with you." She hops out of bed and heads towards the door as if she plans to go to her room and get dressed.

"Thanks, but I don't know how long I'll have to stay. I don't want you to miss school."

"I want to be there. For you." Her eyebrows angle together and cause her forehead to crease.

I step into my jeans and pull them up. "It might be nothing. He might have just been thrown from his horse. If it's something more serious you can come out later."

She crosses her arms over her chest as if she's just remembered she's nude.

I pull one of my t-shirts over her head and then bring her in for a hug. "I miss you already," I whisper into her hair.

She clutches my jaw. "Phone me as soon as you know how he is."

I feel like an asshole to run out on her right after we slept together. But I can't not go. Maybe I should let her come with me. What if he's laid up for weeks? I'll have to stay there. God damn it. The timing couldn't be worse. Maybe he just had a dizzy spell from heat exhaustion and fell off his horse. Hopefully I'll be back by Sunday. I don't want to think about what will happen if his condition is serious. Shit. I'm getting choked up. I gotta go.

I pack a week's worth of clothes and then rush out. She follows me down the stairs and kisses me one more time before I head out and get in my truck. I know it will be a mistake to look up at her standing in my t-shirt, face etched with concern. But I can't help it. I throw the truck into park, leave the engine running and hop back out. She runs across the grass and jumps into my arms.

"I'm sorry for leaving."

"Don't be," she says softly. "He needs you. I'll be here waiting." She reaches around and slaps my ass. "Go. I'm worried about your dad."

I walk backwards and point at her. "Be prepared to go another round when I get back."

She smiles and hugs her arms around her body. "Looking forward to it."

As I drive away, the high of being with her is replaced with worry.

The nurse at the reception desk sends me to a room at the end of the hall. Dad is awake and the head of the bed is raised so he's resting in a semi-seated position. His forehead is bandaged and his arm is in a full cast from his knuckles to above his elbow. Crystal and our head ranch hand named Luke are standing by the window. Dad shakes his head when he sees me and shoots a glare at Phil, who's seated in the corner. "What are you calling everybody for, jackass? He can't afford to miss more school. And I'm fine in case you hadn't noticed."

"He's your son. All I did was tell him what happened. He's the one who decided to drive all the way out here and check on your sorry ass." Phil looks at me apologetically. "Unfortunately, the bump to the head didn't improve his disposition at all."

Dad isn't the hugging type so I just slap his shoulder lightly. "What happened?"

"Don't remember. Zorro must have spooked."

I look over at everyone else in the room to check if Dad's downplaying something that he doesn't want me to know about. Phil's expression twitches subtly as if there is more to the story than that, but he's not going to be the one to tell me. "What did the doctor say?"

Dad's eyes roll slightly as he shifts in the bed to delay answering. "Broken arm. I'm fine."

"Except that you fell off your horse for some unknown reason and knocked yourself unconscious."

He reaches over to grab a glass of water and sips from the straw.

A doctor enters the room and apologizes for interrupting the conversation before she flashes a penlight in Dad's eyes. "All right, Mr. Lewis. Looks like you're good to go home now. But no horseback riding for three weeks. And no TV either. I don't want your brain to work too hard."

Phil laughs. "His brain never did work all that hard, Doc."

She smiles as Dad chucks the straw at Phil, then she hands him a list of concussion tips. I've had my share of concussions from bronc riding, so I'm familiar with the protocol, but I tell her I have a few questions and escort her into the hall so we can talk in private.

"Why do you think he fell?"

She shrugs and writes something on a chart. "His cardiac and neurological tests all came back normal. His blood work is fine. Most likely the horse acted up and threw him."

I nod, not convinced. Zorro doesn't even flinch at most things, and he stood by Dad. If he had spooked he would have taken off, not stayed there.

"Monitor him for the concussion symptoms. The elbow fracture will probably take six to eight weeks to heal. I don't think there is anything else to worry about."

"Okay. Thanks."

When I step back into the room, Dad is already dressed and struggling to button his shirt with one hand. "Let's go," he says. "The animals aren't going to feed themselves."

"Luke can go back and take care of everything." I nod at Luke and he takes that as his cue to leave. "You're supposed to take it easy," I remind Dad

"I am. I'm going to let you drive."

I shake my head and let Crystal and Phil walk ahead of me as they follow him out. I'm glad he's feeling well enough to be a pain in the ass. But he knows as well as I do that he didn't fall off that horse for no reason.

Chapter 17

Della

Easton called. His dad has been released from the hospital, and they're back at the ranch now, but Easton is still worried about how he fell in the first place. He's going to stay for a few days to make sure everything's okay. I'm going to miss him, but it's probably not a bad idea to spend time apart. The healthiest relationships are ones where each person has at least a few separate interests, or so I've heard. And since I already want to spend every second of the day and night with him, it's probably better to set the tone of independence now so I don't turn into a suffocating psycho girlfriend.

BJ is making pancakes for us and Chuck is sitting on a lawn chair in the backyard, staring at the reflection of the sun in the pool. He never did move his things out of his room, but we hadn't seen him all week, so I thought he was in the process of finding somewhere else to live. Apparently not, since he's here now. And if the six empty beer cans scattered around the base of the lawn chair are any indication, he's obviously been out there for a while.

BJ glances at Chuck through the glass patio door and then checks my expression as he slides a plate of blueberry pancakes across the counter for me. "Do you want me to ask him to leave? Or should I invite him in?"

I shovel a forkful of pancake into my mouth to give myself time to think about it as I chew. I don't know what to do. Just because he looks completely dejected and pathetic doesn't mean he's going to change. Generating pity is probably his goal. He wants me to feel sorry for him. He knows my heart will bleed for him. He might even know that Easton is out of town and it's the perfect time for him to weasel his way back in by playing on my sympathies. Or, maybe he hit rock bottom and really needs a friend. Come on, Della, he's not a puppy. He's a grown man who can take care of himself. And, he's a jerk who took what he had for granted. He needs to feel the loss so he learns how he should treat people. Oh dear, he just leaned forward to rest his elbows on his knees and cradle his head in his hands. He needs a hug. Poor thing. No. Stop it. Be strong. He made his bed, he needs to lie in it. Even if he technically doesn't have a bed at all and possibly needs to sleep on the street.

Stop caring about his feelings. He doesn't care about anyone else's feelings. But maybe deep down he does? Maybe that's why he developed such an abrasive outer shell? Maybe he's super sensitive and he needed to protect himself from the cruel world by lashing out first? He's mean, though, remember? We can at least let him in to pack up his things.

And his rent is paid until the end of the month, so if he hasn't got anywhere to go, he could technically stay until he gets it sorted. But it might just cause more problems. What should I do? My breakfast is completely consumed and I still haven't answered BJ's question.

"Let me talk to him first," I finally say.

BJ nods and serves up another helping of pancakes.

"How did you do on your assignment?" I ask to take my mind off Chuck's suffering.

"Barely scraped by. I have a mid-term this Friday that's going to decide my fate."

"Do you feel prepared?"

He shrugs and dribbles syrup over the stack on his plate. "I've been studying, but there's one unit I still don't get."

"Is Easton in that class? Maybe he could explain it to you."

"No, he doesn't take this course. Chuck took it last year. He's too depressed to tutor me, though."

I glance over my shoulder at Chuck. He's still hunched and holding his head in a vice grip. "Is that pathetic thing all just an act so I'll forgive him and invite him back?"

"No, it's not an act. He's legitimately messed up over Janine dating that surfer dude. Chuck's been following her around campus and sitting in his truck outside her apartment building every night. She finally called me to say that if he doesn't stop stalking her she's going to call the cops."

Yikes, stalking is bad. Illegal, possibly crazy, and humiliating. Someone needs to do something. Save him from himself. Or not. He's in charge of his own choices. If he makes a decision that gets him thrown in jail that's his problem. But then again, if I went crazy over Easton breaking up with me to date someone else, I would hope that one of my friends would step in and stop my jealous acts of desperation before I violated any laws. Do unto others as you would wish them to do unto you. "So, if he's this broken up over her does it mean he actually liked her?"

BJ nods.

"I would have never guessed that. He's obviously more complex than I thought." I stand and make a plate of pancakes for Chuck. "Okay. I'm going out there. Wish me luck."

BJ's face locks into a grimace as if he's not sure it's a good idea but can't think of a better plan. "I'll stay right here in case you need me."

I give him a thumbs up to show my gratitude, then after a breath, I head outside and approach Chuck cautiously. "Hey, Taylor. Bailey made breakfast if you're hungry." I extend my arm to offer him the plate, but he doesn't move or even acknowledge my presence. Undeterred, I place the dish on the patio table and pull a chair around to sit next to him. The muscles in his arms and up the side of his neck are so tense it looks as if he's literally straining against something. I have a million things to say, but it feels like the best thing to do is to just sit with him in silence. He's torturing himself. I can feel the self-loathing anger emanating off him. BJ is still seated at the kitchen island, reading from his textbook, so I lean back in the chair and angle my face up to the sun to wait. No idea what I'm waiting for. What was I thinking? Even if he does talk to me, I don't know how to fix his problems with Janine. He was right when he said I was too inexperienced to give advice on dating. Maybe if I just be a friend to him my kindness will rub off on him. Maybe he'll start to appreciate the people he cares about and actually show them how important they are to him. If not, oh well, at least I can say I did the right thing and tried my best to be a good person. That's all that matters anyway, right? No, it shouldn't be all about me. It's about him. And he doesn't feel like talking. Gah. How does anyone solve anything if they don't talk about it? Stop over-thinking everything, Della. Just be. Silence is golden. It feels like at least half an hour has passed. Maybe it's only been ten minutes. Either way, it's got to be a record for me to remain silent for this long. Yulia would be so proud of me right now.

When I was fourteen, Yulia took me to a yoga class with her—once. She was so embarrassed because even though she shushed me repeatedly, I kept forgetting that it's supposed to be a silent practice and I blurted out about a thousand questions. If it wasn't for the non-talking part I'd probably really like yoga. Needless to say she never invited me again. Probably best for everyone involved.

Hmm. Chuck's muscles just relaxed. He doesn't look like he's bracing to fight the world anymore. And the anger is gone. Replaced with sadness. Heartbreaking sadness. My eyes begin to water from the intensity of the vulnerability I can feel radiating off him. I knew it. He has a sweet side down there somewhere. Slowly, so as not to startle him, I reach over and slide my arm across his shoulders. He takes a deep breath to hold back his emotions but lets me hug him.

"I screwed everything up with Janine," he says, fighting to keep his voice steady.

I nod because it's true. But everyone makes mistakes. And regretting it means he cares on some level. I don't know if he deserves a second chance with Janine. At least he still has an opportunity to learn from his mistakes, and become a better person, and be more respectful to the next girl he meets. There's still hope, I hope. "It's going to be okay," I finally say.

He huffs as if he's not sure that's true. But he wants it to be true. I can tell.

Not wanting to push my luck with too much sympathy, I let my arm drop away from his shoulders. There's nothing more I can say or do at this point. What happens next is up to him. That was probably enough Chuckie time for one day anyway, so I bend over to pick up three of the empty beer cans.

Before I turn to leave he says, "Thanks, Della."

I stop and make eye contact with him. His expression is genuine, and obviously I'm too much of a Pollyanna, but I can't kick someone when they're down. "Eat something. And you need a shower. If you help BJ study for his exam I'll talk to Janine for you and see if there is any way for you to get her back. No promises on my end because if she wants nothing to do with you, that's her choice. But I'll try. Deal?"

He nods.

As I head towards the house he says, "I'm sorry about how I treated you, too."

"Prove it. By changing," I say, leaving the sliding door open behind me so he knows he's welcome back in the house. For now.

BJ looks up from his reading. "How'd it go?"

"He's going to help you pass your exam. And I'm going to see if there's any way to help him win Janine back. My odds are not that good, so make sure you pump him for as much information as you can before he finds out that he's burned his bridges with Janine."

"Nice negotiation skills. Thanks for making me the bene-ficiary."

"It's for your mom and your sisters, too. If you graduate everyone benefits."

He stands and walks around the counter to hug me into his side "You're such a good girl."

I smile and squirm away from him as he tousles my hair. There was a time when I would have been insulted by being called a good girl, like it was a bad thing—goody-two-shoes, suck up, hall-monitor, or prude. But now I'm proud of who I am. I mean, I'm not perfect by any stretch of the imagination, but there's nothing wrong with being who I am. Plus, for the record, I'm technically not a prude anymore. I scored with the hottest guy on campus. Can I get a woot woot? Next thing I know I'll be getting a lower back tattoo or something. No, actually, I would never do that. Not judging, but I'm worried the needles might be contaminated with hepatitis. And what if when I'm fifty years old, my flabby, stretched-out skin distorts the image into a grotesque blob of ink? Okay, I'm still a prude. Whatever.

Next item on the agenda, meet up with Janine. Actually, I have an assignment due on Monday. Amendment to the agenda: homework first, then meet up with Janine.

Chapter 18

Easton

Something's not right about Dad's fall. No matter how many times I go over it in my mind, I can't put my finger on the piece that doesn't fit. If the doctor was right, and Dad's fall wasn't because of a medical issue, it means Zorro spooked and then wandered back and stood by him until help arrived. Dad's ridden Zorro for eighteen years, so it makes sense he would stand by him. It's the spooking in the first place that doesn't fit with the Zorro I know. Dad shrugs it off and blames it on Zorro getting older. And maybe he is injured or losing his sight or something, but I'm almost positive there's more to it than that. Dad's not telling me everything.

After lunch, Dad falls asleep on the couch, so I decide to take Zorro for a test-ride and head out to where they found Dad. I can't remember Dad ever being thrown from a horse while he was working. A few times he got tossed when saddle-breaking a new horse, but Zorro is a seasoned work horse. The only other possibility I can think of is they stumbled on a rattlesnake or wasp's nest. But even if that is what happened, Dad should have been able to ride-it-out if Zorro reared up. And if he can't hold on anymore when something unexpected happens, he probably shouldn't be out here riding alone. Not that he'll ever admit to that.

It's a forty-five-minute ride from the house. Zorro is moving fine, relaxed and not favoring anything. No welts from bee stings. No blood on his legs from an animal bite. His breathing is fine. As we get closer to the valley where it happened, his ears prick forward in the direction of the stream. The trail heads north from here, but Zorro's attention is focused intently to the east. I release the reins and let him lead towards the water, through some low brush, and over some fallen logs. If he did encounter snakes or wasps on their last trip, he's either already forgotten or doesn't give a shit.

Once we clear the brush I notice a series of tire tracks in the dirt. We use quads on the ranch, and it's possible that's how the ranch hands came out to search for Dad, but the wheel bases on these tracks are too wide to be quads. More likely 4x4s, and they stopped upstream. Zorro leads the way to a spot where whoever it was got out of their vehicles. I dismount to study the footprints more closely. They were made by thick treaded boots, not cowboy boots.

While I'm taking pictures of the prints and tracks, Della calls.

"Hi. How are you?" she asks but then starts talking again before I have a chance to respond. "Before you answer, I have something to tell you. Okay, so don't be angry or disappointed or irritated—basically just suspend whatever reaction you're going to have for what I'm about to tell you because chances are you won't be thrilled, but it's already done, so no point getting all worked up over it. I mean, not that I'm trying to boss you around and tell you how to feel. Truthfully, I just don't want you to be upset with me even though I did something you probably won't agree with. Do you promise to have no reaction?"

Not sure if I should laugh at her nervous ramblings or be concerned. "Why? What did you do?"

She sucks in her breath for a second before she blurts out, "I let Chuck move back in. But with conditions. And I'm sorry if you don't agree with my decision to give him a chance to redeem himself, but I think it was the right thing to do. Until he screws up again and then you can say I told you so. I'm pretty confident that won't happen. I hope. But I might be wrong. Are you mad?"

"No. If you think it's the right thing to do, I trust your judgement."

"Really?"

"Yeah. Why wouldn't I?"

"Uh." She hesitates as if she's going through a catalogue of reasons why I shouldn't have faith in her ability to make good decisions. When she realizes she doesn't have to defend her reasons, she relaxes. "Thank you. I promise I can handle it, and I don't want you to have to worry about anything here while you're there taking care of your dad. How's he doing by the way?"

"He's fine but grumpy as hell because the doctor told him he can't ride for three weeks."

"Does he remember what happened yet?"

"No, but I just rode out to the spot where it happened to look for clues. I found some tire tracks. Maybe trespassers."

"Do you think your dad tried to confront them and that's why he fell?"

"Maybe. I don't know." I wander over and grab the horn to get back up on Zorro. "I'm going to call the Sherriff's office and ask if they'll send someone out to take a look."

"That's a good idea. And be careful. Maybe they're still out there somewhere."

Right as she says that Zorro's ears flick to the side to narrow in on the sound of someone riding up from behind us. I turn in my saddle to see who it is, but the sun is in my eyes, so all I can make out is the silhouette of two people on dark horses. "Hey, Della, is it all right if I call you when I get back to the ranch house?"

"Sure. Is everything all right?"

"Yeah. I think so," I say as I reach for my rifle. "I'll call you later."

As the riders get closer, I recognize Tracy and her older brother Mike, so I slide the gun back down into its case. They ride up right next to me. Tracy smiles and combs her fingers through her hair. "Hey, Havie. It's been a long time."

I nod, wondering what they're doing out here. Their family's property borders ours, but they never ride out this way, she didn't even cut through when we were dating because it takes longer than riding on the road.

"You look good," she says as she takes a sip of water from her canteen.

I nod again, only enough to acknowledge that I heard her, not enough to encourage the flirtatious banter that she needs to accept doesn't work on me anymore. "What are you two doing out this way?"

"We heard about your dad." She points at the tire tracks. "The same guys have been poking around on our property, too, and several other properties in the valley. I already made a report of trespassers, but it's a waste of paper at this point since I don't have a tag number or vehicle description. You should take pictures of the tracks to build the case against them."

"I already did. Who are they? Hunters?"

"No." Mike dismounts and pulls a camera out of his saddle bag. "We're not sure exactly who it is yet, but they're not hunters. They've been illegally taking core samples."

"For what? Oil?"

Tracy shakes her head as she scans the rock face just beyond the shoreline. "They aren't drilling deep enough to test for oil. Uncle Lou thinks they're most likely looking for gold." She hops off her horse and trails her finger along a quartz striation in the rock. "Here. See."

I dismount and walk over to check it out.

"This dirty quartz vein is an indication there's iron in the seam, which means there's a good chance there's gold. That's why they chose this spot to test." She follows the tire tracks and climbs up into the brush, then points out a grid of holes in the ground. "They use core drills set up in the back of their trucks to pull samples and it leaves these tube-shaped holes."

I walk through the brush behind her, studying the drill holes. At least thirty are lined up along the landscape in an equally spaced pattern. "I don't get it. Why would they waste their time? Even if they find gold in the sample, they can't mine here."

Her eyebrows lift briefly to indicate she's not sure that's true.

"What? It's private property. We own the mineral rights."

Mike climbs up and joins us. "You might want to double check that, Havie. Two recent court cases ruled in favor of the commodities company because the ranchers hadn't purchased the sub-surface rights when they bought the property."

I frown, trying to remember if I've ever even seen the deed to the property. My dad and his two brothers inherited it from my grandpa and then my dad bought his brothers out. My grandpa was originally given the property as a gift from some rich guy because Grandpa saved the guy's daughter from drowning. I don't know if official paperwork even exists from that original transfer. "If a bunch of guys are driving around town in 4x4s with drills on the back, they shouldn't be too hard to find."

"Nobody in town has seen anything. We think they must drive in at night, work all day, and drive out again at night."

"Look at this," Mike says as he waves us over to the top

of the ridge. He leans over to take a photo of something in the dirt. As I get closer the sun glints off the brass rifle casing.

Tracy catches up and glances at me as if it all makes sense now. "Your dad must have caught them in the act. Those bastards shot at him and spooked Zorro."

Although it's a possibility, and would explain what happened, there's no motive. Worst they'd get for trespassing is a ticket. It doesn't make sense that they'd want to tack on murder charges. "They weren't likely the ones doing the shooting," I say as I take my hat off and wipe the sweat from my forehead with my sleeve.

They both nod to agree that my dad shooting at the trespassers is the more likely scenario.

"So, what now?" Tracy asks Mike.

He shrugs. "Havie needs to trace the mineral rights for the property at the county clerk's office." As we walk back to the horses, Mike hands me a business card for a lawyer. "You might own the rights if the deed is fee simple. But since the prospectors have been out here, my guess is they either own a lease to the rights or think they can get it. This is the lawyer our dad has been talking to."

I slide the card into my shirt pocket, wondering how I'm going to come up with the money for legal fees if things aren't solid with the deed and the mineral rights.

We all mount up and head back to the trail. As Tracy trots to pull up next to Zorro, her horse Cheyenne rubs her forelock against my leg because she remembers me.

"So, Havie, how you been?" Tracy asks.

I nod to indicate that I've been fine but don't make the effort to elaborate or ask about how she's doing. Maybe I'm being rude, but today is the first day since the break-up that we've said more than two words to each other. And I know it's not casual chit chat. She has an agenda.

We ride in silence for a while before she says, "Everyone's been talking about your new girlfriend."

And there's the agenda. "Yeah? So?"

"You don't have to get snarky. They're saying nice things about her." She laughs at my defensiveness. "I'm not sure when sweet and innocent became your type, but whatever. If she does it for you, to each his own. Is it more than a fling?"

I glance at her, in disbelief. She's deluded if she thinks I'm going to talk with her about my relationship with Della.

When I don't respond, she shrugs and adds, "Well, must be pretty serious to bring her home to meet your dad, huh?"

"Yup," I say before riding ahead to end the conversation.

We all ride together in single file as far as the junction in the trail. When Mike and Tracy head towards the road, she turns to wave goodbye. I pretend not to notice because I'm still irritated with her. It would be better if she didn't still get under my skin, and I admit I need to work on that, but she better not make Della feel uncomfortable in any way. I'll be beyond pissed off if she tries to mess with Della.

Transitioning into a gallop I cut through the pasture back to the barn. After untacking Zorro, I cross the yard and enter the house through the back porch into the kitchen.

Dad's standing at the sink, washing dishes with one arm. Brewster was asleep on his blanket but shoots up and jogs over to me for pats.

"How's Zorro?"

"Fine." I scratch Brewster under the chin, then open the fridge and grab the milk jug. "Do you remember anything about trespassers out there?"

He glances over his shoulder briefly, too quickly to read his expression. He doesn't answer the question, which means he does remember what happened and chose not to tell me.

"Okay Dad, you can drop the amnesia act. I found drill holes and a casing. You want to explain that?" I ask as I open the cupboard where he keeps the glasses.

He dries a plate with more attention than it needs and places it in the drying rack. "It was a warning shot. In the air. Just to let them know they should be on their way. Zorro spooked, and I lost the saddle because I was holding the rifle."

"You didn't feel it was important to tell me that?"

Without looking at me, he folds the dish towel and hangs it from the handle of the stove. Then he sits down at the kitchen table. "I didn't want you to get it into your head to quit school and come back home to take care of things. It was just a few trespassers. I handled it."

"You didn't handle it. You ended up in the hospital. And they weren't just trespassers. They're prospectors who possibly have rights to our land. You're not in any condition to be dealing with bullshit this dangerous. You have cancer, remember?"

His face registers a blind-sided shock for one beat but hardens before he shouts, "Yeah, it's hard to forget that. But I'm not a damn invalid. I've been taking care of this land since I was a boy. And you're not quitting school with only one year left because a couple of gold company men were sniffing around."

"You didn't even want me to do my MBA in the first place. What do you care if I drop out and move back now or in a year?"

"I didn't raise no quitter."

Brewster glances back and forth between us stressfully, concerned by the raised voices.

I shake my head and put the milk jug back in the fridge. "If the land is stolen from underneath us because of a loophole in the deed, there won't be anything for me to come back to in a year. You get that, right?"

He nods, but I can tell by the way he's avoiding eye contact that there's more that he doesn't want to tell me. "Go back to school. I'm handling it," he says before he stands and leaves out the back door.

Frustrated by his stubbornness, I swing the door open and shout as he steps out onto the yard; "Lying unconscious in the dirt isn't exactly handling it!"

He spins around to face me. "Why does everything always have to be an argument with you?"

"Me? You're the one who refuses to talk about anything and then walks away when things get uncomfortable. Look in the mirror."

"You know what I see when I look in the mirror? I

see you, twenty years from now. You're exactly like me, kid."

"Yeah. Really? You're forgetting one major difference."

It's a low blow. And I instantly regret it. He glares at me, then walks away and disappears into the barn. Frustrated with myself as much as him, I slam the door shut. God damn he knows how to make me mad. But I have bigger things to worry about right now. I head straight to the laptop to research California mineral rights laws. Brewster stays in the kitchen, not sure which one of us he should follow.

Chapter 19

Della

Janine is late. Maybe she isn't going to show up at all. I wouldn't blame her if she didn't. I shouldn't be meddling in her life anyway. But I'm keeping up my end of the bargain since Chuck did his part and spent hours tutoring BJ this week. Hopefully it pays off for BJ. Fingers crossed. His exam is this afternoon.

I glance around the cafe to make sure I didn't miss Janine come in. I check my phone but no messages, not from her or Easton. He has been keeping me up-to-date on everything going on at the ranch and we've talked every night since he left. But I miss him, and I worry about how all the stress will impact his dad. Easton, on the other hand, is handling the whole mess with the same calm confidence he approaches everything. Except he did mention he lost his cool once with his dad and regretted it. He's talked to a lawyer and hopes there won't be a dispute that requires lawsuits and court dates, which is not only a pain and a financial burden, it will also interfere with his school work.

And, although he didn't say it, we both know it will leave no time for his relationship with me. I mean, obviously I know I'm the lowest priority on his list. And I get it. But I really hope it all gets settled quickly, and in Easton and his dad's favor.

"Hey, Della." Janine swoops in and sits on the barstool next to me, interrupting me from my daydream. "Sorry to keep you waiting. The bus was running late and my phone's dead." She waves her arm in the air to signal the waitress. "Cranberry scone and a latte, please." Janine turns to me. "Do you want another tea?"

"Sure. Thanks. Mint, please."

The waitress nods and turns away. Janine removes her jean jacket and fans her face with the menu card. "So, I was glad to get your text. Getting together was a great idea. But I'm assuming Chuck sent you."

"Oh. Uh. Sort of." I cringe slightly from the truth. "Don't get me wrong, I'm happy to see you, and it was technically my idea, but yes, Chuck is involved."

"I figured." She sighs and thanks the waitress as she serves the scone.

"Don't worry. Honestly, I only told him I'd talk to you on his behalf, so he would help BJ study for an exam, which he already did. If it makes you uncomfortable, we don't need to talk about him. Let's just have tea and chat about other things. What do you study?"

"Medicine. Stem cell research."

I blink, maybe a little too exaggeratedly, since she does not in any way fit my pre-conceived stereotypical image of a med student. "That's really awesome. What made you become interested in stem cells?"

"When I was twelve years old my older brother was injured in a rodeo wreck. A bull came down on him and crushed his spine. He's a paraplegic now, and although he leads a really full life and has kids and everything, I guess I always wished there had been a medical intervention that could have helped him walk again."

"Wow. Your motivations are so noble. I mostly chose engineering because I was sort of good at math and wanted to prove my dad wrong."

She laughs. "There's nothing wrong with that. Did things ever go anywhere with you and Havie?"

"Yeah, actually we've been dating. And he's great. Fantastic. Amazing. But he got called home because there was an emergency with his dad. He's been gone for almost a week, and I'm not sure when he's going to be able to come back. So, things are a little uncertain right now."

"Sucks. But I can tell by the way your face lights up when you talk about him that it's probably worth fighting for. Don't give up."

"Thanks for saying that. I'll fight my hardest. How about you? Are things going well with the surfer guy?"

"Oh, God, no. He's so boring. And he cries over everything. Like literally he shed tears because a pod of whales beached themselves in San Diego on the weekend." She sips her latte. "But he's cute. And that drives Chuckie insane."

"Do you miss Chuck?"

"Yeah. But I don't miss his cheating."

Shoot. I just spilled my tea. Reaching for a paper serviette, I ask, "If he stopped cheating would that be enough for you to take him back?"

She shrugs and breaks her scone apart. "I don't know. I doubt it, especially since the chances of him being faithful are close to zero."

"Hmm." I ponder as I dab the stain on the front of my blouse. "It's weird that he cheats since it's obvious he cares about you."

"He has the attention span of a two-year-old and gets caught up in the moment. He doesn't consider the consequences, for anything, not just cheating."

"I don't mean to pry, but why did you put up with it?"

She spins the advertisement card on the table, lost in thought for a few seconds before she answers, "He slept with other girls but never dated anyone other than me. It felt special to know that I was the one he called when he was upset about something. I was the one who met his parents. I was the one he wanted to take out to dinner and watch a movie with. Those other girls were just meaningless hook-ups. And at first, I was fine with that. But it's not enough anymore. I want to be in a committed relationship now, and he can't give me that."

"Well, losing you made him realize what you meant to him. Moving on was the best thing you could have done to help him see that." I tap the counter, thinking. "He's book smart. Maybe he could learn strategies to be less impulsive and not cheat."

"Maybe. If he wanted to. I doubt he really wants to."

"He wanted me to talk to you, so he must be at least somewhat motivated."

She tilts her head with a less than convinced one-shoulder shrug.

"Okay, let's approach this analytically." I pull out a note pad and pencil from my bag to start a pros and cons list. "What qualities are on his cons lists?"

"Liar. Cheater. Immature. Selfish. Rude. Forgetful. Judgmental. Moody. Emotionally guarded. Not responsible enough to be a father." She counts them off on her fingers and stops when she hits ten. "Those are the main ones."

"Okay. That was easier than it probably should have been. And his pros?"

She stares out the window as she racks her brain. "I can't think of any right now."

"He's educated. And he's dedicated to rodeo." I point the pencil in her direction. "And he's kind of funny."

She wrinkles her nose, so apparently those qualities don't really tip the scales for her.

"How is he in bed?"

"Mediocre at best." She laughs. "And you can tell him I said that."

I shake my head. "I don't think I will."

"Not sure if it's a pro or a con, but he walks like a cocky penguin."

"I know, right?" I chuckle at the fact that I'm not the only person who noticed. "That's a con," I say as I write it down.

"Ooh." She clasps my arm excitedly. "He's rich. But—"

She releases her grip as the glow from the one pro quickly fades. "It doesn't mean much if everything else about him screams asshole."

"Chuck's rich? Why didn't he offer to help cover the rent when the guys were desperate?"

"Well, to be more specific, he comes from a wealthy family. His parents don't currently let him have access to the money because they know he'll blow it all partying."

I bite down on the pencil and study the list. Things are not looking good for old Chuckie. "What made you fall for him in the first place?"

She folds her napkin into a tiny fan as she sorts through her memories. "I don't know. I guess because he's so strong, not just physically, but his attitude when he sets his mind to accomplish something is unstoppable. The first time I ever saw him was at a rodeo and he seemed invincible to me. His strength and confidence always made me feel safe." She takes another sip of her latte. "Blinded by the buckle. Stupid, right?"

"No. It's not stupid. Everyone wants to feel safe." I write 'strong' and 'determined' in the pro column.

She chuckles with regret. "I went from a guy who would rather die than cry in front of someone to a bleeding-heart tree-hugger who feels the planet's every pain."

"Chuck cried over losing you."

Her head snaps back and her eyes open wide in shock. "He did?"

"Well, more like his eyes watered and his voice wavered."

"Wow. For him, that's basically equivalent to bawling."

The news sinks in, and based on how she's nibbling her lip, the revelation is plucking at her sympathy strings. "Poor Chuckie."

"Um, Janine." I hold up the list of ten cons. "Which part of this list wasn't clear?"

She laughs and pops a chunk of scone in her mouth.

"Seriously. I can't in good conscience support any type of reconciliation when the results are this tragically lopsided. You deserve better."

"I know. You're right." She spins on the bar stool and signals the waitress for the check, then leans her elbows back on the counter. "Normally, I shake my head at those stupid bitches who think they can change a guy. Imagine my horror to realize I am one of those stupid bitches."

"You're not dumb. You put your foot down."

"But I didn't want to, and it's killing me to stay away from him." She hands the waitress a twenty to pay for both of us and waves off the change.

"I'm sorry he's not good enough for you."

"Yeah." Janine stands and puts her jean jacket on. "Me too. I wish I could stay longer, but I have to get to class."

"No problem. Thanks for meeting me." I stand to give her a hug. "It was nice to see you again."

"I'll see you around. Just because Chuck is out of the picture doesn't mean you and I can't be friends."

"Yeah. Okay. I'd like that." I give her another hug before she rushes down the street. My classes are done for the day, so I head to the library to get some studying done. I probably shouldn't be surprised to find Chuck leaning against the door of his truck a block down from the café.

"How'd it go?" he asks, arms folded.

I pull out the note pad and add 'stalker' to the cons list before I tear off the sheet and hand it to him. "I'd say it didn't go well."

His forehead creases with anger as he reads the list. I'm not sure if he even finishes it before he crumples the paper into a ball with his fist, then throws it through his open window into the cab of his truck.

"This" I point at him from head to toe to indicate his anger management problem "Is also part of the problem. You need to learn how to control your temper. It's off-putting."

He inhales deeply to stifle his rage. It's taking every ounce of his restraint. "So, there's no hope?"

Ah, man. He sounds so dejected. I don't want him to impulsively jump off a bridge or something. There isn't any hope for him and Janine but maybe for him and the next woman he dates. Possibly. Remotely. If he doesn't give up. "Despite your atrocious record of conduct, Janine still inexplicably has a soft spot for you. Maybe that means you have a miniscule redeeming quality somewhere deep down inside. To be perfectly honest, I don't know what that quality is, but if you can find it and dig it up that would be your best bet."

His face lights up with a glimmer of optimism. "What does she want me to do to prove to her I'm willing to change?"

"She doesn't want you to do anything. She's moving on. And she should. My recommendation for you is to completely change everything about who you are and then maybe you'll have a chance at love at some point in the future. With someone else. Sorry to be harsh but, even though the truth hurts, I don't think it would be fair to lie to you."

He nods as he lets the message sink in. I can tell he's still scheming to win Janine back. Whatever. At least if he has something to work towards he won't give up on life and step in front of a train.

"Good luck." I turn and head down the sidewalk.

"Thanks for doing that for me, Della."

Surprised at how well he's taking the bad news, I turn and walk backwards. "You're welcome. And by the way, politeness and manners are good first steps. Keep it up, you might actually be able to redeem yourself."

With his hands in his pocket and a genuinely vulnerable look on his face, he asks, "Will you help me?"

"I can't help you be a better person, Taylor. You have to do that for yourself."

"I'll do the work." With a renewed sense of hope that comes from having a plan, he walks towards me. "I just need someone to ride my ass and keep me focused. You're good at nagging, right?"

"Seriously? Nag yourself." Already offended by him, I turn to leave.

He runs to catch up and matches my stride. "Nag was a bad choice of words. I should have said coach. I need a coach. You understand women. You're nauseatingly nice. And you're not afraid to stand up to me." He hops in my way and stops me in my tracks with a goofy, enthusiastic grin. "I would really appreciate it if you'd be my coach."

Admittedly, I am the perfect person for the job. And the chances of him succeeding without help are astronomically small. But I have more important things to focus on. Oh, who am I kidding? After sizing him up, I roll my eyes in surrender. "Fine. I'll coach you. But not so you can win Janine back. I'll do it because I want to one day be proud to call you my friend."

He pumps his fist, and I already regret that I agreed.

Chapter 20

Easton

Just before midnight a car rolls in and parks in front of the barn. We aren't expecting anyone, so I get up and open the loft window. When I make out the Volkswagen Beetle, I smile and lean against the window frame.

"Surprise," Della whisper-shouts up to me as she springs out of the car and flings her arms out to the side. She's wearing a fluffy, pink rabbit costume, which doesn't faze Brewster. He runs over, wagging his tail. Della crouches down to give him some love.

I can't help but laugh at the sight of a bunny reluctantly patting the stomach of a dog. "Get up here, you goofball."

Della says something I can't quite hear to Brewster, then grabs her bag out of the back seat of the car and hops towards the stable door with Brewster following and jumping, too. I meet them at the bottom of the stairs and Della launches herself into my arms for a hug. A hug I really need. It's been a long week. Meetings at town hall, at the police station, and with the lawyer. Doing all my

214

dad's work on the ranch. Falling behind at school. God, I've missed the way she makes me feel when I'm with her. I can't even explain exactly what it is that she does. She just makes me happy. With her arms still wrapped around my neck, I reach down to hook her plush-covered legs up around my waist, so I can carry her upstairs. It's hard to blindly judge the steps and she squeals, worried I'm going to trip and kill us both.

"I've got you. Don't worry."

She clings tightly to me like a baby monkey, or a bunny in this case. Once we reach the top of the stairs safely, she presses her lips softly to mine. Then she steps back and drops her bag to the floor before spinning around and wiggling her butt to show off the white puff tail. "Do you like your surprise?"

"A midnight visit from an adorable five-foot-five Easter Bunny?" I snap and point to the stairs so Brewster will head back to the barn. He mopes because he's being banished from the fun but turns and disappears down the stairs.

"It's too weird, isn't it?" She glances down at her giant fuzzy body and frowns. "It seemed like a good idea when I was wandering around Walmart, depressed because I missed you so much, and also because I needed staples— as in literal staples for a paper stapler not like the flour, sugar, and butter type of food staples, although we did need salsa, which is arguably a staple here in California—and I was also looking for a new hairbrush. Anyway, they had their Easter products on clearance. Which I'm just realizing is not sexy. Unless you have one of those fetish things."

I scoop Della up in my arms and gently place her on the bed to unzip the costume. "I love my surprise." She's not wearing anything underneath, which makes me grin "You drove four hours like that?"

"No, silly. It's too hot. I drove nude for four hours and then stopped at the beginning of your five-mile-long driveway to put it on."

"Ah. That makes way more sense."

She laughs and shimmies out of the bunny suit.

Pulling it off over her bare feet, I toss it onto the chair, then kiss her toes. "I thought you had to meet your study group to work on your project tomorrow?"

She smiles and inhales deeply as I leave a trail of kisses from her belly button to her collarbone. "I told them I have a contagious skin virus and offered to participate via video call instead. They were all more than happy to oblige."

I slide down next to her and run my fingers along her waist and up to cup her breast. "Your skin looks contagion-free to me."

She rolls and leans in until her lips are hovering seductively close to mine. "I lied."

"What? Not possible. Della Koskov doesn't lie."

"Hmm. Apparently when a bunny suit and a boyfriend she misses desperately are involved, she'll stoop to all sorts of devious lows." Her hand slides across my abs tentatively as if she's thinking about making the first move but instead pops up on her knees and straddles my waist. "Speaking of devious lows, this disobedient version of Della might even use a curse word."

"Really?" I run my palms over her thighs. "Let's hear it."

She slides her hair over her shoulder and then drops forward until her breasts are pressed to my chest and her lips caress my ear. "Just kidding," she whispers. "I would sound weird if I swore. But it starts with an f and ends with a k, and I want you to do it to me. Please."

Wow. That was unexpectedly hot. "Naughty girl."

She winks, and I flip us both over until she's on her back. I push my boxer briefs down to expose my erection but then freeze because I don't have a condom.

"In my bag," she says, breathlessly. "I brought the ones from your room."

So glad that she thought ahead, I reach over the side of the mattress to grab her bag and then hand it to her so she can find the box of condoms inside. Along with the box she timidly pulls out a satin blindfold and a pink feather.

"I don't know if you'll like this," she says and tickles my chest. "I went to a sex shop, thinking I could find some things you'd like, but honestly I was mostly just confused and embarrassed because I had no idea what anything was. The sales clerk could tell how out of my comfort zone it was to even buy the blindfold. She threw in the feather for free."

"You don't need to pretend to be someone you're not comfortable being just because you think it's what I would like. You're already everything I could ever ask for just by being you."

Her lips pucker in a sexy way from the compliment before she whispers, "Thank you." Then her eyebrow lifts with a mischievous arc as she rolls the condom on me. "To be honest, though, I'm kind of into trying the blindfold. If you are."

Man. She's awesome. How did I get so lucky? I love everything about her. Seriously. Love her. Whoa, Havie. Do not tell her you love her in the middle of sex. She won't believe it's genuine. But say something. If you don't, she's going take the silence as a rejection.

Her smile fades as she notices my hesitation. "Is everything okay?" she asks.

Damn. Speak, dummy. But not I love you. Not now. And swallow back whatever that emotion is that's threatening to choke you up. I nod so she won't worry. Then after admiring how beautiful she is for a little longer, I finally find the right words. "I'm really glad you're here."

Her eyes sparkle with a smile as her gaze blazes into my soul. A million thoughts seem to flicker through her mind as she studies my expression. Her mouth opens slightly as if she's going to speak but then she presses her lips together to stop herself. When she starts again, she says, "I'm really glad I'm here, too."

I reach for the pink satin blindfold and stretch the elastic over her head, kissing her before drawing the fabric over her eyes. Knowing it will heighten her other senses, I run the feather over her skin. Then touch my tongue to her nipples, one at a time, and watch them react. As I continue to explore down her midline with my mouth, and make my way between her legs, she clutches at the bedspread, her body writhing from the sensations. Bathed in the moonlight, the curves and angles of her body are so beautiful—the arch of her back, the flex of her legs, the extension of her neck, and the slope above her upper lip as her mouth opens in a gasp. God. I need to be inside her. Now.

She inhales sharply, head falling back onto the pillow as I enter her, and she bucks her hips up to meet my thrusts, enticing me in deeper each time. I lace my fingers with hers and lift both her arms over her head, watching her breasts bounce in rhythm to our movements. It's a huge turn on, especially the soft moans that escape from the back of her throat each time I penetrate fully into her.

Propping her up by the hips into a bridge position, I kneel and, with my knees wide, extend her legs to rest on my shoulders. It's a position that brings us even closer together. Our movements synchronise and her muscles quiver as I feel her start to come. At the peak of her wave I release, and she screams in unbridled ecstasy.

God damn. It doesn't get any better than that.

After soaking up the high for a few extra beats, I pull out, slide her legs off my shoulders, and flop down beside her. She pushes the mask up onto her forehead before leaning over to kiss me. In between rapid breaths she says, "That was fun, right?"

I nod, unable to form words quite yet.

Super jacked, she drums my chest with her palms several times and then shoots up to stand on the bed. "I'm going to hop in the shower. Do you want to join me?" She bounces up and down on the mattress, trying to get me to move.

"Jesus. Did you take speed before you got here or something?"

She holds up two fingers on her left hand and one finger on her right hand. "Two green tea lattes and one Red Bull." She blinks exaggeratedly and then opens her eyes wide. "I'm going to be awake for a while. And probably super annoying."

I sit up and spank her bare ass, which makes her jump off the bed and run to the bathroom. I laugh as I follow, throw the condom in the trash and then step into the shower behind her.

"Sorry I'm hyper. I didn't want to get sleepy while I was driving."

"It's okay. I like the hyper you as much as the calm you."

"And the grumpy me?"

"I like all of your yous."

She bounces up on her tiptoes and kisses me. "Have lots of women slept over here?" she asks as she lathers my back with shower gel.

"No. I stayed in my childhood bedroom in the house up until I built the loft apartment last summer. You're the one and only guest I've ever had up here."

She nods in a satisfied way and hands the shampoo bottle to me, so I'll wash her hair for her. "I've been avoiding asking you the next question because I'm afraid to know the answer, but we have to talk about it at some point."

"Okay," I say, worried that it's not something I'll want to talk about.

She leans back and lets the water pour over her head,

then wipes her eyes as her forehead creases. "How much more school can you miss before they kick you out?"

I curl my finger under her chin and tilt her head up to make eye contact with me. "Don't worry. I've emailed all my instructors and explained my dad's medical situation and that I need to run the ranch. All of them except for Cavendish have said that as long as I get the assignments in on time, and do well on the exams, they'll waive the classroom participation mark."

"What are you going to do about Cavendish's class?"

I kiss her forehead and then slide conditioner down the length of her hair. "Show up on Wednesdays and Fridays, I guess."

"That's so much driving back and forth."

I shrug and kiss her shoulder. "I'd be driving out on weekends to spend time with you anyway."

She smiles and reaches up to squeeze my face. "That makes me happy. But your dad needs you."

"And I need you, so either way, I'm going to be putting a lot of miles on the old Silverado. I don't want you to worry about any of that. I'm going to make it work, no matter what it takes. Okay?"

She nods, and after rinsing her hair for her, I step out of the shower to get two clean towels from the linen cupboard. She twirls her towel into a whip and snaps it at my ass, then sprints out of the bathroom. I chase her, and she squeals as I spin her around and toss her onto the mattress.

Straddling her legs, I tickle her mercilessly. She laughs

franticly and squirms, then rips a huge fart. Her face immediately freezes in a horrified, shocked expression, which makes me buckle over in hysterics.

"Oh, my goodness. I want to die." She covers her face with both hands to hide the embarrassment. I try to stifle my laughter, but it's not going that well. And she's completely mortified, so she flips over and crawls under the sheet to hide. "I knew that giant burrito from the taco stand on the side of the road was a mistake," she says, muffled under the fabric.

I pull the sheet back and kiss her cheek. "Don't worry about it. You're dating a cowboy, remember? I rip them way better than that. Especially after I eat eggs."

She crinkles her nose. "Uck. I smell bad."

I start laughing again because it really is a rank refried bean fart. Seriously decent.

She swoops the sheet back over her head. "I'm going to sleep with the horses and sneak out in the morning. It was nice being your girlfriend while it lasted."

I spoon up behind her and drape my arm over her waist. "You're going to have to come up with something better than epic room-clearing burrito gas to get rid of me, Della Koskov."

She pulls the sheet down to reveal her face. "Sorry for being gross."

"Be as gross as you want to be. I'm not going anywhere. But your new nickname might be Tootie."

She rolls over to face me and wraps her hands around mine with a big grin on her face. We stare at each other for a long time without speaking until eventually she says, "My sister told me about guys like you."

"Yeah, what did she say?"

Della smiles and kisses the tip of my nose but doesn't answer before she rests her head on the pillow and closes her eyes. I have a fairly good idea that whatever her sister told her, it was good, so I close my eyes too.

A minute later, Della says, "It smells really bad in here. Maybe we should crack a window or something."

Now we're both laughing again.

Chapter 21

Della

Easton woke up before the rooster this morning. Literally. The rooster crowed after he was already gone. Insanity. He and some ranch hands are fixing a fence somewhere out on the range, or whatever it's called, and it's going to take all day, which is fine since I have my conference call with my classmates this afternoon anyway. He and I made plans to have a picnic dinner date and watch the sunset later, which I'm excited about. I'm more than a little worried, though, about what will happen if he has to stay here permanently instead of coming back to school.

At eight o'clock, I get dressed and then sit cross-legged on the bed to call my sister. Brewster hops up next to me and rests his head on my leg, then looks up at me as if to ask, "Is this okay?" He'd be borderline cute, if it weren't for the fact he's a dog.

"Hey," I say to my sister when she picks up.

"What's wrong?" she asks, half-distracted by something else she's doing.

"Why would you assume that? Can't I call my sister just to say hi?"

"We talked on Wednesday. I told you everything about Tabitha and Alex. You told me everything about school and the boys you're shacking up with. My life isn't exciting enough to talk more than once a week and have fresh material. So, you must have something new. What's wrong?"

"Okay, fine. I want to tell Easton I love him." Brewster lifts his head and cocks it to the side as if he knows how momentous a statement like that can be, and he is intrigued. "Maybe you think it's too early and I'm naïve because I haven't dated before, but I know for a fact I love him. So much. Plus, I farted in front of him and he basically thought it was cute."

Yulia laughs. "I'll use that in my speech at your wedding."

"Ha ha. Seriously. The problem is, even though we are totally compatible, he might have to drop out of school and move back home to help run the family ranch. I don't know how the relationship would survive if we had to live that far apart. So, I'm freaking out about laying all my feelings out the on the line only to have my heart stomped on. What should I do?"

She says something away from the phone to Tabitha, then says to me, "Wait for him to say it first."

"Are you sure?"

"Positive."

"But what if he's not sure I feel the same way, and he's reluctant to say it because he doesn't want to get rejected. And neither one of us ever says it, then we drift apart never knowing what could have been if only one of us had taken the risk to say it? If I just say it first, he'll know for sure. No awkwardness."

"Awkwardness if he doesn't say it back. Jesus Christ. Where did you get scissors?" Yulia drops the phone and runs to save Tabitha from a bloody mishap of some sort. When she returns to the phone, Tabitha is crying because she wants the scissors back and Yulia is swearing under her breath. "Where were we? Oh, yeah, right. The L word. Let him say it first. Just send lots of signals about how happy you are and how much you enjoy spending time with him, and maybe drop a few hints about the future. If he's feeling it, he'll say it. If he's not, well, you probably have a problem on your hands."

"What kind of problem?"

"You're going to get your heart broken."

"Ugh." I flop back on the mattress of his bed and stare at the loft ceiling. Brewster takes that as a signal to stretch out and get comfortable next to me. "How long am I supposed to wait for him to say it before we can declare my heart officially broken?"

"He'll say it. Don't worry. If things are going even half as good as you think they are, and Mom and Dad are right, he's in for the long haul."

"What did Dad say?"

"Oh my God, he wouldn't shut up—in front of poor Alex, I might add—about how Easton's a specimen of physical fitness, has a great business mind, is a true gentleman, understands the value of hard work, smiles at you like the earth revolves around you, blah blah blah, and so on and so on."

"Dad said all those things?"

"Yes. He practically made Alex cry. So, I'm sure Easton will tell you he loves you. Just be patient."

"Okay. And thank you. And tell Alex I'm sorry. And tell Tabitha I love her."

As soon as I hang up with my sister I receive a text from Chuck: *What's my assignment for today?*

I type back: *Don't offend anyone.*

You need to be more specific. I want to learn something I can practice.

I don't know what to tell him so, instead of replying, I get up and tap my leg to summon Brewster. "Come on, boy. Let's go get something to eat." Brewster and I head downstairs and through the stables to make our way over to the main house as I think about what my response to Chuck should be. I didn't realize he was going to expect specific lesson plans. I should probably do some research on how to teach someone empathy and integrity, if there is such a thing. In the meantime, I can only come up with one thing, but it should keep him busy for a while.

Here's a link to a series of articles. Read them. Memorize them. Put them into practice.

I knock on the front door of the ranch house and Mr. Lewis answers. "Hey, good morning. Easton told me you got in last night. Did you sleep all right?"

"Yes. Thank you." I hug him, sort of awkwardly because his cast makes his arm angle out in an unnatural way.

"Since you only have one arm to work with, can I interest you in some pancakes? My treat."

"Well, Easton has me on a strict cancer-fighting diet that doesn't include carbohydrates unless they come from vegetables, but I'm sure it won't hurt to sneak a couple pancakes in if you swear not to tell him. And I'm happy to have the company. Come on in."

He leads the way to the kitchen and my phone buzzes with a text from Chuck: *The complete how-to of great sex? Seriously? I don't need to learn that!*

Yes, you do! It's about respect and caring about the other person. Read. Memorize. Practice. And don't question my teaching methods or I won't help you.

His response is a GIF of an eye roll.

Disrespectful. Try again.

He sends another GIF of a person flipping feverishly through the pages of a giant textbook. *I'm reading. But only so I can skip to the practicing part.*

Good. I'll send your second assignment tomorrow.

Mr. Lewis shows me where he keeps everything for making pancakes and I get to work. Brewster lies down on his blanket in the corner to watch. "Have you been getting headaches from the concussion?" I ask as I pour batter on the skillet.

"Nah. The head's fine. The cast is a pain in the ass, though."

The elbow cast does look awkward, but he'd likely be out riding if he didn't have it, so it's probably for the best. "Just think how good you'll be at ballroom dancing after six to eight weeks of holding your arm out to the side like that."

"Good point." He winks.

When the first batch is done I stack three pancakes on a plate, along with a scoop of sliced strawberries, and place it on the table in front of Mr. Lewis. After a quick knock, the porch door opens behind me. Thinking it's Easton, I spin around with a big grin on my face. But the joy disappears when Tracy walks in without waiting for an answer, acting like she lives here.

"Oh, hey, Jack." She sizes me up with her eyes and removes her boots at the door. "Sorry to interrupt. I didn't know you had company."

Really? The car parked out front wasn't a clue? My internal monologue sounds jealous. Why am I jealous that Easton's former girlfriend is chummy with his dad and walks into the house with nothing more than a cursory knock? Gee, I wonder. At least Brewster doesn't like her. He glanced up and then put his head back down on his blanket when he realized it was her.

"Tracy, this is Easton's girl, Della."

"Yeah, we met once before." She nods a slightly dismissive greeting and sits down at the table. "Nice to see you again."

"Uh huh." I don't know what else to say. I'm making it more awkward than it needs to be. They dated ages ago. He doesn't have feelings for her. Why is she here? Maybe she's been here every day. Why do I care?

"Pancakes?"

"Oh, no thanks. I already ate."

I nod and continue making more pancakes than we need, partly because there's leftover batter and partly because I don't want to sit at the table next to her.

"What brings you by?" Mr. Lewis asks, which, to my relief, probably means she doesn't drop by unannounced every day.

"Mike dug deeper into the background of the commodities company and found out they used to be registered under a different name." She slides over a stack of papers for Mr. Lewis to read through. "The original company has lawsuits pending against it in several states. I thought you guys might be interested."

After scanning the documents, Mr. Lewis says, "Easton has been handling all the conversations with the lawyer. You should probably talk to him about it."

"Is he around?"

"They're working on the fence past the north ridge. Won't be back 'til dinner. You can come back then if you want."

Wait. What? No. He and I have plans for a picnic under the stars. I don't want her to come back later. Or ever for that matter. "Or you can drive out to the north ridge now," I blurt out. "I'm sure he'll want the update sooner rather than later." Stop talking, Della. You sound like an idiot. Why would he care when she told him? Why are you encouraging a beautiful woman to head out and meet your boyfriend in an isolated location?

Mr. Lewis shakes his head and finishes swallowing a mouthful of pancakes before he responds, "There isn't road access out that way, but you two could take some horses.

It's only about a thirty-minute ride each way if you cut across the river."

She raises her eyebrows at him as if she's not overly keen about the idea.

He bobs his head as if the more he thinks about it the more he believes it's a good idea. "Della wanted me to teach her how to ride today anyway. It will be better if she's out there with someone who knows what they're doing."

Tracy's smile is definitely forced. "Sure." She looks across the kitchen at me. "You up for it?"

Um. I can't even swallow properly right now let alone ride a horse into the wilderness with Easton's former lover. But I don't want to seem like a wuss. Or petty. Or unfriendly. And I do want to learn how to ride a horse. Mr. Lewis isn't supposed to ride anyway. "Sure." Swallowing is still not functioning, so I have to choke out the next part, "I need to be back by one o'clock for a conference call."

"No problem." Tracy stands and frowns at my flip flops. "What size are your feet?"

"Seven."

"I've got another pair of boots in the truck. I'll get them and meet you in the barn."

I quickly wolf down a stack of pancakes, and as I clean the kitchen, Mr. Lewis disappears down the hall. He returns with a cream-coloured cowboy hat that has a beautiful turquoise beaded band around it. The feathers arranged on the front give it almost a tiara look. "This belonged to Easton's mom. She would have given it to you if she were here."

"Wow. It's so gorgeous." I admire it briefly but then extend my arm to return it to him. "I can't accept it."

"She would have been offended if you didn't accept it."

"Are you sure?"

"Positive." He places it on my head like he's crowning a princess.

I'm completely honored. "Thank you."

He nods, then walks over to shout out the door at Tracy. "Take a rifle with you."

Oh my goodness, what have I gotten myself into?

Mr. Lewis turns around and notices my horrified expression. "There's nothing to worry about. Tracy's a great shot."

Not helping.

He wraps his arm around my shoulders and gives me a squeeze. "Plus, you don't have enough meat on your bones to interest a bear."

"I'm not worried about bears," I mumble as I follow him outside.

Tracy's spare pair of boots are turquoise blue and match the beads on Easton's mom's hat. Mr. Lewis talks me through all the steps of saddling a white horse named Hemingway. He ends up helping more than he probably should with one arm because the saddle is ridiculously heavy and I can't manage it myself. Tracy tacks a speckled horse named Hobelia—she's completely proficient and self-sufficient.

"Have you ridden before?" Mr. Lewis asks me.

"On a pony at the fair when I was seven."

He crouches over and holds his hand out. "Give me your ankle. And hop. There you go. Up and over."

Okay I'm on the horse. Not sure how I did that, but I'm definitely a good five feet off the ground and have no idea how to steer this thing. Mr. Lewis adjusts my stirrups to the correct length and then shows me how to hold the reins properly. Tracy leans forward on the horn of her saddle in boredom as she waits for my tutorial to be over.

"Okay. Just take it easy. Hemingway will take good care of you. He likes the water, so you won't have any trouble crossing the river. Hobelia might shy, though," he says to Tracy.

She nods, not concerned in the least. And then we're off. Slowly. More of a mosey than a walk, as if the horses really don't want to go. Maybe they're picking up on Tracy's and my reluctant attitudes. Brewster follows us until Mr. Lewis whistles to call him back.

For the first ten minutes or so I concentrate on holding the reins properly and pointing my toes up and out in the stirrup. Hemingway is doing all the work and following the trail without my help, though, so I relax and glance over at Tracy. "So, what do you do for a living? Are you a rancher?" I ask.

"Midwife," she says matter-of-factly and with no elaboration as if she's filling out a government form.

I should probably just accept that she doesn't want to make small talk with me, but my nervous chatter is kicking in. "That's a great career out here, so far from a hospital. How many babies have you delivered?"

"On my own, only one. I assisted quite a few while I was still training but only got certified last fall. My first solo birth was last month."

"Congratulations."

"Thanks."

This is painful. I don't know which is worse, stilted conversation or uncomfortable silence. We ride for another five minutes—she's pretending to be enthralled by the scenery, I'm feverishly editing every discussion topic that comes to mind, searching for one that isn't too odd to discuss with the ex—and the empty air time is especially awkward now since we are travelling so slowly. The horses are probably rolling their eyes at each other and commenting in horse language about how you can cut the tension with a knife.

"Easton mentioned that you are half-Mexican and half-Norwegian. Were you born in California?"

"Yeah." She glances at me and then surrenders to the fact that we are stuck out here together and making polite conversation is better than ignoring each other. "What about you? I can't place your accent."

"Born in Russia. Grew up in Canada. I moved here to study engineering at Stanford."

"So, you'll be moving back to Canada after you graduate?"

The question ignites my face. I can't help it. The underlying insinuation that Easton and I will only be together temporarily makes me feel embarrassed. Who knows what the future might hold? If things work out with us, I could apply for residency in the United States. Or we could get married. Or, maybe things won't work out. I don't know. Why does she care? Is she wondering if she'll have an opening to navigate her way back into his life? I'm taking too long to answer the question. Afraid that she's going to feel smug for putting me on the spot, I impulsively form a completely unsubstantiated statement in my mind and vomit it out, "All of the best jobs for the field I'm training in are located in California, so I'm planning to stay and build my career here."

She doesn't react, maybe because the random spewing of falsehoods doesn't require a response, or because we've reached the river and Hobelia starts to prance sideways. Tracy nudges him with her right leg to straighten him up. He rears his head back as if she's asking him to step into lava. Hemingway ignores the drama and wades into the water without me even asking him to. I glance back over my shoulder as Tracy coaxes Hobelia with gentle words to the edge of the river. As soon as the water touches his legs, he rears up and Tracy has to heel him harder to let him know who's boss. He protests with head flips every step of the way, but she is a confident rider and he has no choice but to obediently follow her commands. Once he's made it through the deepest part of the crossing, which isn't even up to his belly, he races past Hemingway and me and leaps up onto the far shore as if a crocodile is about to snap at his butt. I must admit that the gracefulness of Tracy's horsemanship is impressive. Strong. Calm. Brave. It's painfully obvious why Easton fell for her. I mean, come on, I'm practically crushing on her. She looks over her shoulder to see if I'm following and notices that I'm gawking at her with way too much admiration to be considered normal.

Fortunately, Hemingway hops out of the water effortlessly, and once Tracy sees that I'm fine, she continues on ahead and disappears over the ridge. Twenty minutes later, we clear the summit and I can see the men working on the fence. Four men, all shirtless, glistening with sweat in the hot sun. Easton has a red bandana tied across his forehead and the ends of his hair dance in the breeze like a horse's tail. He swings a sledgehammer-y thing over his head and drives the fence post deeper into the ground, causing the muscles in his chest, abs, and arms to simultaneously flex into an awe-inspiring geometric tapestry.

"Oh my."

Tracy glances at me and chuckles.

Wait. Did I say that out loud? I meant to say it in my head. Oh my is exactly the right sentiment, though. Mmm. Mo' Havie. Who wouldn't want to see more of that? I totally get the nickname now. Easton glances over at us and wipes the sweat from his eyes with his forearm. He frowns when he recognizes Tracy, then half-smiles with a perplexed curiosity when he realizes I'm the person on the horse next to her.

He clicks his tongue, then calls, "Hemi." Hemingway trots eagerly towards Easton, bouncing me along with him. Easton climbs up on the stack of fence posts to make himself the same height as me, then kisses me on the cheek. "You found my mom's hat?"

"Your dad lent it to me." I study his face to see if he's uncomfortable that I borrowed it, but it seems like he hasn't yet decided how he feels about it. "Do you mind?"

He smiles and tugs the brim down lower. "Not at all. It looks nice on you." His eyes glance sideways over at Tracy. "You found a new buddy to hang out with?"

"I wouldn't say we're buddies. She wanted to share some legal information with you about the gold-digging trespassers. It was your dad's idea to make me tag along."

"Well, I'm glad you did."

"Me too." I point at his chiselled physique and lift my eyebrows. "The view was worth the ride."

Easton smiles and shoots me a swoony model-worthy wink. After introducing me to his staff and telling them to take a break, he talks to Tracy for about ten minutes. I stay on Hemingway and let him rest under the shade of a tree because I'm not one hundred percent sure I'd be able to get back on him again if I got off.

Tracy hands Easton the papers that her brother gave her and then he walks back over to me and pats Hemingway's shoulder. "I'm looking forward to our picnic later."

"Me too." I point at the papers. "Anything important in that?"

"Possibly. I'll call the lawyer on Monday."

I lean forward onto Hemingway's neck to give Easton a kiss. "You do realize that for the rest of my life I'm going to have very pleasant dreams about you mending fences without a shirt on."

"Good." He smacks Hemingway's butt. "Now, get out of here so I can actually concentrate on my work and get home in time for our date."

Hemingway is already trotting to meet Hobelia and Tracy

up the trail, so I just give Easton a thumbs up over my head and keep going. Once we catch up to Hobelia, Hemingway slows to a walk, with no instruction from me whatsoever.

Tracy says, "You guys make a nice couple."

I glance over to check her expression, not sure if she's being facetious. It seems like she genuinely means it. "Thank you." We ride for a while and I work up the nerve to say, "I don't mean to pry, and you don't need to answer if it makes you uncomfortable, but Easton said you were unfaithful to him. I was just curious, if it's true, why you made that choice?"

She shrugs and stares off at the trail ahead of us for a while as if she's contemplating whether she wants to share her reasons with me or not. Obviously she wouldn't want to. Why did I even ask? So inappropriate. Such a dork. Oh well, her opinion of me probably wasn't very high to begin with.

Just when I'm about to apologize for being nosey, she takes a deep breath and starts to speak, "When Easton went to Stanford, I didn't have a job or even any idea of what I wanted to do for a living. He has always been so driven. I imagined him at college, meeting a bunch of really smart Southern Cal. girls who all had ambition and money and were throwing themselves at him at fraternity parties. I mean he was a hot model and rodeo stud. I was in a bad place emotionally. I felt stuck here, small-town, nothing to offer him once he graduated. We only saw each other every other weekend and I had convinced myself he was cheating on me, so I made a desperate and stupid decision to boost my self-esteem with a guy we went to high school with. Easton found out, and as soon as I saw the look on his face, I knew for a fact he had never cheated on me and likely never would have. But it was too late. I wrecked us." She glances over at me. "And it was over for Easton the second he found out. He never looked back." She shrugs remorsefully and mumbles, "I don't blame him."

I nod to the rhythm of Hemingway's stride as I let it all sink in. I don't know what to say, but I'm glad she told me. It makes me feel sorry for her. That's not normal. Right? I have got to be the only person on the planet who can feel sympathy for the cheating ex. First Chuck now Tracy. Yikes. I really hope I never do anything to give Easton the expression she described. It would break my heart if I disappointed him. And it would kill me to be in Tracy's shoes. Well, literally, I am in her shoes. Figuratively, it would kill me to be the second love of his life to screw up and lose him. Is it a bad omen to borrow an ex's boots? I hope the universe gets the difference between literal and figurative. Maybe I should have worn my flip flops.

Thankfully, we reach the river, which interrupts my completely ridiculous train of thought. Instead of balking, Hobelia abruptly sprints full-speed past me and Hemingway and lunges into the water. Hobelia loses his footing and throws Tracy head first over his shoulder. She lands on her back in the water and Hobelia leaps up onto the shore. Hemingway, who looks a little stunned, stops in the middle of the river.

Tracy stands up, soaking wet and looks as if she's going to lose it on Hobelia, but then her expression changes to something I would describe as calm apprehension. "Della. I need you to ride over to Hobelia and get the rifle from my saddle."

"What?" Rifle. Why? She's not going to shoot the stupid horse for bucking her off, is she? That's crazy. I won't let her. Bizarrely, Hobelia wades back into the water on his own and crosses back to the other side with Hemingway following. "They're going the wrong way."

"Della. Grab the rifle. Slowly. There's a mountain lion."

Pardon me. Come again. Did she say lion? As in giant carnivore? I don't want to look. Maybe if I pretend it's not there, it's not there. Or, maybe there really isn't a mountain lion right behind me, and Tracy's pulling a practical joke to scare the bejeezus out of me. It's working, by the way. I turn in the saddle to check if she's laughing at her prank. She's not. She's watching the shore behind me intently and the increasingly alarmed look on her face is also working to sell the joke. The horses are both jittery, so I know it's not a prank. I just don't want to admit it. Hemingway spins all the way around, and yup, it's a frickin' mountain lion.

Holy Hannah. Its paws are the size of my face. My palms instantly saturate with sweat, and my throat pulse pounds ridiculously hard. Crouched on a rock and ready to pounce, the massive, tan cat looks up at my jugular and blinks its yellowish, mascara-like framed eyes as if it's intrigued by how much delicious human blood is coursing through my veins. Or it can smell my fear, oozing out of every pore in my body. The mountain lion growls somewhere deep in its chest and shows a glimpse of his giant vampire fangs as it eyes Tracy. She's thigh-deep in the water and can't even run or play dead if that's what you're supposed to do. The horses are antsy and definitely going to bolt if the cat makes a move. Hobelia spins around and bumps his butt against Hemingway's, so I lean over and reach for the gun. But miss. On the second swipe, I catch the handle and slide it out of the leather case. "I don't know how to use it."

"You have to release the safety first," Tracy says slowly, not taking her eyes off the mountain lion. "Slide the black lever on the side of the handle until you see red. Then aim and pull the trigger. It's going to kick back, so brace it against your shoulder."

"I can't kill it."

"Just shoot in the air. It should run. If it jumps on me, you have to shoot it, though. And pray you hit it and not me."

Eek. I close my eyes, aim the rifle in the air, and squeeze the trigger. I forgot to brace it against my shoulder. The kick blows me backwards off Hemingway and into the water.

This is bad.

Chapter 22

Easton

Della hands me the picnic basket with a trembling hand. She's barely spoken since I got back to the loft. And her face is paler than normal, too. "Everything okay?" I ask as I load a lantern and a blanket into the truck bed.

"Mm hmm." She nods and then hops into the passenger side.

After sliding behind the wheel, I study her face. She's definitely off. "We don't need to go for a picnic if you're not feeling well. We can stay in and have a quiet night instead."

"I want to go."

Okay. Doesn't seem like it, but I'm not going to argue with her about it. I reverse the truck and then turn onto the dirt road that cuts through our property and leads to a good spot to watch the sunset.

"How did your conference call go?"

"Fine. Inefficient. Group work. You know how it is. Too many cooks in the kitchen and nothing actually getting done." She runs her palms over her thighs to straighten her cotton skirt. "Two people didn't even call in, so we have to meet again Monday evening. How about you? Did you get the fence repair finished?"

"Yup. Tomorrow we'll be inseminating heifers if you want to help?"

"Did you bring a rifle?" she asks randomly, missing my insemination invitation.

"Yeah, why?"

She stares out the side window at the scenery to avoid making eye contact with me. "No reason. Just wondering. Actually, there is a reason."

"What's going on, Della? You're acting weird. But not your normal weird. Did something happen when you were out with Tracy today?" Her head rotates to look at me and her eyes start to water, so I stop the truck and turn the engine off. "Spit it out."

Her cheeks turn scarlet and her breath hitches in her throat. "Okay, don't be mad. I need to tell you something. If possible, I'd like you to pretend as if it's no big deal, even though it was a big deal. Huge deal. I actually wish it was some bizarre bad dream that didn't really happen, but it did, so here goes. Brace yourself. Like ripping a bandage off, I'm just going to say it. Go. Okay. On our way back, Tracy and I encountered a mountain lion." She holds two hooked fingers up and hisses to imitate the teeth of a mountain lion. "Like a big, healthy, male one. Ferocious. Yellow eyes. Smelly, too. Hobelia spooked and threw Tracy, so I had to grab the rifle from her saddle, but I don't know how to fire a gun. I panicked, and she had to talk me through the steps of how to release the safety. I didn't want to shoot the cat, but Tracy was worried it was going to pounce on her, so I fired. Just a warning shot. In the air. But it was loud, which made Hemingway freak out, and I forgot to brace for the kick, so I fell off, and fortunately I landed in the water, but unfortunately it still hurt a lot because my hip hit a rock and it's bruised, badly." She waves her hand in a circular motion from her ribs to her thigh to indicate the size of the bruise. "And your mom's hat got wet, which I feel horrible about, but it's drying out nicely. Fingers crossed. And I have a wicked headache, so I probably got whiplash, or maybe the throbbing pain is from the stress-vice digging into my temples from knowing I had no choice but to tell you at some point. To make it worse, the gun somehow went off again when I hit the ground and I have no idea where that bullet went. Thank God it didn't kill Tracy or one of the horses. It might have killed something. Not the lion. Tracy said it headed for the hills, but she was worried it would come back for a calf, which is why she insisted I tell you. During the chaos, Hobelia took off in a sprint, so he made it back to the barn before we did. He might be scarred for life. Me too. We all survived, though, so that's a good thing." She pauses and shakes out her arms as if it somehow removes the post-traumatic stress from her body, then she continues talking, "And since I'm already divulging secrets, I might as well come clean about a few other things, like the fact that Tracy and I talked about the reasons why she cheated on you. Not that I should have pried into your private life, but she shared the details, and now I feel sorry for her because I can empathize with how devastating it must be to live with the regret of ruining the chance to be with someone as amazing as you. Sorry if you don't like the idea of us talking, but since we are now also bonded over the lion incident, cordial feelings would have likely developed between us anyway. And even though you would have likely never found this out because he made me pinky swear not to tell you, I fed your dad carbohydrates in the form of pancakes. And he loved them. And lastly, I'm teaching Taylor to be a good lover." She inhales and then lets the air out slowly. "Okay. Phew. I feel better."

I blink several times to let my brain catch up. "Teaching Chuckie how?"

"Really? That's the one that bothered you the most?"

I nod. "The mountain lion was likely more afraid of you than you were of him. Falling off a horse is a rite of passage for beginners. The water broke your fall, luckily. Cowboy hats get wet and dirty, that's what they're designed for. As soon as I saw you and Tracy together I knew you were going to end up knowing more about what happened than I do. And Dad cheats on his diet all the time. But if Chuck lays one finger on you, I'll have to break both his arms. So, yeah, that's the one that bothers me the most."

At first, Della's eyes widen in disbelief at my questionable priorities, but slowly a smile creeps onto her lips and eventually reaches her eyes, making them sparkle with amusement. "You're jealous."

I turn the engine back on and continue driving. "Call it whatever you want. There's not a guy alive who would be okay with his girlfriend teaching some other guy how to be a good lover."

She shoves my shoulder playfully. "It's not hands-on instructions. Janine said he was mediocre in bed, at best, so I sent him all the articles that I read when I was preparing myself for our first time. They were very informative. Might as well share the wealth of knowledge since I already did all the research, don't you think?"

"No. Don't waste your time on him. He's a lost cause."

She pokes my thigh and laughs. "You're jealous. It's cute."

I back the truck in and park at the top of the ridge, then get out to open the door for her. She wraps her arms around my neck and lets her body slide slowly down mine until her feet hit the ground.

"Don't worry, Havie. No matter how much Chuckie studies, he will never be as good of a lover as you because he only cares about himself. And he doesn't have the biggest rig."

I smile and kiss her forehead. "What do you know about the size of his rig?"

"I live with three men who wander around in their boxer briefs all the time. I'm practically an expert." She skips over to hoist herself up into the truck bed, kicks off her flip flops, sits on her knees, and opens the basket to unload several containers. "You're in for a treat. Potato salad. Raw veggies. Fried chicken. Your dad showed me how to use the deep fryer, and now that I'm hearing it out loud, he probably volunteered that idea so he would have an excuse to make fried chicken for himself. Presumably it's not on his cancer-fighting diet."

I join her and stretch out on the blanket, propped on my elbow. "He bamboozled you."

She nods and feeds me a carrot stick. "So, how many mountain lions have you encountered in your lifetime?"

I chuckle and steal a piece of chicken before she has a chance to get it on the plate. "None. It's extremely rare to see one."

Her mouth drops open. "You stinker." She slaps my arm with a paper serviette. "You acted like battling a mountain lion was no big deal, like it happens all the time, and we were perfectly safe."

"You literally told me to act like it was no big deal." I laugh. "I would have shit my pants if I saw one that close up."

"So, we were in danger?"

I reach over and tickle her waist. "You could have been killed."

She squeals and squirms. "Ow. Ouch. My ribs. I'm injured, remember?"

"Sorry." I stop tickling and pull her shirt up to examine the damage. Her skin is reddish-purple and swollen. "That's definitely going to develop into a respectable black and blue bruise."

"I can't believe you made me believe we overreacted like sissies."

"The fact that it was potentially dangerous and that you

overreacted like a sissy aren't necessarily mutually exclusive."

"That sounds like an asshole-ish type thing Chuckie would say, not an encouraging and supportive thing Easton would say."

I point at her in feigned shock and fake a gasp. "You swore."

"No, I didn't."

"You called me asshole-ish."

"Nope. You misheard." She shakes her head from side to side. "Maybe you heard me say apple crisp. Your dad showed me how to make his famous apple crisp for our desert. It's your favorite, right?"

"Definitely my favorite." The sun has dipped below the crest of the hills and the explosion of color in the sky tints her skin pink. She's beautiful. And hilarious. And she went head to head with a big cat. I'm dreading tomorrow when she has to leave. I lean over to kiss her ear, then whisper, "I'm proud of you for scaring off the lion. It took a lot of guts. Like a real cowgirl."

"Thank you." She reaches behind her for the container of potato salad and grabs two forks. Then she pauses and looks around. "Do you think mountain lions like potato salad?"

"No. But I heard they go crazy for fried chicken."

"I'm serious. Is it stupid to sit out here eating in the open when a beast is on the lose somewhere?"

I pat the rifle next to my leg. "If we get any visitors bigger than an ant I'll protect you."

As we eat, the sky turns to dusk and the wildlife sounds come to life—the screech of an owl, a coyote off in the distance, and a noise I can't identify. She scans the environment, then frowns at me.

"I'll protect you."

She smiles as she opens a bottle of water and passes it to me. "I know you probably feel like a beer or a glass of wine after working so hard all day, but your dad came shopping with me at Crystal's store, so I wanted to respect him."

"Water's good."

"Tomorrow, will you teach me how to shoot a rifle?"

"Sure." I tip the bottle back and relax as the stars start to appear.

"And at some point I should probably learn how to steer a horse properly, too." She pops a celery stick into the corner of her mouth like a cigarette as she uses both hands to attempt to open a jar of veggie dip.

"I'm happy to teach you whatever you want to learn about ranching." I reach over to open the jar for her, then turn the lantern on.

"I might pass on cow insemination." She hands me another piece of fried chicken.

I laugh. "I thought you didn't hear that."

"Oh I heard you. However, I determined that the shock of a mountain lion attack took precedence over cow sperm curiosity."

"Yes. According to the rancher's handbook, you're correct."

"I'm totally going to study that handbook and end up a ranching expert. You know that, right?"

I nod and smile. "I wouldn't expect anything less." After finishing two more pieces of chicken, I say, "This is nice. Thanks for coming out for the weekend."

She leans her upper body forward to kiss me. "My pleasure."

"You have no idea how much I'm going to miss you after you leave tomorrow."

"Not as much as I'm going to miss you. I'm going to cry all the way back to Palo Alto, and if we talk about it now I'm going to start bawling, so maybe we shouldn't talk about it. Okay?"

"Okay."

I sit up and pop the lid off the container with the apple crisp in it. After fishing around at the bottom of the picnic basket I find a spoon. She leans in and lets me feed her the first helping, then we alternate, taking turns until it's all gone. She stacks the container back into the picnic basket.

"Della."

"Yeah?" She spins around to face me and uses her thumb to sweep her hair away from her eyes, then tucks it behind her ear.

"I love you."

Her face lights up and she digs her upper teeth into the flesh of her lip. Then she presses on my shoulders to make me lay down, folds her arms on my chest, and rests her chin on the back of her hand to study my expression. "I love you, too. But you probably already knew that."

"I had my suspicions." I hug her close, then turn the lantern off so we can watch shooting stars.

"My sister is really smart," she says in a dreamy way. "And I'm not wearing any underwear under my skirt, in case you were wondering."

Definitely love her.

Chapter 23

Della

My mood is foul. Partly because I miss Easton. And partly because my period just started—bloated, crampy, pimply, and irritable. And I have a test this morning that I'm really not prepared for. BJ is already sitting on a barstool, eating oatmeal, when I shuffle into the kitchen and turn the kettle on to make tea. "Fair warning, I'm not going to be good company for a couple days."

"Noted," he says as he loops his neck tie and pulls a knot.

"Why are you all dressed up?"

"I have an academic probation hearing this morning."

"But you passed your exam."

He shakes his head with restrained frustration. "I did, but now they're saying I needed to get seventy percent." He shoots back some orange juice and then clears his dishes to the sink. "I got sixty-eight."

"Oh, my gosh, they're being ridiculous. Two percent. Really?"

"It's Cavendish. She's chair of the committee, and she hates me."

"Why?"

He winks but doesn't smile. "In my first year, she had too much to drink at a faculty function and tried to take me home. Even though she's hot, I turned her down. Because, believe it or not, I have some morals. And she's been screwing me ever since."

"That's sexual harassment. You could file a report."

"The timing will look suspicious now. And it's my word against hers. But at least they're letting me plead my case before they make their final decision."

"Is there anything I can do to help?"

"Pray."

"Here." I reach up to straighten the knot on his tie. "Don't forget to mention how you're doing this to support your sisters and provide them with a better future. That will play on the committee's heart strings." I wrap my arms around him for a quick hug and then pat his shoulder like they do when they are about to ride their broncs. "Good luck."

"Thanks," he says, sounding less than optimistic. He grabs his bag and then leaves.

It's so unfair. I can't believe Cavendish would be so malicious about something that happened years ago, especially since it was inappropriate for her to make an advance towards BJ in the first place. Maybe if Easton ever dumps me I'll turn into a mean witch like Cavendish. I'll fire employees willy nilly from my imaginary future engineering firm because they are late to meetings, or my tea is too cold or something. Probably not, though. I really can't imagine wanting to ruin someone else's life simply because I was bitter and jaded. But never say never, right?

I sit down at the table to eat a plain piece of toast as I stare out the window in a hormonal brain fog. Chuck runs through the kitchen, wearing only his underwear, and cannonballs into the pool before swimming a few laps. "What's my assignment for today?" he hollers at me from outside.

I don't answer because I don't have the energy to participate in a conversation that requires shouting. Eventually, he climbs out of the pool and comes back inside.

"You're dripping on the floor."

"It's only water."

I turn my head just enough to glare at him with a scary amount of disdain that's surprisingly easy to produce. Probably evidence that I could become a bitter and twisted Cavendish if someone catches me on the wrong day.

"Whoa, someone woke up on the wrong side of the bed." He crosses his fingers and holds them up like a crucifix warding off evil. "That time of the month?"

I roll my eyes and stand to leave.

"I'll take that as a yes. What's my assignment?"

"Don't ever talk about a woman's menstrual cycle. And three random acts of kindness. If you don't know what one is, Google it." I slip my feet into flip flops because I don't feel like bending over to put on proper shoes. Walking to school is out of the question, so I head to the bus stop. So lazy. Or depressed. I don't know which. The bus driver does a double take as I board, so I must look even worse than I feel.

One good thing is that Easton is coming back to go to Cavendish's class on Wednesday. And if he can get a lot done at the ranch today and tomorrow, he might stay straight through until next Monday. I'm trying to be cool and not get my hopes up too high just in case it doesn't happen. I'm going to be freaking cartwheel level giddy if it does.

My first class is Atmosphere, Ocean, and Climate, which I actually like, but I don't feel like making small talk with anyone, so I sit at the back of the room. If I had my way I'd go home and crawl into bed. Unfortunately, my test is next block.

Walking like Eeyore, I cross the campus and sit at the back of the room to take my exam. Grr. On any other day this test wouldn't be that hard, but my brain is sluggish and my irritability makes my tolerance for frustration non-existent. Is that clock faster than normal? Other people are already finished and leaving. I'm not even half done yet. Why did I want to take engineering again? I can't remember anymore. Do baristas need to take stupid exams? I'm pretty sure I'd like to work in a hip café. Then again, what do I know? I thought I'd enjoy classes on structural integrity. Come on. Della. Focus. You need to prove that girls are smart enough to do these idiotic questions. Time's up. Great.

Two other women from the class are standing outside on the front steps of the building. They wave me over as I exit.

"How do you think you did?" Kate asks me.

I shrug, honestly not sure. "I definitely screwed up the fourth question on variance reduction techniques. And I didn't have time to finish the last question. At least it's only worth five percent of the whole grade."

"Thank God, since I blew the whole thing," Lizzie says. "The project is way more important. Do you want me to pick you up for our group meeting tonight?"

Oh right. I forgot about that. "Sure. Quarter to seven?"

She nods and Kate raises her eyebrows at something behind me. "There is a very sexy man across the street, staring at us, and he's not waiting for me."

Lizzie looks and smiles. "Not waiting for me either, sadly."

I spin around, and after the initial surprise wears off I mutter a quick goodbye to the girls. I run down the steps, carefully since everyone is watching and it would be an epic fail if I tripped. Easton's hair is tied back in a neat ponytail at the base of his neck and he's dressed in dark grey trousers and a tailored, form-fitted, white dress shirt that make him look like he just stepped off the runway. He lunges forward to catch me as I launch myself at him for a hug. He squeezes me tightly before lowering me back down to the ground. "You look very handsome. I thought you weren't coming for another two days?" I lean back to admire his snazzy outfit.

"That was the plan." His forehead creases and he reaches to hold my hand as he escorts me across the grass, away from the audience of my classmates. "I've got bad news. Do you want upsetting, crushing, or shattering first?"

"Uh." I glance sideways at him. He's not joking. "None of the above." I stop walking and face him in an attempt to predict the content of the impending blows before he delivers them. My heart races, and since my blood pressure is already low from my period, I'm suddenly light-headed. "I need to sit down."

Easton leads the way to a bench and digs my water bottle out of my bag to offer me a drink.

"Am I going to cry?"

He blinks slowly and sits back against the bench, then inhales deeply as he massages the tension in his temples. So, that's a yes, obviously. Just the thought of what the news might be causes pressure to build behind my eyeballs. He drove four hours to tell me in person, which is a bad sign. My nervous system fires with an intense impulse to get up and run away so I don't have to face whatever it is. His hand tightens around mine as if he can sense my irrational desire to bolt.

"Okay. Just do it." I close my eyes and brace for impact.

"There was a special academic hearing this morning that I only found out about in an email last night."

"The one for BJ? What did they decide?"

"He was expelled. And, even though I'm getting over ninety percent in all my classes, Cavendish also kicked me out of her class."

"What? That's not fair. Why? If you're getting great marks what difference does your attendance make?"

"She argued that it shows a lack of professionalism and that she can't in good conscience pass someone who doesn't respect the time of fellow students who made the effort to show up."

"Is she joking? I'd much rather work with someone who can attend half the classes and still pull top grades over someone who never misses a lecture and is barely passing."

"Yeah, well, she didn't appreciate it when I made that point."

He looks so deflated, which makes me want to confront her and maybe accidently spill a coffee on her laptop or something. What is her problem? Why make things more difficult for students when they are already hard enough? "Did you turn down one of her sexual advances at some point?"

"No, but when BJ rejected her she decided she hated all of us."

I tip back the water bottle and drink nearly all of it. "Luckily it's only one class."

"Except I can't take next term's classes without her course as a prerequisite, so I have to repeat hers next term and put all my other credits on hold. Which means I'd graduate later than I'd hoped."

That's definitely a wrench in his plans but not as tragic as BJ's verdict. Thank goodness. "I know this sounds selfish, but the bright side of you having to stay at school longer is that we'll graduate at the same time. It's kind of a silver lining on a less than ideal situation."

He scratches the back of his neck. "I'd be happy about that part, too, but I haven't budgeted enough money to be a student and carry the rent at the Palo Alto house for that long. I'd have to fit work in somewhere, either by taking a term off or by taking fewer credits and working part-time as I go. Either way, it delays my graduation even more. You'd be done before I am."

My eyes narrow as my brain absorbs the gravity of his tone.

"Ready for the shattering news?"

Terrified, I shake my head, and as soon as he notices my eyes water, his start to too.

He takes a deep breath to compose himself, then leans forward to rest his elbows on his knees and stares at the ground between his feet. "So, the one piece of good news is that we do own the mineral rights. But I just found out that my dad took out a reverse mortgage and deferred our property taxes to pay for the medical expenses that aren't covered by his insurance. The lawyer thinks the reason the commodities company targeted our property is because they somehow knew we owed the bank. And we got a notice in the mail that the bank is going to force us into foreclosure if we don't come up with all the late payments and penalties in thirty days."

"That's not much notice. How much do you owe?"

"Close to three hundred thousand. And they did give more notice. My dad just failed to tell me about it."

Both of us are quiet as I feverishly generate solutions. "You could take another loan."

"I can't. I've already tried. There's too much debt."

"How about we set up a Go Fund Me campaign?"

He almost winces before he shakes his head. "I'm not

taking charity. I'd rather lose the land than beg for money."

"It's not begging. It's asking for help."

"Asking for help would kill my dad. He'd more likely walk off the land penniless just to save his pride."

"Stupidly stubborn, but okay, if there really is gold on the property just dig it up and sell it yourself."

He responds quickly, so obviously it's a possibility he's already considered. "It requires specialized equipment and costs a lot of money to extract minerals. Even if I could set up contracts to have someone come in, it wouldn't get done in thirty days."

I sigh and fidget with the empty water bottle as I brainstorm more options. "Chuck's family is apparently rich. Maybe they would loan you the money?"

Easton hesitates long enough to consider it but then shakes his head. "His dad cut him off financially. If he were ever to change his mind it wouldn't be to bankroll one of his rodeo buddies."

"It doesn't hurt to ask."

Again, he takes his time to mull it over. "Even if we could get a private loan from someone to cover what's due right now, I'll still have to work to pay back the loan on top of paying all the on-going expenses we already have."

I clench my eyes closed to force back the tears. It doesn't work. "So, either way, you're not going to be able to keep going to school next term?"

He doesn't answer, but I can tell by the way his jaw muscle twitches that the answer is not what I want to hear. I don't know what to say. This is devastating. To him. His

Dad. Us. I wish I had a brilliant idea that would solve everything. Unfortunately, I don't. Overwhelmed and scared, I slide closer to him and wrap my arm across his shoulders. "When are you going back to the ranch? Is there anything I can do?"

He shakes his head and kisses my forehead, holding his lips against my skin for an extra beat. "I need to leave right away. I have a meeting with the bank tomorrow morning to request an extension until after we can sell the cattle. And my dad has a treatment scheduled in the afternoon."

"If you won't be coming to campus for Cavendish's class, you don't need to waste money on rent at the Palo Alto house. Are you going to move your things out?"

Pain etches across Easton's face. "I haven't figured out all the details yet. It's complicated. I don't know what to say."

I examine the darkness in his eyes, and I can see what he doesn't want to say. What I don't want to hear. "This is us breaking up, isn't it?"

He hugs me into his chest, heart thumping. It takes a long time before he finally says, "I'm sorry, Della."

Ow. That hurts. Like being shot in the back or t-boned by an eighteen-wheeler. Only hours ago we said "I love you" to each other for the first time. How can everything change so quickly from "I love you" to "We're breaking up?"

To maintain composure, I nod and swallow hard. An emotionally immature, primal part of my brain wants to freak out and blame him for everything. But the more evolved part of my brain knows that none of it is his fault. And dumping all my heartbroken pain on him is the last thing he needs right now. Come on, Della. You're a big girl. Suck it up. He needs you to be strong. Say the right thing.

"Don't be sorry. You have to do what you have to do to take care of your dad and save your land. I understand. And I admire you for it."

He hugs me even tighter, and when he eventually speaks his voice is choked. "If there is any way I can come back to school, I will do whatever it takes. But no matter what happens, I want you to always know that you're the best thing that's ever happened to me."

And that does it. The final thread that was holding me together unravels. My tears smash through the floodgates with massive force—convulsing-type weeping. I can't help it. It's been such an awful day, and I don't want this to be the end of us, even though I really do understand that his other priorities are more important right now. And the fact that it kills him too makes it even more tragic. There are a thousand coherent things I'd like to say, but the most I can manage to squeak out is a weak and pathetic, "no." And then I collapse into a complete breakdown.

Chapter 24

Easton

That was the hardest damn thing I've ever had to do. I haven't cried since my mom died, but I've been on the verge ever since I left Palo Alto.

After I drove Della back to the house, she helped me pack the truck with my things. Despite the fact that she fought hard to keep her composure as we said goodbye, there was no hiding that she was crushed. And her body trembled as I hugged her. The guilt of knowing I'm the cause of that pain feels worse than a bronc stomping on my chest.

I slam my palm against the steering wheel in frustration. Not that it improves my mood. The ranch has been my entire life so far, everything that made me who I am. But Della's everything I imagined for my future. When she asked if we were breaking up I couldn't force myself to say yes. I didn't say no either. It kills me to let her go, but it's what's best for her right now. She needs to focus on school, not worry about my problems or jeopardize her scholarship. Neither one of us can afford the time or money it would take to make a long-distance relationship work. And I don't want her to pass up internships because she feels tied down to me when I'm in Three Rivers. Hopefully I'll get back on campus next year.

Shit. What was I thinking? Letting her go is a mistake. I need her in my life. What if my dad doesn't beat the cancer? I'll literally be left with nothing—no family, no education, no home, no money, no past, no future. Or, maybe it would be easier that way. No attachments to anything.

Cut it out, Havie. Depressing yourself while driving on a dark, desert highway is probably not the best idea in the world. Great, they're playing *Tennessee Whiskey* on the radio. Seriously? Stop playing the victim. Shitty things happen sometimes. Dust yourself off and get back on the horse. First, change the damn radio station before you lose it. Second, come up with an action plan. Okay, getting kicked out of Cavendish's class is not the end of the world. I can still finish off my other credits for this term by working from home and driving to campus for exams. I'll worry about getting Cavendish's class done later. Then I'll eventually get back on track. It's a delay, not a fatal blow.

Next, come up with the money to pay off the bank and get rid of the vultures circling to pick our bones dry. Cattle prices are below average right now, but if the bank gives me an extension, I can raise enough to cover the amount owed. It won't leave anything left for ongoing and future expenses at the ranch and Palo Alto house, but I'll have to worry about crossing that bridge when I get to it.

Finally, figure out how to make things work with Della.

Eventually. Or, figure out how you're going to survive if you have to live without her.

This sucks.

The lights are still on in the ranch house when I pull up at midnight. Dad might still be awake since his cast is making it hard for him to sleep. More likely he fell asleep on the couch. Brewster saunters off the porch to greet me. "Hey, boy." I pat him under the chin. "Was your day better than mine?"

He looks up and cocks his head as if he's actually trying to understand, then follows me to the front door. Dad's awake and sitting in his chair, watching TV.

"How'd things go around here today?"

He turns the TV volume to mute. "The mountain lion got two calves and a heifer."

I don't want to take my shoes off, so I sit on the arm of the couch. "Did you apply for a depredation permit?"

He smiles and turns the volume back on. "Don't need to."

I assume that means he already killed the lion illegally, but to make sure losing valuable livestock is not another problem I need to worry about, I ask more specifically, "Are we going to lose more of the herd, or not?"

"Not." He gets up and carries his empty coffee mug into the kitchen. "How'd it go at the hearing?"

"One instructor kicked me out of her class for missing too many lectures. The rest gave me permission to work from home and finish the term."

"So, does that mean you flunk the course you got kicked out of?"

In his mind, quitting is the worst. Failing is a close second. He raised me not to quit. And I pushed myself not to fail whenever humanly possible. Cavendish knocked me on my ass, but she can't keep me down forever. "I'll take it again."

When he returns to the living room, he hands me a plate with a slice of chocolate cake on it. "Crystal came by earlier to check in on me and brought some leftovers from the diner."

"Thanks." I haven't eaten anything since the drive-thru breakfast I grabbed on my way to the hearing. Crystal's chocolate cake is almost as famous as her root beer floats, and her timing couldn't have been more perfect. But even this can't make me feel better right now.

"How's Della doing?" Dad asks as he sits back down.

"She's been better."

He nods as if he already figured that, then he flips through the channels. Without looking at me he says, "Everything's going to work out. We've made it through worse times."

We? Who the hell's he trying to kid? I've made it through worse times. He went off the rails and got stuck in the past. Whatever. I don't have the energy to get into it with him tonight. I stand, still eating the cake, and leave. Brewster follows me up to the loft and hops up to sleep on the bed. Normally I wouldn't let him, but he can obviously tell I'm going to let it slide tonight.

Chapter 25

Della

It's raining. Not like Vancouver rain that hangs around relentlessly for four days. California rain that completely dumps everything it has in the course of an hour and floods the street culverts in biblical proportions.

I failed an exam, which is the first thing I've ever failed in my life. And I'm on a roll. A downward roll. I've been so out of it since Easton moved out, I also forgot to hand in one of my assignments. I finished it. I just forgot the due date and got a zero. I've missed two group meetings, too, because I was at home crying. And to top it off, the scholarship committee chose this week to review my marks. Hopefully they realize it's just a blip. I'm a mess. Wrapped in a blanket, I curl up on the window seat in my bedroom with a warm cup of tea. I went to my classes today but came straight home, had a hot shower, and changed into pyjamas. Hopefully I won't feel like hibernating every day for the rest of my life, but right now, it's all I can manage.

Easton was originally messaging and calling to check in

on how I'm doing, but hearing his voice made missing him harder for me. So, I asked him not to contact me, which I vehemently regret now. Especially since no-contact hasn't helped at all, and I'm still just as devastated.

There's a soft knock on my bedroom door, then it swings open and Chuck pops his head in. "Hey. How you feeling?"

Not in the mood to talk, I sip my tea and stare out the window.

"Can I get you anything?"

"No thanks. I just want to be alone, please."

Ignoring my request, he enters my room and sits against the edge of my desk. "What's my next assignment?"

"Respect the fact that I told you I'd like to be left alone."

He tilts his head side-to-side in a conflicted gesture. "Easton asked me to check in on you. And he can beat me up, so I have to do what he asks me to do. Sorry."

Although hearing Easton's name piques my interest and I want to know what else he said when he called, it's better if I don't torture myself with hearing about how he still cares even though we can't be together. "You checked in, I said I want to be alone, if you leave now you'll satisfy both requirements."

Chuck wraps one arm across his body and rubs his chin with his other hand as he studies me in a pensive way. It's obvious that he wants to figure out what might make me feel better. To give him credit, the fact he's even making an effort to care about someone else's feelings is progress. Too bad there's nothing anybody could say to make me feel better right now. Maybe he'll just get bored and go away. I sip my tea and draw a heart in the fog on the window. Easton's absence makes the house feel like it was hit by a tornado and it left a huge gaping hole that's letting the wind and rain in.

Chuck sits patiently, staring at his socks, as I finish my tea. When I eventually glance over at him, surprised that his ADHD hasn't kicked in and made him either say something or walk out, he smiles in a way that could almost be interpreted as sympathetic. Okay, I have to admit it does feel somewhat reassuring to know that I'm not completely alone in the world right now. He's going to screw it up, though. Any second now. Something insensitive is going to shoot out of his mouth. Wait for it.

Wow. Shocking. He's just sitting there quietly. It doesn't even seem like he's itching for me to surrender and let him off the hook. He must have prepared himself to wait for as long as it would take. It's amazing what a person is capable of when they really want to do something. I don't know why, but the fact that he's trying so hard to be sweet makes me cry. I place the mug on the windowsill and cover my face with my hands as the tears stream out.

Chuck walks over, sits next to me, and stretches his arm across my shoulders. "It's going to be okay."

"It hurts so much," I mumble.

"I know. It gets better, though. I promise."

Right now, I can't imagine feeling happy ever again. Why did the universe send me the perfect person only to rip him away? Am I supposed to quit school and go be with Easton? Am I supposed to focus on my studies and move on with my life as originally planned? Does every breakup feel like someone reached into your chest to rip out your still beating heart? It is comforting to know that Chuck understands the pain, though. I sniff and blink up at the ceiling to push the tears back. Unfortunately, all I can focus on is how sweet it was for Easton to ask Chuck to check in on me. How am I supposed to turn off my feelings when I love him so much, and he loves me?

After sitting with me for about twenty minutes, Chuck gives me one more squeeze around the shoulders, then stands. "BJ is heading out soon if you want to say goodbye. He'll understand if you're not up to it."

"I want to." Wiping the tears from my cheeks I step out of the blanket and follow Chuck downstairs.

BJ's duffel bag is on the floor next to the stack of rubber bins that are filled with his other belongings. His truck is backed into the garage, so Chuck helps him load it up to the top of the canopy. His rodeo gear is the last thing they put in, then he closes the tailgate with a sigh. When he notices my red and watery eyes, his expression transitions into empathy. "Come here, darlin'." He pulls me in for a hug. "No more crying allowed. Everything's going to be fine. You hear?"

I nod.

"Seriously. When the world knocks you on your ass, you can't lose faith. You have to get up. Dust yourself off. Then prove how tough you are to everyone who doubted you."

"Cowgirl up," Chuck adds.

I've never been knocked on my butt by anything. And

if I did ever stumble, my mom and dad were always right there to catch me by the elbow and prevent my fall so I would never get hurt. The boys are right. I need to be tougher. "Okay, but you have to promise to do the same," I say to BJ.

"That's the only way I know." He hands me his key to the house. "Pick someone Chuck won't want to sleep with for your next roommate."

"So, a guy," I say.

They both laugh, and it makes me sadder to realize that their light-hearted banter is what I'm going to miss the most.

"I didn't plan to move in with three men, but I'm glad everything worked out the way it did. You guys have changed me. In a good way. And I'm thankful for that."

"You were the best roommate we ever had. Think of me whenever you two-step." BJ hugs me again.

"I'll think of you more often than that. I wish you and your family all the best. Call me if you or your sisters ever need anything."

He bends over to grab his backpack and slings it over his shoulder, then slaps Chuck's hand. Chuck grabs his arm and pulls him in for a proper hug. Their male bonding moment makes tears well up along my eyelids again. Geez. Who knew that living with three guys would be so emotional? BJ slaps Chuck's back and climbs into the cab of his truck. I press the garage door opener and it rolls up. The weather is still brutal. BJ probably can't even see me waving as he pulls out into the storm.

"How long will it take for him to get home?" I ask Chuck after the truck has disappeared down the road.

"Three days if he takes it easy. Two if he pushes through." He presses the button to close the garage door. I stand, staring at it. "You coming?"

"Yeah." I turn and follow him into the house. "Your next assignment is to find a roommate you don't want to sleep with."

"Two roommates."

"No. One. I'm going to pay Easton's share of the rent."

His eyes narrow as if he's worried I'm insane, but he's apparently smart enough not to say anything about my fiscally inadvisable decision. Maybe I underestimated his capacity to read people.

I'm close to caving in to call Easton, just to hear his voice. But I know if I do I'll just feel worse after. So I head upstairs and video call my mom instead.

"Sweetheart. What a nice surprise." She raises her eyeglasses and squints into her iPad screen to examine my appearance, which is dishevelled. "Is everything all right?"

I'm not ready to admit out loud that Easton and I had to break up. And I definitely can't handle explaining why, so I dodge the question by saying, "I'm a little homesick."

"Aw. *Myshka*. We miss you, too. Hold on. I'll get Dad. Viktor! Della is on the computer to say hello." She turns back to face me. "He got a puppy."

"Really?"

He shows up behind Mom and leans into the camera proudly holding out a ball of fluff.

"Cute." If one likes dogs, that is. "What is it?"

"A Pomeranian," he beams.

"Named Cha Cha," Mom adds as she pets its head. "She's not entirely house broken yet. But who can stay mad at a face like that? Your father is so smitten he lets her sleep in the bed."

"Excuse me," Dad protests. "Who was already curled up with her on the pillow when I finished brushing my teeth?"

"You didn't kick her out." Mom winks at me, then goes on for at least twenty minutes about all the antics of the adorable puppy, who gets away with everything from shoe chewing to carpet pooing because she's cute. Wow. They weren't even this excited when Tabitha was born. I've been replaced. Why not throw some acid in the wounds?

"Hey, Mom. Would you mind shipping my camera down?"

"Oh." Her face contorts. "Hmm. That might be tricky. I'm not sure which box it's in."

"It's on the top shelf of my closet. In a black camera bag."

She waves her hands in excitement. "Ooh. Didn't I tell you? We packed up all your things and rented a storage unit because we converted your room into a home gym. Rubber flooring. Mirrored wall. Universal weight set. It's great. Just what I've always wanted. It's the perfect space to do my yoga every morning. But your father hogs the treadmill, not for himself of course, to train Cha Cha to walk herself." She rolls her eyes. "Can you believe that?"

No. Really. I can't believe that. Definitely replaced. All

right, I guess I'm officially flying solo. Not the best feeling in the world. They waited until Yulia was married before they converted her room into an office.

"Oh my gosh. Cha Cha just piddled on me." Mom stands and rushes off to put the dog outside and then heads upstairs to change her clothes.

Dad sits down in front of the screen, then studies my expression more closely. "You feeling okay?" he asks.

I shrug and chew on my fingernail out of habit.

He smiles sympathetically as if he's already guessed that I called because something is wrong. "You know, Della, sometimes you can be too stubborn."

"Thanks, Dad. But I'm not sure pointing out my flaws is going to make me feel better."

"Let me finish. Sometimes you are too stubborn, but sometimes that's what it takes to succeed. Like your mother."

"Mom has a law degree that she doesn't even use and works at a flower shop instead. How is that succeeding?"

"Because the shop is what she loves to do. She chose that. Maybe you don't know, but your mother is very brave. She always did exactly what she set her mind to. She went against her family's wishes to go to school in Moscow. Then they threatened to disown her when she decided to marry me. And she nearly left me when she decided to come to Canada."

"What? You almost got divorced?"

"I didn't want to emigrate. I was dead set against it— afraid to take the risk, I guess. Not willing to start over from scratch. But your mother is like you. She knew you girls would have better opportunities here. And that I would grow to like it here as well. She was right. And without her stubbornness, I'd probably still be poor a farmer in rural Russia right now."

"So, are you admitting that moving to California was a good choice for me and that maybe I'm smart enough to be an engineer?"

"I never said you weren't smart enough, *zvezda moya*. That isn't why I was against Stanford." He sighs and looks at me with pride. "It was selfish of me, but I knew once my little girl left home you wouldn't be back. And I wasn't ready for you to go. I'm glad you did, though. Just like your mother, you take risks. You work hard. And when you set your mind to it, you can do anything. Whatever it is that has got you down, I'm sure you'll figure out a way to sort it out. But if you need my help, just ask. You will always be my *myshka*, no matter how far away you are."

Aw, man, now I'm crying again. "Thanks, Dad."

Chapter 26

Easton

There's a rainstorm on the horizon and coming this way. I'm taping my arm, not that I feel like riding. But the payout at the Madera rodeo is good relative to the competition. Plus, I was already registered and didn't want to lose the entrance fee. And there's an off chance Della might show up since it's only two and a half hours from Palo Alto. My knee isn't in great shape. Hopefully, if I wear a brace it will be stable enough to ride—and more importantly, stable enough to land after the ride.

When Chuck finally pulls into the participants' lot and parks next to my truck, my heart rate speeds up in the hope that Della made the trip with him. Unfortunately, nobody else gets out of the truck. Disappointment hits me like a sack of feed, but it's probably better if we don't see each other. Better for her, since she specifically asked me not to contact her. Not better for me. I'm dying. A constant battle is going on inside me between the need to reach out to her and honoring her request for space.

I'd like to try to make it work long-distance, if that's what she wants. I just don't want to hold her back or screw anything up for her.

"Haaaavieeee." Chuck wanders over and shakes my hand. "We miss you back at the house. How's it going, buddy?"

I glance over at his truck again, hoping Della really did come with him and I just didn't see her. Nope. "I've been better. How's Della?"

Chuck sits on my lawn chair and tips his hat back to relax. "She hasn't eaten anything more than toast since you left, she flunked a few assignments, and she cries herself to sleep every night. Other than that she's awesome."

"Shit." My heart sinks.

"Don't worry about it, man. It's her first break up. It's hitting her hard, but she'll get over it."

"I don't want her to get over it. I want to figure out a way to be with her." After tightening the straps on my knee brace I hop off my tailgate and pace to vent my frustration.

A group of five barrel racing competitors walk by on their way to the arena. One stops. It's Tracy. "Hey, Havie. I didn't know you were going to be here." She frowns as she gives me the once over. "You seem tense. Everything all right?"

"Yup," I say to keep it short and blow her off.

She looks over at Chuck, who was never her favorite person, and she purposely doesn't say hi to him before she focuses back on me. "Is Della here?"

"Yeah." Normally, I wouldn't lie about something like that, but I want Tracy to leave me alone. "She's in the stands."

Chuck scratches his head as the slow wheels in his brain turn.

"Cool," Tracy says. "Maybe I'll run into her before I race. Good luck."

"You too," I mumble as I buckle my chaps.

She struts away. Hard to tell if it's for my benefit or Chuck's.

"Daaaaaamn," he says as his eyes follow the sway of her hips. "I always loved that girl. Is it weird that the fact she still hates me is giving me a boner?"

"Yes."

"Did she get even hotter?" He stands and makes a show of watching her walk away.

"She's exactly the same as she's always been. And so are you, obviously. You better watch yourself."

"Tracy wouldn't give me the time of day." He slaps my back and hops up to sit on my tailgate. "What do you care anyway?"

"I'm not talking about Tracy. I'm talking about the girl you live with. She thinks she's helping you become a better person, but you and I both know that isn't what you're really doing. You need to stay inline or you'll be sorry. You hear me?"

The grin falls off his face as I stare him down. He probably deserves a shot to the head just for considering it. Since he hasn't actually tried to make a play at Della, I leave it at a warning.

He stands, genuinely offended. "You think I'm trying to move in on Della?"

I nod once and then lift my foot to wrap my boot ties.

His mouth drops open as he shakes his head in disbelief. "Wow. I admit I can be an asshole sometimes, but I can't believe you'd think I'd try to steal your girl." Just like that, his short fuse is lit and he kicks over an empty feed bucket. Then he spins around and points at me. "I've been there for her, man. As a friend. And maybe you haven't noticed, but I don't got a lot of friends." He holds up one finger at a time to count them off. "Her, BJ, and you. At least I thought we were friends." His voice cracks from emotion, and out of frustration, he makes a motion as if he's going to throw his water bottle on the grass. But then he doesn't. Instead, he just walks away.

Holy shit. That's a first. Maybe Della really has made progress with his humanity makeover. That was the realest thing I've ever heard him say. And he controlled his temper. I watch him sulk off like a sad penguin and actually feel bad for jumping down his throat. Maybe I was wrong.

Chapter 27

Della

I climb the bleachers and find my seat as the first bareback bronc cowboy nods to open the gate. There is a fairly big crowd here, considering a thunderstorm is closing in—and I suddenly wish I brought a jacket. The first rider holds on for all eight seconds but then falls off awkwardly afterward. It looks like he hurt his collarbone based on how he's cradling his arm.

Easton is scheduled to ride third. As he climbs up and gets ready I try to catch his attention with my burning stare, but he's focused, and all the way on the other side of the arena. Neither he nor Chuck knows I'm here because I changed my mind a thousand times. I finally settled on coming because the bottom line is I want to see Easton. Maybe hug him. Possibly kiss him. Definitely tell him that I'm willing to also drop out of school if that's what it would take for a relationship with him to work. He would never let me, of course. But I want him to know that I don't care if we live four hours apart or across the planet from each other. I wrote out what I plan to say to him, practiced it, and ran it by my sister. She thinks it's sweet, but she's not convinced that a long-distance relationship can work. In my opinion we have to at least try. If it doesn't work, I'll be crushed again, but at least I'll know that I tried everything humanly possible and didn't quit at the first sign of adversity. I really wouldn't be happy with a life that didn't include him. Hopefully he feels the same way.

Oh shoot. No, no, no. My breath catches in my chest as Easton gets bucked off right out of the chute—head over heels, flying through the air bucked. After what feels like an abnormally long time, he lands hard and the horse kicks him in the shoulder. The entire crowd lets out a collective gasp. My hands fly to my mouth as I stand and wait for him to move, but he doesn't. The arena cowboys run across the thick dirt and crouch next to Easton. They ask him questions, but I can't tell if he's responding.

Eventually, to everyone's relief, he rolls to his hands and knees and then takes his time to get up. Two cowboys help him to the gate, carrying most of his weight by his belt so he doesn't have to put pressure on his leg with the bad knee. I don't know what to do. My heart is telling me to run to the backfield and make sure he's okay. My head is telling me that he's all right and he doesn't need someone nervously hovering and making things worse. Chuck looks concerned, but he's next to ride, so he climbs into the chute.

After Chuck successfully completes his ride, I make my way through the crowd towards the medical tent and peer in the open door flap. A guy who's maybe a doctor or a physio is examining Easton's shoulder, so I hang back and loiter in the area that's technically only for participants, surrounded by a bunch of cowboys. A bunch of bull riders to be specific. An intense mixture of excitement and apprehension buzzes off them. I bought proper cowboy boots, so I don't feel quite as out of place at a rodeo anymore. Who am I kidding? Everyone here can still tell I'm a poser.

Now Easton is lying on a treatment bed. The medical guy is testing the stability of his knee. Whoa. I turn my head as the first bull ride starts. From this perspective, on the ground, and right up against the fence, it's even crazier. How do they convince their bodies to do that? Oh, my goodness. He was launched against the fence. What a horrific noise that makes. Eek. The bull is charging him but gets distracted and lifts a bull fighter up in the air instead, spinning him like a propeller. Idiotic. Why does everyone in the ring look like these near death experiences are fun?

As they try unsuccessfully to coax the bull to leave the arena, I turn back to check on Easton. He's gone. How did I miss him leave? I wander around the grounds to look for him as the crowd cheers for the bulls. Mmm. Mini donut food truck.

Even though I haven't talked to Easton yet, he obviously wasn't injured that badly and just being in his general vicinity makes me feel better. My appetite is back. I buy enough donuts to share with him, hoping it will cheer him up after getting bucked off. But I still can't find him as heavy rain drops start to fall. Rushing to avoid the downpour, I head towards the parking lot to check if he went back to his truck to change.

I spot him in the distance. So sexy. Wait. No. He's getting in the cab. I break into a sprint to cross the field, but he's already backed out. Shoot. In an attempt to get my phone out of my purse, while running, I end up dropping the entire bag of donuts which roll across the wet grass. I'm about to dial his number when a voice speaks up beside me, "Don't take it personally, Della. They all get pissy and want to be alone when they shit the bed and get hurt."

"Tracy?" I'm confused. She's dressed in a pink shirt and white cowboy hat, staring at me amusedly. And Easton is getting away. What is she doing here? "Hi. I didn't know you competed in rodeo."

"Barrel racing." She ducks under the pop-up canopy tent next to her truck to get out of the rain, then pulls a bottle of beer out of a cooler and holds it up to offer it to me. "I tried to find you to say hi but couldn't see you in the crowd."

"No thank you," I shake my head in response to the beer offering and also because I'm confused. "How did you know I was here?"

"Easton told me."

What? "He knew I was here?"

"Yeah, he said you were in the stands." She takes a sip of her beer and studies my rain-soaked face as I attempt to assemble the pieces together. A burn flares across my chest and rushes up my neck to heat my cheeks. He knew I was here and took off without even saying hello? That is unnecessarily cruel. And embarrassing. I don't want to cry in front of Tracy. But she must be able to tell I'm on the verge because she's giving me a pity smile. Maybe it's a smug smile, or a genuinely kind smile. I don't know. Doesn't matter. I'm leaving.

"Nice seeing you again," I say quickly so my voice won't break. "I have to go."

Chapter 28

Easton

Stuart left another message. He has some work for me in San Francisco. Unfortunately, as much as I'd like to earn some quick cash modeling, it wouldn't be enough to justify taking time away from the ranch. Right now I'm worth more if I stay here and work. Plus, we're less than a week away from the bank's deadline. I need to move the last hundred-thousand-dollars' worth of cattle to auction on Wednesday and transfer the money by Friday. The only reason I've been avoiding calling Stuart back to turn down his offer is because it means talking about Della if I do, and I don't think I'm emotionally strong enough to do that right now

I climb up on the small wheel loader to get back to work. The engine clicks. Nothing happens. Try again. Nothing. Damn it.

Seriously?

Of course the tractor would choose now to breakdown. What's one more kick to the nuts? I climb out on the hood and stomp my foot down, leaving a dent with the heel of my boot. Then do it again, and again. Good thing it was already beat up because I've got enough pent up frustration to do this all day. Piece of crap. Why does every single thing in my life turn to shit?

I try to do the right thing. I work my ass off. And for what? Nothing. I want to switch feet and stomp again, but I can't because my bum knee will give out. And the reminder that I need knee surgery at some point, which will lay me up and put me out of commission, pisses me off more. There's no time for surgery. I don't have time for anything, good or bad. Why is it that whenever I make progress with one thing in my life something else goes wrong? All of the successes I've ever achieved have been paid for with some sort of heartache. I've never complained. I've always just fought harder. The problem is I'm tired of fighting for every single damn thing only to end up right back where I started. I close my eyes and shout at the wind as I drive my heel into the hood again.

"Everything all right?" Tracy asks as she leans out the open driver's side window of her truck. I didn't hear her drive up during my stomping fit.

"Perfect," I mumble and jump off the loader to lift the hood and figure out why it won't start.

"You sure? You sort of did a number on the hood. And since I've never, in all the years I've known you, seen you lose your cool, I'm going to assume things are not going that well for you right now."

There's no way I'm going to talk to her about it, but I

could really use her help. Her uncle trained her to be a mechanic and she knows more about engines than I do. As I stare blankly under the hood, she gets out of her truck and hops the fence to take a look.

"Try to start it again. I want to hear what's wrong."

Wiping the sweat from my forehead with my sleeve, I climb into the cab. It makes the same dead clicking sound, which feels like poetic irony. She leans under the hood and signals with her arm for me to try it again. Despite my encouragement, when we were still in high school, she never got her mechanic's ticket because she didn't want to end up working as a grease monkey for the rest of her life. She's also a qualified aesthetician, she completed a baker's apprenticeship, and she's a registered massage therapist, but she lasted less than a year in each of those professions. Not that there's anything wrong with that. At least she has options. I just wasted five years focusing on one goal and still have nothing to show for it.

After a few minutes of tinkering, she sends me to get the tool box out of the back of her truck. Then she ties her hair into a braid and leans over the engine. I sit on the fence and drink water as a truck flies down the gravel road and kicks up dust in its wake. The driver slows as the truck approaches us and then stops. "Wow. Lucky guy." My dad's friend Phil hangs out of the driver's window. "When my mechanic bends over, all I see is crack," he barks out in a chesty laugh.

"Shut up, Phil," Tracy hollers.

"What? That's supposed to be a compliment."

She pops her head up from under the hood. "That type of sexist remark is exactly why I'm not a mechanic. I'm a midwife."

"You're a midwife this week." He laughs. "What are you going to be next week? An astronaut?"

She gives him the finger and then gets back to work.

He winks at me, but I don't encourage him because I need her to not get pissed off and leave. "By the way, kid. The auction on Wednesday is cancelled. You're not going to be able to sell anything locally until the week after next at the earliest."

"Why?"

"It's a damn scam. Someone, AKA a person who has a vested interest in the Lewis family forfeiting on the loan, made an anonymous tip to the town hall to complain that the electrical in the auction hall isn't up to code. They shut it down until the work is done to upgrade it."

"Are you being serious?"

"Yup. I was just heading over to talk to your dad about how to come up with the rest of the money that's owing to those bank cocksuckers. There's another auction about three hours away, but it's not until Saturday."

Tracy glances over at me nervously. Surprisingly, I don't feel anything. Not shocked or angry or worried. Nothing. I must be too emotionally exhausted to care about another setback.

Phil waits for me to respond. I just don't have the energy. Eventually, he says he'll see me at the house and drives off.

Tracy wipes her hands on a rag before she closes the

hood. "I can't fix it right now. It needs a part. Good news, it's an inexpensive part. Bad news, it needs to be ordered, so might take a few days to get here. I'll order it for you and come by to put it in once it's here."

I nod and stare out over the pasture. Maybe it doesn't even matter. We don't need a working loader if we don't own a ranch. It's hard to imagine not owning the land since all the memories of my mom are attached to it. It will kill my dad to leave here. Literally. He'll give up and let the cancer take him. But me? I can start over somewhere else. Wherever Della is. Great, now I'm choked up again. I guess it means I'm not completely emotionally dead inside. Yet. I can't give up. If my mom were alive, she would be devastated that we lost it to a greedy corporation with questionable ethics. Actually, she'd be livid. They'd have had to get past her shotgun before they removed her from the land. There's got to be a way to save it, for her.

"Havie?" Tracy waves her hands in front of my face to pull me out of my daze. "Do you want me to give you a lift back to the house?"

Without answering, I hop off the fence and walk around to the front of her truck and slide into the passenger seat. "There must be a way to uncover the collusion between the bank and the commodities company," I say to her as she slides in behind the wheel.

"Probably, but not before Friday. The only way to screw them at this point is to pay off the debt." She glances at me before she turns onto the driveway. "The town will pull together if you want to ask for help."

"They wouldn't be able to raise a hundred thousand by Friday."

"Every little bit will help."

I don't respond.

It's obvious she wants to say something else but doesn't until she stops in front of the barn to drop me off. "I know you think it was all my fault that we broke up."

Really? She wants to go there when I've got a shit ton of other problems on my mind? I close my eyes and take a deep breath. "You cheated."

"I know I cheated, but have you ever thought about why I did it? There were two of us in the relationship. When things got hard, you stopped talking to me. You shut me out and pushed me away. That's why I panicked."

"What difference does it make? We're ancient history. I don't want to talk about it."

"Taking off on Della at the rodeo was a shitty thing to do. She drove all that way out there to see you and you shut her out because you were in a bad mood. That's exactly what you did to me. And sorry for getting in your business, but I just thought maybe you wouldn't want to make the same mistakes again."

What the hell? "Della was at the rodeo?"

"Yeah, dummy. And she started to cry when you abandoned her there."

I glance at her and jump out of the truck. "Thanks for the ride."

Damn it. Della must think I'm a complete dick. I hate to admit it, but Tracy's right. I did push her away. I know that. I've always known that, even though it was easier to blame her for cheating than admit that I played a part in it. But I didn't mean to push Della away. I didn't even know she was there.

I grab the banister and lunge to head up to the loft to call her but then stop because Chuck steps out of the tack room.

"Hey, buddy," he says with a big grin. "What do you want me to do? I'm all yours until tomorrow night. I'd stay longer, but I gotta to go back for Cavendish's class on Wednesday." He winks and points at me. "Word on the street is she kicks assholes out if they don't show up for her lectures."

At first, I don't know what to say because I'm surprised he would drive out to help. "Did Della send you?"

"Sorta. She hinted at it like sixty-five times before I finally clued in that she wanted me to offer to lend a hand." He laughs and picks up a shovel to muck a stall. "I'm still slow on the uptake, but I'm trying to think of other people. Which reminds me." He reaches into his shirt pocket and hands me a folded check. "I told my dad what you've been going through and asked him for a loan. This is all he would give me. Hopefully it helps."

The check is made out for twenty thousand dollars. I'm stunned. "Wow. Thanks, man. I appreciate it." I cross the floor to hug him. The sentimentality makes him uncomfortable, so he shoves me away and throws a rough-housing punch at my shoulder.

"You're welcome."

"I'll pay your dad back as soon as I can." I glance at the check again in shock. I can already imagine Della's face glowing with pride from whipping Chuck into a half-decent human being. "I'm sorry I got on your case about Della. I was wrong."

"It's fine." He punches me again. "We're cool."

"Thanks. I'll be right back. I just need to make a quick phone call."

He nods. "Tell her I've been working my ass off, and I'm the best ranch hand you've ever had."

"I'll tell her you showed up. You'll have to prove the rest," I grin as I take the stairs two at a time.

Chapter 29

Della

As I'm heading to class, Easton calls. Yikes. I'm not prepared for this. Maybe he's calling to apologize about the rodeo. Or maybe he's not sorry that he left without acknowledging me. Maybe he's mad that I showed up in the first place. Or maybe Tracy was lying. Either way, I want to know. But I might end up in tears, and I don't want to miss more school due to emotional instability. Avoid? It's going to go to voicemail if I don't decide quick. Just do it, Della. Like a bandage. Find out where you stand. "Hi."

"Hi. You were at the Madera rodeo?"

"Uh, yes. Sorry if I was a distraction. I hope that's not why you fell off and got injured. I should have called you to ask if you wanted me there."

"I did want you there. I didn't know you were there."

"Oh. Tracy said you did. Did she lie?"

"Not exactly. I'm so sorry. It's my fault. I told her you were there, even though I thought you weren't, because I didn't want her to think we weren't together. But then you really were there, which I only just found out, and she said you were crying because you thought I bailed without talking to you. If I had known you were there I would have stayed. You know that, right?"

"Yes. Maybe. I thought I did." I massage my temple with the heel of my hand. "Lately, I'm confused about every-thing."

With unwavering certainty, he says, "I love you, Della. Don't ever doubt that. And I will try to see you every chance I get, if you want me to."

"Really?" I abruptly stop walking, and the guy behind me has to quickly side-step to avoid bowling me over. Okay. Wait. What? I literally stuck a sticky note on my mirror that has *It's never going to happen. Give it up, Della* written on it to condition my feelings to turn off. Now my brain is jammed up with the mixed messages, and my heart is trying to hammer through my chest. "So, would you be open to trying to date long-distance to see how it goes?"

"That's what I want. I just can't promise anything until I find out what's going to happen with the ranch. Can we sit down and talk about everything after my meeting at the bank on Friday?"

I lean against a tree, hugging myself with one arm to contain the excitement inside. "I'd like that. Very much."

"I wish I could drive out to see you right now, but it will have to wait until after Friday. Pray for a miracle before then. We need all the help we can get."

"Um, speaking of help. I did something without asking you first that I assumed would be helpful, but after I did it I started to worry that my brilliant idea will mean more work for you. I didn't consider whether it was really the help you needed or the help I assumed you needed. It's too late to cancel the surprise now, though." My eyebrows crease together as I slide down the trunk of the tree and sit on the grass. "He's probably almost already there."

"Chuck?"

"Yeah." I wince. "Sorry. He's probably a nightmare to supervise. I hope he doesn't end up causing more problems."

"He won't. He knows his way around a ranch. It was a good idea. And I can definitely use the extra set of hands. Not that getting the work done will matter if the bank forces us to forfeit on Friday."

"How much is still owing?"

"More than what you have in your savings account, so don't get any bright ideas."

Hmm. Uh oh. I stand and start walking again. "So, I wish I could talk longer, but I need to get to class since my grades took a tiny slip. One more thing before I go." My eyes dart around as if I'm avoiding eye contact, even though he can't see me. "I kind of did one more thing without running it by you first. It's already done, so there's nothing either one of us can do about it now."

"What?"

"I transferred seventy-five thousand dollars to your account. I love you. Bye."

Oh my goodness. Shoot. My heart is pounding in my throat from hanging up on him. He's going to be so mad that I used all my savings to help him out. It's the right thing to do, though. He's too proud and stubborn to accept the money any other way. Hopefully he doesn't hate me. Yulia worried it might make him feel like he can't support his family, but I don't look at it that way. Her other concern about how I was going to pay my own bills made more sense, but it's only a loan. I know he'll pay me back, whether I ask him to or not, he will pay back every cent. Probably with interest. I know he'd insist on helping me if the roles were reversed. It's the right thing to do, whether he agrees or not. Fingers crossed that my loan and Chuck's dad's loan are enough.

I rush to class and sit down in my lecture hall, out of breath, then turn to the guy sitting next to me. "Would you feel emasculated if I gave you a seventy-five thousand dollar loan to save you from losing your property?"

His eyes narrow, debating whether I'm insane. "No?" he says with a cautious tone as if he's attempting to gauge which answer I was hoping to hear.

"You'd feel grateful, right?"

He nods with uncertainty. "Sure."

Forget it. It was the right thing to do, no matter what anyone else thinks. I care what Easton thinks, though. Please be man enough to not feel threatened by what I did. If he has too much pride to accept it, I'll just have to convince him it takes courage to ask for and receive help.

What if it isn't enough to pay off the entire debt? They'll still lose the ranch and he'll resent me for my unsuccessful attempt to bail him out. Grr. Did I make a mistake? Maybe. But really, do I want to be with someone who can't accept my support? That's what a relationship is, right? Give and take. I'm strong when you need me and you're strong when I need you. Fingers crossed on both hands that I didn't screw things up immediately after they got unscrewed.

I might as well not have gone to class. I didn't pay attention to one word the instructor said. Everyone else took at least four pages of notes. I doodled a picture of Easton shirtless and swinging a sledgehammer. Oh well. I wonder if they need any baristas in Three Rivers. Or, I could make sandwiches at the racist Russian's deli. But I'm only allowed in the country because I have a student Visa. Gonna have to at least go to community college to keep that. So complicated. While I go over my back-up options for when I flunk out of engineering, I pack up my bag and file out of the lecture hall behind my classmates. Maybe I should call Easton back and apologize for dropping the news and hanging up on him. That was rude. But necessary. Or, on second thought, it might be better to give him time to get used to the idea.

"Della!" Janine waves from the steps of a building across the street, then jogs over to me.

"Hi. You look happy," I say as I hug her.

"Ecstatic actually. I just found out that I got chosen for a residency in New York. I've always wanted to live there. I thought it would be a long shot, but I got the acceptance letter today." She unfolds the official letter and shows it to me.

"That's fantastic. I'm so happy for you. When do you leave?"

"At the end of the month." She nods knowingly as if she can read my thoughts, but she doesn't mention Chuck, so I don't either. "I need to challenge one course before I go."

"What does that mean?"

"The New York program wants me to have a specific stats course. I already took a similar stats class in second year and don't want to re-take it. I requested to challenge the one New York recognizes as a prerequisite. All I need to do is take the final and prove that I know the content. Then I get the credit."

"Really? Can anyone in any department do that?"

"I think so. You just need to make a request."

Interesting. "How would I go about doing that?"

She digs through her purse and hands me a pamphlet. "This is the information they gave me at admissions. Ask for Sarah. She was really helpful."

"Thanks." I feel giddy.

"No problem. Where are you headed?"

"Green library."

"I'll walk with you. I have to go that way, too. How is BJ, by the way?" We start to walk in sync. "I heard he got expelled."

"He called to tell me he made it home safely. His mom and sisters are excited to have him there, and he's going to be able to transfer most of his credits and finish his MBA at the University of Houston."

"That's great. How's Easton?"

I shrug and take a sip from my water bottle. "We'll know for sure on Friday if they're going to lose the ranch or not. He's pretty stressed."

"That sucks. If I had anything to lend him, I would. Hopefully it works out." She glances at me as we cross the courtyard. "I know you're dying to ask me whether you should tell Chuck that I'm moving away."

"I am. I didn't want to bring it up if you didn't want to talk about it. I'd prefer not to be the person who tells him, but I will if you think that's best. If you don't want him to know, I won't say anything. Fair warning, though, I'm horrible at keeping secrets. There's a high probability it will blurt out of my mouth without my consent at some inopportune moment."

She digs through her bag again and pulls out a granola bar. She offers the bar to me. "Bite?"

"I'm okay thanks."

She breaks off a chunk of granola and pops it in her mouth. Eventually she says, "I'll tell Chuck about New York. We dated for three years. He deserves a proper goodbye."

I nod and honestly feel sad for him. He has worked really hard to complete every assignment I've given him. And even though I still think the way he treated Janine can never be erased, he has changed. And the New York news is going to gut him. Hopefully it doesn't make him regress back to who he used to be. He's come so far.

When we arrive at the library she points to the building across the street. "My next class is over there."

"We should go out for dinner to celebrate your residency. Are you free Thursday?" I ask.

"Yeah. That would be great. I'll pick you up at the house

at seven and then that will give me a chance to talk to Chuck when I drop you off." She exhales sharply. "That's going to be a fun conversation. I might chicken out. If I do, I'll write him a letter."

"Whatever works. Don't torture yourself over it."

"See you Thursday." She hugs me and then rushes away.

My phone buzzes with a text. It's from Easton: *Thank you for the loan. I love you.*

So grateful that he has decided to accept it, I hug my phone to my chest and literally skip up the library steps. People are staring at me funny. I don't care.

Chapter 30

Easton

The bank manager has kept Dad and me waiting for more than half an hour. The ranch hands, Phil, and every member of Tracy's family all chipped in a thousand dollars each. So, combined with Della and Chuck's loans, and the earnings from the last auction, we have enough to cover the debt.

It's making me nervous that they're forcing us to wait. Dad's been pacing in the waiting area since we got here. He's pissed that we had to ask our friends for the money, but whatever, it was either that or lose everything. My entire life was on the line—losing the ranch, all the memories of my mom, and Della. We had no choice. Just like we had no choice that Dad got cancer.

I've been thinking about my relationship with him a lot. Seeing how Della is with Dad makes me miss the easiness I used to have with him when I was a kid. Before the accident. When Tracy pointed out the part I played in wrecking our relationship, it got me to thinking about how

I've pushed a wedge between my dad and me, too. I've blamed him for a long time for killing Mom. And maybe I needed to at first. But it was an accident, and if he could have traded places with her he would have. I don't want to hate him anymore, and I don't want our relationship to be strained. We've both suffered long enough. Life's too short.

"Hey," I say without looking at him.

"What?"

"I forgive you."

He stops pacing and turns to face me. His stare rests heavy on me as the full meaning of what I said sinks in. After a long silence he says, "Thank you."

I nod but keep staring down at my boots with my elbows rested on my knees. I should probably get up and hug him or something. But he would hate that.

He steps closer and cups the back of my neck. "Love you, kid."

"Love you, too, Pop."

With perfect timing, a woman crosses the floor and extends her hand in greeting to my dad, then she shakes my hand as I stand. "I'm Isla. I'm the district manager for the bank. I'm going to be handling your paperwork today. Sorry to keep you waiting, I wanted to review everything before we meet."

"Where's Brad?" Dad asks.

"He's been removed from your account."

Dad and I exchange a glance. Isla turns and walks ahead of us to lead the way to Brad's office with her high heels clicking on the tile. She invites us to sit and then she slides behind the desk and opens a folder.

"You'll have to excuse me as I catch up with your account. I was confused because the note on my schedule says you are here to pay off what's outstanding on a reverse mortgage loan."

"We are," Dad says.

"Okay. That's strange. There must have been a miscommunication between you and Brad." Her eyebrows angle together as she opens our account on her computer screen. "The payment was made in full earlier this week."

"By who?" I ask.

She shakes her head. "It doesn't show that information."

Dad is suspicious, which makes me wary. A manager we've never met before suddenly shows up and tells us the account is mysteriously paid off and we don't need to make a payment. Then Brad comes back to work tomorrow and all of a sudden we've forfeited? She must think we're stupid.

"We'd like to make another payment anyway," I say.

"There's nothing to apply it to. I can put it into a savings account or stock fund if you want."

"Where's Brad?" I ask.

"He's on administrative leave while head office conducts an investigation. That's all I am at liberty to say about it."

I honestly don't know how to feel. Should I be happy that it's magically paid off and get her to sign off on the paperwork before they figure out their mistake? Or should I assume that she's trying to dupe us into missing the deadline? Dad doesn't trust her. He's giving me side glances.

I don't even know anybody who could have paid off the full three hundred thousand dollars. It has to be a mistake. "Are you sure you can't figure out where the payment came from?" I ask her.

She scrolls down on the screen. "It was transferred from another account at this branch. Hold on. Maybe I can search it." She opens a different screen and types on the keyboard. "Looks like the account belongs to C. Mathers."

What? The shock literally blows me back against the chair. With a huge grin on my face I spin to look at Dad to see if he can believe it, but instead of making eye contact with me, he gets up and walks out of the office. Ah, that's priceless. He's never going to live that one down. I chuckle and sign the papers. Then I transfer Della's money back to her account and rip up the checks from everyone else.

Dad is waiting for me outside, leaned up against the truck.

"You want to explain why Crystal paid off our mortgage?" I ask to tease him.

"Nope."

I laugh and climb behind the wheel. He sulks all the way home, and then gets downright bitter when he sees a red Chevy parked beside Della's VW in front of the house. I'm so pumped to see Della I've got the door open before the truck even stops rolling. Dad's acting as if he would rather wrestle a mountain lion than follow me inside. Della must have heard us drive up because she swings the front screen door open and bounds out onto the porch. She leaps off the steps and runs to jump in my arms. I spin her around and then place her back on the ground so I can kiss her.

"Hi." I smile.

"Hi." She gazes deep into my eyes. "How'd it go at the bank?"

"Really well," I whisper in her ear. "And we didn't need to use any of your money."

"Really?"

We both turn as Crystal steps out onto the porch with two bowls of homemade ice cream. "A little bird told me a celebration is in order," she says as she winks at me.

Sill holding Della's hand, I lead her up onto the porch and kiss Crystal's cheek. "Thank you for paying off the loan. We'll pay you back as soon as we can."

"Don't mention it," she says as she hands me one of the bowls. "And I know you will pay me back when you can. I'm not worried about that."

I stretch my arm across Della's shoulders and feed her a spoonful of ice cream. God, I've missed her. "What do you say to Crystal, Dad?"

He's still lingering by the truck with his hands jammed in his pockets and kicks the tire before he mumbles to Crystal, "I didn't ask you to do that."

"No kidding?" Crystal jokes as she slides onto a rocking chair and dips a spoon into the ice cream. "You didn't even tell me you were about to lose the land. I would have paid it off a long time ago and saved Easton a bunch of headaches if you'd told me about it yourself. But instead I had to hear about it from gossip."

"We had it covered." He says, sulkily.

"Mm hmm," she says. "Turns out Brad the banker has

been taking kickbacks from the commodities company in exchange for confidential client information. Did you also have that covered? Or, is it a good thing that I filed a report with the bank?"

Dad grumbles.

"How did you know that about Brad?" I ask Crystal.

"It's a small town. People talk." She lifts her eyebrows in an animated way. "Specifically, the woman who was formerly sleeping with Brad talked." She shrugs and eats another spoonful of ice cream. "He probably won't be charged with anything, but he might get fired. And the company won't try to bully anyone else around here." She points at me. "And that lawyer of yours was talking to some out-of-towners in trucks in front of the diner, so stop paying him for doing nothin' for you."

Dad ventures up onto the porch and sits on the railing with his arms crossed.

"Stop being such a grump, Jack. I brought pie, too."

"I'll get it," Della says as she breezes inside.

"Why are you being such a baby?" Crystal chuckles. "I got nothing better to do with my money than help your sorry ass out of a bind."

Della returns and hands Dad a piece of blueberry pie.

"And while we're on the topic of your less than exemplary communication skills, this is probably as good a time as any to tell Easton," Crystal adds.

Dad rolls his eyes and balances the plate on the railing as if he's lost his appetite.

"Tell me what?"

Della glances between Dad and Crystal in amused antic- ipation.

"Jack," Crystal says to prod him.

He mumbles something under his breath, then says, "Crystal and I have been dating." He picks the pie plate back up and shovels a huge forkful into his mouth, so he won't have to say anything else.

"For four years," Crystal adds and shoots me an apolo- getic look. "He wouldn't let me tell you. Lord knows why."

Okay. Wow. Not sure how I didn't suspect anything. I always knew he had a thing for her. I'm totally fine with it, but I don't know what to say exactly.

"That's fantastic news," Della answers for me and claps excitedly as she walks over and bends at the waist to give Dad a kiss on the cheek. "Don't screw it up," she whispers to him. "We can't let anything come between us and the ice cream supply."

He shakes his head, embarrassed.

Della spins around with her arms in the air and then crouches to scratch Brewster behind the ears. "Guess what, boy? It's been a great day. Everybody gets to still live here. Jack and Crystal are in love. Della and Easton get free homemade ice cream. And my sister is pregnant again. Life doesn't get any better than that. Does it?" She rests her forehead on his for a second and then she skips over and throws her arms around me. "I also applied for you to get permission to challenge Cavendish's class, so you don't have to re-take it." She hands me a confirmation letter of the request from the school and grooves her neck and shoulders back and forth in a pseudo hip hop celebratory move.

It's so goofy it even makes my dad smile. It's impossible not to adore her. "You guys don't mind if we excuse ourselves, do you?" I say and grasp Della's hand, so she'll follow me.

Crystal smiles. Dad shrugs, like he'd rather not know the details, before he takes another bite of pie. Della rushes with me across the yard to the barn, then I press her up against the wall at the bottom of the loft stairs. Her hair is wild and she's breathing heavy. Without a doubt she is the person I want to spend the rest of my life with.

"Is now a good time to talk about the future of our relationship?" I ask.

She dips her finger in the ice cream bowl that I'm still holding and touches my lips so she can kiss it off. "I want to always feel the way I feel when I'm with you," she whispers. "That's all the talking I need to do."

Sounds good to me. I smile, swoop her up, and carry her to the loft.

Epilogue

Della

Two Years Later

"Yeah, baby!" I shout, jumping up and down on the spot and whistling with my fingers in my mouth. Whoops, just spilled my popcorn. Easton winks up at me from the middle of the arena as he waits for his score. Eighty-seven. "Woo!" That should be good enough for the win. Chuck and BJ might not be thrilled, but hopefully they're also going to place. Just like old times.

"Hey." Chuck plops down next to me on the bleachers and wraps his arm around my neck for an embrace that is half hug, half headlock. I nearly didn't recognize him when I first spotted him. He has a completely normal haircut now. He's actually kind of handsome. "How's our Little Miss Oh My Gosh?"

"I'm great. Thanks for flying in for our roomie reunion." BJ and Easton also climb up the bleachers to join us to watch the bulls. Easton sits on the bench in front of me, so I lean over his shoulder to give him a congratulatory kiss on the cheek before I stand to hug BJ. It's the first time I've seen him since he moved back to Texas two years ago. "It's nice to see you, Bailey Congratulations on finishing your MBA."

He nods and sits next to me. "Thanks. I also landed a job in Houston, close to my mom and sisters."

"And close to your lady lawyer friend, too?" I needle him in the ribs to tease him. "Easton said you've being seeing her for almost a year. Sounds pretty serious?"

His eyebrows flick. "Yeah. She's great. Y'all will have to come down and meet her sometime."

"Definitely." I slide one arm over BJ's shoulder and one over Chuck's. "How's it going working for your dad in Portland, Taylor?"

He shrugs less than enthusiastically. "It's fertilizer. Not exactly exciting."

"Lucrative, though," BJ says as he watches a rider get thrown from a bull.

"True." Chuck says. "But I want to get out of Portland."

"Still no serious girlfriend?" I ask.

He shakes his head.

"So, my efforts to train you didn't have any lasting effect?"

All three of them laugh as if it was a lost cause in the first place. On the bright side, Chuck hasn't said or done anything crude so far. So I'm still going to hold out hope. It's so nice to be all together again. It would have been fun to go back to the Palo Alto house all together instead of staying at a hotel, but Easton and I have new roommates, so unfortunately, there isn't room for the guys to stay over.

I love that house. It's going to be heartbreaking to say goodbye to it at the end of this term.

"Excuse me," I say to a boy who is about twelve years old and staring at the guys as if they are Gods or something. "Would you please take a photo of us?"

He hops up excitedly as I hand him my camera. "Yes, ma'am."

We all pose in front of the railing with a bull ride going on behind us. "Thank you," I say as I take the camera back and check the shot as we all sit back down. It's such a great picture. They all have their chaps on, and it brings back so many memories as I stare at it—a mixture of happiness and sadness. I guess that's what nostalgia is. I've never felt nostalgic for anything before.

I still think rodeo people are lunatics, but Easton loves it. Even though he didn't need to, he wanted to graduate when I did, so he took time off school to tie up all the loose ends at the ranch and to have his knee surgery. He went back to modeling after his surgery, while waiting for his knee to heal enough so he could compete again. That work with Stuart parlayed into a bunch of international runway shows, several endorsement deals for bronc riding, and more print contracts with a cologne company and a watch brand. He did a lot of traveling, but I was lucky enough to tag along for some of the trips.

He cut back on modeling when he came back to school full-time. He still goes out to the ranch one weekend every month to help, not that he needs to. His dad's cancer is in remission and Crystal moved in. They also hired two extra ranch hands, and everything is running smoothly. As soon as Easton graduates, he's going to hire a company to come in and start extracting the gold on the property. Fingers crossed they'll strike it rich.

"Oooh," all three of the guys groan and wince simultaneously as a bull rider bites the dust. Literally. He landed face first and his back is bent in an unnatural way. He doesn't seem to care that he has a mouthful of dirt. He waves at the crowd to let them know he's okay. Although, based on how he is stumbling towards the fence, I'm guessing he's not okay. Crazy cowboys.

Chuck leans back against the bench behind him. "Man, I miss shooting the shit with you guys. Sorry for cursing," he adds without looking at me.

I wave my hand to indicate that I'm not as uptight and prudish as the first time we were at this rodeo. "Cursing, manure, serious injuries and all, I miss you guys, too. And I'm glad we decided to do this."

"I also miss my mullet," Chuck laments.

"No!" we all shout at the same time.

I rub his sandy blond curls. "Don't ever disrespect your head like that again. This is much better."

Easton leans back from the bench in front of me and rests his elbows on my knees. "What do you say we go to that same steakhouse we went to the first time we brought Della here?"

"Yes." I lean forward and remove his hat to kiss his forehead. "And can we go to that bar with the longhorn thing on the dance floor?"

He smiles and pretends to debate it in his mind before he eventually agrees. "Sure."

Both Chuck and BJ grin, oddly enthusiastically, as if the three of them are in on something together. "What?" I ask, suspicious of any time that all three of them are smiling like that simultaneously.

"I get the first dance," BJ says.

I hold up my hands in surrender. "I still can't dance. Fair warning."

It's only ten o'clock when we arrive at the country bar, so it's not busy yet. It's weird to be here. It looks exactly how I remember it, but it feels different. The first time we were here I felt like such an outsider in a world I knew nothing about. Now, it's a part of who I am, so familiar and comfortable. Easton even called ahead to reserve the exact same table we stood at two years ago. So, sweet.

"Virgin margarita," Chuck says as he places a drink in front of me.

I sip it and it actually is a virgin.

BJ clinks his glass with mine and says, "Cheers to the good girl."

With a grin I hold my glass in the air. "To all the cowboys I've loved before. Great roomies and best friends."

After enthusiastically toasting to that, Chuck wraps his arm across my shoulders and squeezes me into a slightly jarring sideways hug. "You're finally proud to call me a friend. I'm touched."

I shove him away playfully. "I haven't seen you in a while.

Maybe the secret to getting along with you is not spending any time with you."

He laughs. "Whatever it takes. You called me a best friend. You can't take it back now."

Oh. My. Gosh. My jaw drops as I catch a glimpse of a familiar face in the doorway. That can't be a coincidence. She smiles and waves as she makes her way across the bar. "Janine!" I squeal and rush to hug her. "What are you doing here?"

"Havie invited me to the reunion." She glances at Chuck, who is frozen in stunned shock with his beer bottle suspended halfway to his mouth. She smiles demurely. "Hi Taylor."

"Hi Babe." He blinks repeatedly, sort of dumfounded. "You look great."

She does look stunning. Her hair is silky straight and shorter than she used to wear it. And although she is wearing simple dark jeans and a white blouse, it's a sophisticated Manhattan casual look. Way different than the Oklahoma farm girl casual look that she used to have. Her cheeks blush from Chuck's compliment and she tucks her hair behind her ears. "You look good, too."

He stares at her, completely thrown off. It's as if he's seeing her for the very first time, like he never truly noticed her before. BJ and Easton exchange a look, amused by the sparks that are flying. The staring with no speaking goes on too long and Janine turns away from the awkwardness to hug Easton and BJ. They ask her about New York and her residency. Chuck hangs on to every word she says, not distracted, not interrupting, and genuinely interested. Eventually she sneaks a side peek at him, clearly as shocked by his uncharacteristic quietness as the rest of us.

"You want to dance?" he asks her.

She glances at me and then back at him. After a long hesitation she says, "Sure."

I silently clutch both Easton and BJ's arms to contain my excitement. Chuck and Janine hit the dance floor and start to two-step, just like they were meant to be together. I bounce up and down on the spot. Yay. I love happy endings. I smack Easton's chest. "Why didn't you tell me Janine was coming to the reunion?"

His eyebrows angle together comically. "You can't keep secrets."

"True." I chuckle as I pick up my margarita to sip the slush. Over the rim of the glass I notice another unexpected guest standing at the other end of the bar—a very pregnant Tracy. She's with her husband Jeff, her brother Mike, and, "What the what?" she's also with Jack and Crystal. I spin around to face Easton. "Why is everyone from Three Rivers here?"

"It's a reunion," he quips and turns to greet them.

Okay, what's going on? I'm confused. Jack and Crystal are here, in a bar five hours away from where they live. Jack doesn't even like driving from the ranch to Three Rivers if he doesn't have to. And he's only visited us in Palo Alto once. Bizarre. I hug everyone and then make eye contact with Easton to question him. He winks.

What has he been up to? I love it. I just can't believe it.

I had no idea he'd been planning something so elaborate. It's a nice surprise. Too bad they didn't come earlier to watch the rodeo.

Arms circle around my waist from behind and I know instantly who it is as she screeches, "Surprise, Dee Dee!"

I whirl around and squeal as I hug Yulia so hard we almost fall down. I kiss both her cheeks and then reach over to hug Alex. He's very preppy and stands out terribly in a country bar. I can't believe he even agreed to come. "What are you doing here, I can't even, how did you not spill the beans, who's watching the girls?"

"Alex's parents are spending the weekend at the house," she says before she takes a sip of a beer. "God, I needed this break."

I shake my head, so overwhelmed. "And you decided to come here?"

Yulia shrugs innocently. "Easton wanted to surprise you. Aren't you happy to see us?"

"Yes, but." I scratch my head and search for Easton. He glances at me from across the crowd and nods towards the door, so I'll shift my attention. Okay. This is too strange. Am I in the Twilight Zone or something? The only two people who could possibly stand out worse than Alex are by the bar with their coats still on. Mom is trying to move to the music. Dad looks like he wants to impale himself with the longhorn to put himself out of his misery. When Mom spots me she waves excitedly and it makes me burst into tears. I don't know why. I'm just so happy to see everyone. I don't understand it, but I love it. They make their way across the dance floor to join us. And I hug them repeatedly as I fluctuate between crying and laughing.

Then Stuart pops up out of nowhere and says to Easton, "What is this gay heaven that you call a country bar and why have I never been invited here before?" After we all screech, he air kisses cheeks with me, mom, and Yulia.

Seeing how ridiculously ecstatic I am makes Easton grin. If someone had told me yesterday that I would love him more today, I would have sworn to them it's impossible. I would have been wrong. And now I'm crying again. "How did I get so lucky?"

He reaches out to hug me into his chest. "I'm the lucky one. Della, will you marry me?"

"Whaaaat?" I'm choking. I can't breathe. Did he just? What? The tears are making my vision really blurry, but I think he's holding up a diamond ring. I wipe my eyes. Yes, it's a very big, gorgeous engagement ring. What is happening? He's proposing. I feel like I'm dreaming. Everyone is looking at me. Agh. Easton just knelt down on one knee. People in the bar are cheering. I'm taking too long. He looks slightly worried. Speak, Della. Don't leave him hanging. "Yes. Yes. Of course I'll marry you!" I drop to my knees and fling my arms around his neck. We're on the floor of a bar. It's sticky, ew. We just got engaged. Everyone's whistling and clapping. I can't believe it. Holding his face between my palms I lock eyes with him. Everything about this moment is so perfectly surreal and wacky. "Easton Everley Havie Lewis, you are a very unusual person." I kiss him and then add, "The good type of unusual."

"So are you Della Koskov." He slides the ring on my finger. "I can't wait to have some unusual half-Russian and half-Mohave kids with you, so we can take them to the racist Russian's deli and order some delicious sandwiches."

I rest my forehead on his, grinning as *Tennessee Whiskey* starts to play on cue. "I can't think of any better reason to have children than to rub it in the face of the racist Russian."

He laughs. "Would you like to dance with me, funny girl?"

"I can't dance, but I'll press my body against yours and sway back and forth."

His eyebrow flicks in a sexy way as he wraps his hand around mine to help me to my feet. "That's the best dancing. Why do you think I fell for you that night two years ago?"

"I thought it was because I was going commando under my dress."

His eyes open wide, then he bursts out laughing and leads me to the dance floor. Guaranteed all my blood relatives are currently having flashbacks to the Koskov wedding inferno incident from the last time they witnessed me attempt to dance. Yup. They're all checking for the nearest fire extinguishers and emergency exits.

I pull Easton by the belt buckle to step closer. "You're my first fiancé, by the way."

"I figured." He nods over my shoulder to make me look. His dad and Crystal are dancing.

"Oh my goodness. So cute. Do you think your mom is happy right now?"

Easton's eyes water and he swallows hard before he nods. Then he hugs me against his chest and we sway to the crooning of Chris Stapleton.

Best.

Night.

Ever.

Acknowledgements

When I set out to write this project, I didn't intend for it to be a romantic comedy. Then Della started talking and kept making me laugh. I sent the draft of the first four chapters to my mom and asked, "Is this funny? It wasn't supposed to be." My mom agreed that Della was an amusing goofball, then she urged me to write quickly so she could find out what happened next with Easton. Sadly, my mom passed away before I completed the manuscript. So, now, this story will always hold a special place in my heart and remind me of those last light and lovely laughs with my mom. I hope you enjoy Della and Easton as much as we did.

I'd like to thank Denise Jaden, Paige Gregory, Laura Jones, Romy Sommer, Rasa Cortes, and Erica Ediger for reading early drafts of the manuscript and providing invaluable feedback. Thanks to Brian Tingle for technical advice on prospecting. And thank you to Elley Gunter who named Della after winning a RodeoChat contest. Bridget Thomas won the contest to name Easton. My editorial director Charlotte Ledger is a superstar—I owe her so much, and more people should aspire to be as kind and professional as she is. Thank you also to Kate Ellis and the entire team behind the scenes at Harper*Impulse* and HarperCollins *Publishers*.

And thank you to Sean, the hero of my own personal romantic comedy.

HELP US SHARE THE LOVE!

If you love this wonderful book as much as we do then please share your reviews online.

Leaving reviews makes a huge difference and helps our books reach even more readers.

So get reviewing and sharing, we want to hear what you think!
Love, HarperImpulse x

Please leave your reviews online!

And on social!

/HarperImpulse   **@harperimpulse**
@HarperImpulse

LOVE BOOKS?

So do we! And we love nothing more than chatting about our books with you lovely readers.

If you'd like to find out about our latest titles, as well as exclusive competitions, author interviews, offers and lots more, join us on our Facebook page! Why not leave a note on our wall to tell us what you thought of this book or what you'd like to see us publish more of?

/HarperImpulse

You can also tweet us @harperimpulse and see exclusively behind the scenes on our Instagram page www.instagram.com/harperimpulse

To be the first to know about upcoming books and events, sign up to our newsletter at: http://www.harperimpulseromance.com/